"Ben, we c
relationship

"What am I to
asked challeng
convenient lay

Susan gestured miserably. "You're being unfair –"

"Am I?" he asked, his eyes flashing accusingly at her. "Am I unfair to want a long-term commitment? To want this to be . . . " Staring down into her flushed face, Ben almost said "forever." But he wasn't sure she was ready to hear those words yet.

"You arouse something very primal in me, Susan," he said instead, gathering her into his arms, as if to soothe her. "I look at you and start thinking about homes and children –" As he spoke, he started nuzzling her ear, his teeth nipping the flesh lightly.

"Are you sure this isn't just lust?" Susan argued feebly. She felt herself melting under Ben's expert touch.

"Whatever happened to *love*?" Ben murmured huskily, his mouth seeking her lips.

Love. She'd been waiting all her life for that one word . . .

To my sister Wendy –
with love and thanks
for sharing her expertise
on so many subjects

———— 🐝 ————

EUGENIA RILEY
is also the author
of this novel in
Temptation

LOVE NEST

The Perfect Mate

EUGENIA RILEY

MILLS & BOON LIMITED
ETON HOUSE, 18-24 PARADISE ROAD
RICHMOND, SURREY TW9 1SR

First published in Great Britain in 1991 by Mills & Boon Limited, Eton House, 18-24 Paradise Road, Richmond, Surrey TW9 1SR

© Eugenia Riley Essenmacher 1990

ISBN 0 263 77385 X

21 – 9106

Made and printed in Great Britain

Prologue

EVER SINCE THE CHICKEN had broken Susan's foot, her life had been hurtling toward disaster.

If Aunt Florence hadn't worried so about her and Jamie, the whole mess never would have occurred in the first place. But with Aunt Florence being a neurotic mothering type who always brought them something for the fridge, and Jamie being a slob as well as a compulsive gambler, the appalling chain of events became inevitable.

For six months, the chicken had sat frozen in the refrigerator in the apartment Susan shared with her brother, Jamie. Neither sibling cooked, and yet neither had wanted to offend Aunt Florence by trashing the bird. Vaguely, they had planned to invite their aunt over for dinner some Sunday, but their good intentions had faded off into many a sunset. Finally, one summer day, sick to death of doing Jamie's share of the housework, and his laundry, plus trying to pay off his gambling debts, Susan had insisted that her brother clean the apartment as well as the refrigerator. "And throw out that baking hen in the freezer—no offense to Aunt Florence, but I'm tired of looking at it, and I'm sure that by now it has a terminal case of freezer burn," Susan had declared.

Jamie had made a halfhearted attempt to clean the apartment and the refrigerator. But, in typical male fashion, not only had he forgotten about the hen, he'd left all six pounds of it balanced precariously on a slippery can of frozen daiquiris. And that is why, when Susan opened the freezer section to extract her microwave dinner, the chicken had come sailing out and, true to Newton's law, had landed smack on her foot.

Her scream had rattled the ice cubes.

"Hairline fracture of the metatarsal," her doctor had diagnosed when he met her at the emergency room. Upon learning that the chicken had done the "fowl" deed, Dr. Springer had laughed himself silly. "Tell me, Sue, what did you say when the chicken broke your foot?"

"Well, Dr. Springer, it goes with chicken and it ain't soup," Susan had snapped back nastily. How dare her doctor sit there and laugh his head off while she was in excruciating pain! What about the Hippocratic oath?

For six weeks afterward, Susan had hobbled around on crutches and had worn the cumbersome cast. Jamie had made himself scarce, doubtless realizing that he wasn't exactly in his sister's good graces.

That was probably why the thugs had come around again—Jamie had gone back to gambling and had really gotten in deep this time. In no time at all, Jamie's gambling partners began hassling Susan for money again, showing up outside the apartment, even calling her at work.

But this time, Susan just didn't have it. She'd been in terrible pain that first week and had been forced to stay home on ghastly pain pills that had made her weep incessantly. Her pay had been docked, plus her doctor bills were astronomical.

This she tried to explain to the three menacing strangers in faded jeans and black T-shirts who cornered her outside her apartment, only an hour after Dr. Springer had removed her cast.

"Lady, we want three thousand dollars," their leader—a fierce, bearded type—told her, blowing smoke in her face. "And we want it *now*."

Terrified, Susan choked out, "Please, if you'll just give me more time—"

That's when the leader reached for his back pocket with heartstopping menace. "Lady, how would you like your brother's head on a platter?"

And all three of them began to close in on her, pushing her toward her apartment door.

Thank God for Rumor! At that critical moment, Susan's cat had come sailing out of the apartment window, distracting her unwelcome guests momentarily. Even as the hoodlums instinctively jumped back to escape the black thunderbolt, Susan raced off, Rumor flying along with her, springing up into her arms with a frightened *mrrrrrow*.

The thugs, yelling obscenities, were soon hot on her trail.

Susan was usually a fast runner, but that was before the chicken had broken her foot. Her right leg, unused for so many weeks, had practically atrophied, and within ten yards she was running with a definite—and agonizing—limp.

Thus, all she could think of as the ruffians continued to stalk her—aside from her terror and her certain vow to murder Jamie—was that her foot was killing her.

1

WITH A VAGUE SENSE of unease, Ben Adams watched the sunset emblazon the spectacular Dallas skyline.

He knew he should be in a splendid mood this Saturday evening, standing before a stark glass wall in his Turtle Creek penthouse, perched in the Dallas clouds. The sunset over the city was an awesome sight that rarely failed to move him. And Ben had just landed for his bank the financing of Southbridge Manor, a massive new development being planned south of the city. Only half an hour ago, Ben had shaken hands on the project with Charles Marshall of Marshall Development. Marshall was a relatively young man, he was innovative, and all of his residential projects had been masterfully planned communities that were instant, phenomenal successes.

It was a major coup for Reunion Bank to win the financing of the project, as Marshall had previously dealt with their biggest competitor. However, with shockwaves still being felt in the Texas banking community due to the oil industry downturn, many big banks were being taken over by the Federal Deposit Insurance Corporation and sold to out-of-state interests. Three months ago, when Charles Marshall had heard the rumor that the bank he was doing business with was about to go under, he'd become only too eager to transfer his business to a midsized, privately owned and stable institution like Reunion.

And Ben, as president of Reunion and an old friend of Charles, had been right there to do the persuading. The victory for him was enormous, both personally and professionally.

Then why was it the sunset appeared so tarnished tonight, the expensive Scotch he was sipping tasted so flat, the luxurious penthouse with panoramic glass view seemed so dull and empty?

Ben moved from the wall of glass to the adjacent fireplace with its cold alabaster mantel. On the mantel were perched four priceless Venetian Warriors, all eight inches tall, cast in bronze with silver detailing. Above them was a Picasso line drawing valued in six figures. Ben had never liked the rather dark, abstruse design, but the drawing had been a housewarming gift from his mother, and it did impress the customers Ben entertained.

He frowned, moving one of the warriors a fraction of an inch so that it was in perfect alignment with the others. Mrs. Ramirez must have moved the statue slightly when she dusted, he mused.

He supposed it was the being alone on a Saturday night that unsettled him a bit. It shouldn't—at his age, he was quite accustomed to a permanent state of bachelorhood.

But it had been something of a disappointment to have his plans for the evening curtailed. He'd expected a long negotiating session with Charles Marshall at Marshall's Highland Park mansion. He'd planned to take Charles and his wife out to dinner afterward. Yet Charles had greeted him with a cocktail and a handshake, promptly giving verbal approval to their basic terms. Then Charles's very young, very beautiful, very pregnant wife had come dashing into the study, telling Charles that they must leave at once to go buy a baby bed tonight. With a grin and an apology for cutting the evening short, Marshall had rushed off.

So Dallas's most successful young real estate developer was spending Saturday night buying the most expensive baby bed the posh Galleria had to offer, and Ben Adams was alone nursing his Scotch.

He sauntered over to the bar and poured himself another drink. What was it he had felt at Charles Marshall's house? A stab of envy? A hint of his own mortality? He and Charles had much in common. Both were in their late thirties, both were from old, monied Dallas families, and both were highly successful in their fields. Charles was a high-charged, energetic man who was all business, but he'd lit up like a fifteen-year-old kid when his wife, Jessica, had burst in. Suddenly, the fact that he was about to enter into the most ambitious development of his entire career had mattered not at all to Charles Marshall.

Ben sat down on the couch, stared at the glass wall before him and loosened his tie. Had he known his business would be concluded this early, he would have made other plans for the evening. He was considered one of the city's most eligible bachelors, his name regularly mentioned in the society columns. He dated regularly, but he'd never found the woman who seemed just right for him. He knew he'd been pursued more than once because of his wealth or status. And, he had to concede ruefully, he expected a lot from a woman. He'd decided long ago that if he ever did choose a wife, she would have to be the perfect mate. Ben was a perfectionist, both in his personal and in his professional life. He was very orderly and sophisticated, and he liked his women elegant and well-organized, too.

And perfect. Because of his highly exacting standards, he had never dated a woman for more than a few months. This one would be too abrasive, that one too meek, this one too irresponsible, that one too rigid, this one too jealous or possessive, that one a flirt or tease.

And because of these same standards, here he was, alone on a Saturday night. Remembering his visit to the Marshall house, he had to acknowledge that part of what he was feeling now was envy. Envy, because it looked to him like Charles Marshall had landed the perfect mate—Jessica was beautiful, intelligent, charming and unpretentious. She obviously doted on Charles.

And she was having his baby. There, most of all, Ben found himself feeling jealous of Charles and Jessica's happiness. Ben had recently turned thirty-nine, and he was beginning to realize that if he ever wanted a family of his own—and he *did* want a family of his own—then he'd best get started soon, or he'd end up sixty-five years old with a teenaged son out wrecking his Jaguar.

The phone interrupted Ben's musings, and he decided to let his answering machine screen the call. After the requisite, "Hi, it's Ben Adams, and I can't come to the phone right now..." he heard a sultry voice croon, "Ben, darling, it's Margo. If you're there now, would you please pick up the phone? I was wondering if you'd like to join me for a little supper and champagne. I'm so lonely for you, Ben...."

He almost grabbed the lure, then stopped himself. Margo Pershing was a beautiful twenty-six-year-old who'd been trying unsuccessfully to seduce him for the past four weeks. He was doubtless a fool not to hop between the sheets with the very willing beauty, but something about the girl bothered him.

He didn't like the way she parted her hair, he acknowledged now. It was a silly basis on which to reject her, yet it bothered him, nevertheless. Margo parted her hair on the left, yet it was always curling in the opposite direction. It was, Ben decided, a subtle indication of a very strong-willed nature. Heaven help him if Margo ever really got her hooks into him.

He groaned self-deprecatingly. If he didn't adjust his ridiculous standards soon, he'd find no mate at all—perfect or not. Twenty years from now, he'd still be sitting here, sipping Scotch that would taste ten times as insipid by then. He'd still be all alone, and he'd still feel sorry for himself.

Then, almost as if it were destiny, the doorbell rang.

Scowling, Ben got up. Since his housekeeper was gone for the weekend, he'd have to greet the caller himself. He crossed the room and opened the door, only to stare, flabbergasted, at the most beautiful woman he'd ever seen in his life. Dark-haired, dark-eyed, with smooth honey-hued skin, a wide face, a sensuously full mouth and a firm chin with a small, sexy cleft—mid-to-late-twenties, he quickly assessed. And perfectly shaped. Her loveliness was mesmerizing.

But where the product was perfect, the packaging was all wrong. The girl wore very tight, very faded jeans, and a T-shirt that read, Elvis Lives, although it was a bit hard to read the message behind the black cat she carried in her arms—a sleek, menacing beast with hostile green eyes.

The girl was trembling, Ben noted, and she looked frightened, in pain. After drawing a quick, unsteady breath, she said awkwardly, "Hello. You must be Ben."

"Hello," he replied. "I suppose I must be."

Wincing as she tottered on her feet, she added, "I don't mean to be rude, Ben, but could you please take Rumor? I think I'm going to collapse."

"Rumor?" Ben stammered.

But the girl was already dumping her black cat in his arms, whereupon the green-eyed monster hissed in protest and dug his claws viciously into Ben's gray flannel, Brooks Brothers suit. Before Ben could even react, the girl limped painfully into his penthouse and collapsed, white-faced, on his couch. Grimacing as she pulled off a tennis shoe, she added lamely, "I don't suppose you could scare up a pan of hot water, could you, Ben? My foot is *killing* me."

Ben was too stunned to speak, even when Rumor's claws dug all the way through his jacket and shirt to painfully contact the flesh of his forearm.

He had never seen this woman before in his life.

2

SHE'D REMEMBERED about Ben Adams soon after she clambered onto the southbound bus. The driver glanced askance at Rumor, then shrugged at Susan's pleading look and accepted her money. The door closed with a welcomed *whoosh*.

The thugs just missed the bus. Susan caught a glimpse of them through the window—they were waving their fists and chasing a black trail of exhaust. She nodded to herself with grim satisfaction and hobbled down the aisle, hoping they would gag—and then some.

She settled into a vacant seat, stroked Rumor to calm him down and caught her breath with an effort. Her foot was throbbing, her heart pounding. Damn it, Jamie had gone too far this time—putting her very life in danger. What on earth was she going to do?

It was not until the bus was curving down lush Turtle Creek Boulevard, the prestigious street where Ben Adams lived, that the memory came to her.

It was an old memory, a little-girl's memory, of the most painful letter a child had ever received. Nineteen years ago, just days after she and Jamie had been informed that their father was killed in Vietnam, their dad's last letter had arrived, with the closing words: "If something should ever happen to me and you kids need anything, just get in touch with Ben Adams. He's one of the finest young men I've ever known, and I know he'll help you."

Ironic words, coming from the very grave of a man who had loved his children so dearly. Several months later, Ben Adams had come to visit them at Aunt Florence's home here in Dallas. He'd just returned from his own tour of duty in Vietnam. But Ben Adams had come home on his own two feet, not in a casket.

To Susan, only eight years old at the time, Ben had looked too haunted, too handsome, too thin, and much too young. She remembered asking him bluntly how old he was, and he'd replied, "Twenty." She remembered telling him solemnly that her father had been thirty-six when he had been killed. She remembered him turning away suddenly, avoiding her eyes....

Ben had stayed for only a few minutes, visiting with Susan, her little brother, Jamie, and Aunt Florence, who had just become the children's legal guardian. Their mother had died eighteen months earlier under scandalous circumstances, a few weeks before their father had returned home after his first tour in Vietnam. Susan had often reflected that it was surely her father's grief and anguish regarding their mother's death that had spurred him to enlist in the army for a second term. And, at the time, another term in the army meant another tour of Vietnam.

Her father's second tour had been the death of him.

"If there's anything I can do," Ben had said lamely, that day he came.

What was there to do? Their very lives had been shattered.

And after that one awkward visit, Ben Adams had never come back.

Oh, for many years thereafter, Susan and Jamie had received cards from Ben on each birthday and Christmas, a generous check enclosed each time. For a while, his correspondence had come from Cambridge, Massachusetts, and Susan remembered him mentioning in one of his brief notes that he was studying at Harvard Business School. Later, his return address shifted back to Dallas. Then, when Susan and Jamie became adults, the cards and checks abruptly stopped.

But Susan had never forgotten the posh Turtle Creek address embossed on Ben's stationery, the address to which she had efficiently sent many thank-you notes over the years. She had even driven by his high rise a few times and wondered what he was like now. Half his lifetime had passed since she'd seen him—and two-thirds of her own!

Occasionally Susan had read about Ben's career, his social activities, in the society columns. If the local gossips were correct, he'd become quite the urbane sophisticate, quite the man about town.

So why go see him now? she asked herself bitterly. If he'd truly cared about her and Jamie, he would have come to see them many times, not just during that one token visit.

Yet the bus was heading straight for his address, almost as if it were destiny, and Ben Adams was the only person Susan knew who lived in this part of town. Of course, he might have moved by now, or he might not be home. But if he was there, perhaps she could impose on him for a few hours. She desperately needed a place to crash until it was safe for her to return to her apartment. And there was her father's promise, after all—his last, sacred promise—that Ben Adams would help them.

Perhaps Ben could even do something about Jamie, too, she reflected. At twenty-four, her brother was getting totally out of hand, especially his gambling. Susan was twenty-seven herself now, and thanks to Jamie, she was still living a Bohemian life-style. She had bankrupted her retirement fund at work and had spent every spare dime she could muster rescuing her brother from his various scrapes. At this very moment, she was on the run from hoodlums—and her foot was killing her.

She was getting too old for this nonsense!

Ben Adams would be in his late thirties now, she mused. Maybe he could exert a stabilizing influence on her brother. She had often theorized that a big part of Jamie's problem was the lack of a strong male role model. He'd only been five when their father had been killed. And Aunt Florence had indulged him shamelessly all his life.

Then she frowned. She wondered if she could bring herself to tell Ben about Jamie's problems. For despite all her brother's faults, familial loyalty and pride ran deep between the two siblings—losing both parents had drawn them close at a very early age. And Susan had already discovered that men were not inclined to be supportive regarding Jamie's plight. Indeed, two men she had dated in the past, upon finding out about Jamie, had pretty much said, "Hey, it's him or me." As far as Susan was concerned, there hadn't been a contest either time. And unfortunately she had no real reason to believe that Ben Adams would be any more sympathetic regarding Jamie's troubles than these other men had been.

The bus was now pulling to a halt just half a block away from Ben's high rise, and across from Susan, a middle-aged woman in maid's uniform stood and moved toward the exit. After a moment's hesitation, Susan struggled painfully to her feet with Rumor and followed the woman toward the front of the bus.

They alighted on a shady expanse of the street just a few hundred yards from Ben's building. The bus lumbered off, and the other woman tossed Susan a bemused glance before starting off across the street. Susan hobbled ahead with Rumor in her arms, slowly ascending a slight rise. To her left meandered lovely Turtle Creek, with its lush flowers and verdant jogging trails. But the serenity of the treed setting failed to calm her nerves. She felt another twinge of indecision as she approached the elegant high rise, with its canopied front, impeccable landscaping and the gleaming pool off to one side. Then she squared her shoulders and limped on toward the entrance.

The doorman tossed her a quizzical glance as she approached, shifting his weight to effectively bar her entrance. "May I help you, miss?"

Susan felt a sharp prickle of irritation. "I'm here to see Ben Adams in 22 A."

The man looked taken aback. "Are you expected, miss?"

"Of course," Susan said, sidestepping him, pushing open the door herself and limping inside with as much dignity as she could muster.

The lobby was lined with elegant, trendy shops, but Susan hardly gave them a glance as she made a beeline for the elevator. She breathed a sigh of relief going up in the car, thankful that she and Rumor were the only ones inside. Yet when she emerged on the twenty-second floor and stood outside Ben's imposing double doors, she knew yet another moment of hesitation. Was she really going to crash in on the poor man like this? With Rumor in her arms?

. Then Susan winced as a sharp pain shot up her leg, and Rumor wailed in a combination of hunger and commiseration. She sighed. There was no quick cure for any of these ailments. Her foot was killing her and the cat had to be fed.

She rang Ben's doorbell.

MOMENTS LATER, Ben Adams continued to stare mystified at the woman who had just boldly walked into his penthouse, thrust a mangy cat into his arms and sprawled herself on his couch. Then the cat ended the charged moment by bolting out of Ben's arms and joining his mistress on the sofa, whereupon he began exercising his claws on the expensive designer fabric.

"Do you mind?" Ben asked the girl stiffly, nodding toward the cat.

"Oh, good grief!" the girl said, obviously flustered. "Rumor—bad cat!"

With an indignant *mrrrrrow*, Rumor sprang off the couch and went over to park himself on his haunches against the glass wall, eyeing both humans with ill-disguised contempt.

"That's better," Ben muttered, as he at last gathered the presence of mind to turn and shut the door. Then, once more, he stared flabbergasted at the girl sitting on his couch.

Susan gave him a supplicating gesture and forced a thin smile. All at once, she felt unbearably awkward, especially with Ben Adams staring at her so perplexedly. "Look, I'm really sorry to burst in on you this way, Ben," she began lamely. "I wouldn't have come at all, except that the only bus I could catch came straight by your place, and you're the only person I know who lives in this part of town."

"Oh?" Ben queried. Despite himself, he fought a smile. The girl looked so earnest—and so lost. "I suppose that explains everything, then."

"Well, Rumor and I did have to leave my apartment in something of a hurry," she muttered.

"Rumor?"

"My cat."

"Ah, yes, your cat. If you don't mind my asking, why do you call him—"

"Because he always streaks in and out—"

"Like a rumor?" Ben supplied.

"Right."

"And I suppose no one knows where he came from, either?"

She smiled. "Right again."

Shaking his head, Ben came over to join her on the couch. Susan watched him settle his weight into the opposite end, and her heart quickened its tempo. When she'd seen Ben Adams before, he'd been a thin, lanky, rather self-conscious boy. But now, the Ben Adams sitting all too near her was very much a man—tall, solid and intimidating.

Especially when he raised an eyebrow at her, as he did now. "Would you mind explaining something to me?" he asked mildly, looking her over in an equally unsettling way.

"I'll try," Susan replied tremulously.

"Who are you?" he asked, with an exasperated gesture. "And how did you know who I am, much less where I live?"

"Oh! Sorry." She blushed. "Actually, I—I'm Susan Nowotny."

Ben paled beneath his tan, leaning toward her tensely. He was suddenly hit by painful memories, a powerful wave of guilt. "You don't mean—don't tell me you're Jim Nowotny's daughter?"

She nodded solemnly.

He shook his head, looking very taken aback. "Well, I'll be damned—Susan Nowotny. You've changed."

"So have you," she replied, taking in his chiseled, slightly angular face, the dark hair now tinged with gray at the temples. "You've put on some weight, which looks good on you. And you've grayed a bit. You look rather distinguished."

"Don't put me out to pasture yet," he put in rather grumpily.

She smiled. "Oh, I'd say you still look very much in your prime."

An awkward silence settled between them, then Ben cleared his throat and repeated, "Well, Susan Nowotny. You know, I've often wondered about you and your brother, er—"

"Jamie."

"Ah, yes, Jamie. I really have thought about you both a lot over the years."

Susan automatically tilted her chin. "Have you?"

"Of course."

They stared at each other for another tense moment, then Susan glanced across the room, her expression horrified as she spotted Rumor lasciviously eyeing a potted plant. She bolted to her feet, scolding, "Rumor, no! Bad cat!"

She started after the cat, then screamed in pain as her foot gave out beneath her.

And with a total lack of dignity, she fell smack into Ben Adams's lap.

It was an electrifying moment for both, as Ben caught Susan and held her smartly to him, his bright blue eyes boring down into her bewildered brown ones. Her heart slammed in her chest at his arousing nearness—the hard male arms holding her, the enticing scent of his cologne. Lord, she hadn't remembered Ben Adams as being this sexy. . . .

Of course, at eight years of age, one didn't quite think in terms of sexy. Yet staring at Ben Adams eyeball-to-eyeball now gave Susan a strange, sinking feeling in the pit of her stomach. She noted with wonder that there was not a flaw anywhere on his classically handsome face—the deep-set eyes, straight nose and a mouth with just enough sensual fullness to break quite a few feminine hearts.

And to land right in his lap like a bumbling fool! With him so elegantly dressed and her in her Saturday castoffs. She was making a great start of things!

"You were saying?" he now inquired with a touch of wry humor.

"It was Rumor," she managed breathlessly. "He was eyeing your—er—fern—"

"Dracaena," he amended.

"Well, whatever. I think he was about to eat it."

Ben chuckled. "I suspect your cat is merely hungry. And didn't you say you wanted to soak your foot?"

Before Susan could even react, Ben stood, still holding her in his arms. Her cheeks flamed as he started off with her, his stride long and assured. "Please, Ben, you don't have to carry me!"

"Oh? I'd say that was a pretty dismal demonstration of walking that you gave just now." He was already heading through the dining room toward what she assumed was the kitchen. "Come along, Rumor," he called over her shoulder.

And to Susan's complete surprise, Rumor sprang right into step behind them.

Inside the largest, most lavishly appointed kitchen Susan had ever seen in her life, Ben placed her on a padded Breuer chair, then brought her a panful of warm water. While Susan pulled off her sock and soaked her foot in the comforting warmth, Ben took a piece of beefsteak from the refrigerator, then began chopping it up for Rumor, who was practically climbing Ben's pant leg in shameless anticipation.

"Oh, please," Susan protested from her chair, mentally wincing as she spotted messy tufts of black fur on Ben's perfectly creased gray trouser cuff, "I can't let you feed my cat steak."

At the counter, Ben pivoted to frown at her. "Doesn't he like steak?"

"Oh, of course he does. But I mean, the expense—"

Ben shrugged as he leaned over to give Rumor the saucer full of meat. The cat attacked the steak with unmitigated gluttony. "I don't have any cat food," Ben explained as he rinsed off and dried his hands. He strode over to Susan's side, pulled out a chair and sat down across from her. "How's the foot?"

She smiled. "Much better. The water feels great."

He nodded. "Well, Susan Nowotny, care to tell me how you landed in your current predicament? You did say you had to leave your apartment in something of a hurry."

Susan sighed. She was beginning to feel ridiculous. "Well . . . Actually, I've always had a penchant for the dramatic."

Ben chuckled, then raised that intimidating eyebrow again. "Somehow, I think there's a little more to it than that. Why don't you tell me how you ended up on the lam, as well as on the lame?"

She ran a hand through her short curly hair, took a deep breath, then met Ben's gently probing gaze. "Really, Ben, it's a long story."

"Then why don't you start at the beginning?"

"You don't want to hear this."

"Believe me, I do."

Susan sighed, realizing she was trapped. "Well, it all began when the chicken broke my foot..."

LIKE THE OTHERS, Ben laughed at first. Susan told him about Aunt Florence's gift of the baking hen, about Jamie's slovenly attempt at housekeeping and about how the chicken had subsequently broken her foot. His responses ranged from shock to outrage to concern.

But when Susan got to today's harrowing episode, she found herself freezing up. She couldn't bring herself to tell Ben about Jamie's gambling.

She wasn't sure what held her back. Ben was polite—a sympathetic listener.

Maybe it was pride, not just familial, but personal. By now, Susan was very aware that everything about Ben Adams's world was perfect—his home, his dress, even his fingernails. In fact, staring at Ben's beautifully manicured hands, Susan found herself hiding her own nails—chipped from washing dishes—as they spoke. How could she explain to this man, whose whole universe had not a hair out of place, that her life, and Jamie's, were tottering on the brink of ruin due to her brother's gambling? Ben Adams probably had apoplexy if an ashtray got overturned—he'd clearly be appalled if he learned about Jamie. And why should he care about her problems, anyway? she asked herself with some bitterness. After all, this man had never given her any real indication that he wanted a continuing relationship with her or her brother. She was beginning to feel very foolish regarding the impulse that had brought her crashing in on him in the first place.

"So you had your cast removed today," he was now remarking. "And then what happened? What made you start running, Susan?"

She bit her lip. Maybe she could tell the truth, yet not really tell the truth. Minimize things, then get out of here quickly and gracefully. "Well, Ben, when I got home today—you see, my brother has fallen in with a rather loose crowd. Some of Jamie's friends were there, and they sort of—you know, began hassling me and—"

Now Ben was scowling, the very picture of outraged male chivalry. "You need say no more, Susan. I can't believe your brother would let you be subjected to such a threat."

"Oh, Jamie had nothing to do with this. I mean, he wasn't even there, and—"

"Still, he should watch who he associates himself with, for your sake," Ben put in sternly.

No lie, Susan thought ruefully. To Ben, she said casually, "Oh, it wasn't—that terrible—"

"Then why did you run?"

Susan didn't have an answer for that.

"And why don't you have a place of your own?" Ben continued.

Susan felt a flush of embarrassment creep up her neck. "Jamie and I share an apartment for—well—for economic reasons, and really, we're the only family either of us has left now." She cleared her throat and glanced awkwardly at the cat, who had devoured the meat and was nonchalantly licking his paws and washing his face.

"I see," Ben was saying with a deep frown. "You need your own apartment, Susan. I'll help you."

"Oh, no," she protested. "I wouldn't dream of—"

Ben reached out and took her hand, and despite herself, Susan was rendered speechless. His warm, firm touch was so compelling, especially when his bright blue, deep-set eyes locked with hers and held her captive.

"Look, Susan," Ben said, "I've felt guilty as hell that I haven't done more for you and Jamie over the years. Your father—" he paused to clear a strangely raspy throat "—Jim was the best friend I ever had when I went to Nam. I was just a kid, a green pilot, and more than once, Jim's wisdom saved my life. Now the least I can do for you is to help you find a respectable place to live."

Before Susan could reply, Ben had gotten up and gone over to a cabinet. He pulled out a bottle of brandy and two glasses, half filling the two snifters. "Here," he said as he returned a moment later, handing her a drink.

"For medicinal purposes?" she asked.

"Of course," he concurred, sitting down across from her again. Taking a sip, he went on thoughtfully, "Susan, I want you to stay here until we find you a place of your own."

"Ben, I wouldn't dream—"

"Oh, yes you will. I'll not leave you at the mercy of your brother's lecherous friends—you with a lame foot, no less. Now drink your brandy, then I'll see about getting us some dinner."

Yet Susan was biting her lip, staring at her lap. "No, Ben. I can't. Look, I'm really feeling foolish that I've imposed on you. I should leave."

"But why? You came here, didn't you? Why do so if you were planning to rush right off again?"

Susan sighed heavily, setting her drink down on the table. "To tell you the truth, Ben, I wouldn't have come at all, except for my dad's last letter—"

"Letter? What letter?" Suddenly Ben was all attention, sitting ramrod straight in his chair, his eyes riveted on Susan.

Susan felt her throat tightening painfully. "It came a few days after we were notified of—of his death. He said if ever we needed anything, to go see Ben Adams."

"Oh, Susan," he said with a groan. "Poor babe. Bless your heart."

But Susan wasn't ready to hear Ben's words of sympathy. Abruptly she got to her feet, almost tipping over the pot of water. Distractedly wiping her foot on a nearby kitchen rug, she began to pace unsteadily, and her next words to Ben burst forth with surprising bitterness. "But you never cared about us, did you, Ben? That's the real reason I'm wondering what the heck I'm doing here. I mean, you sent us cards on Christmas and our birthdays, along with such generous checks. But you never came to see us—you were never there for us. What were we to you, anyway? Just a couple of kids I'm sure you just wanted to forget."

"Susan, you don't understand," Ben said, gesturing his own frustration as he got to his feet. "I did care. I cared—too much, perhaps."

Susan paused, staring at Ben intently, feeling confused by the turmoil she spotted in his eyes. Then she winced, tottering and grasping the edge of the nearby counter as her foot threatened to give out again.

Ben rushed to her side and took her arm. "Susan, please, quit pacing and come sit down. It makes me wince just to watch you limp around."

She nodded, in too much pain to argue as he led her back to her chair. Her foot and leg were throbbing horribly, and she was beginning to feel quite foolish regarding her emotional outburst.

"Put your foot back in the water," Ben directed as he settled her into her chair. As she complied, he added worriedly, "Maybe I'd better call a doctor."

Susan managed a pained smile. "You forget—I've already seen a doctor today. He pronounced my fracture completely healed. Only he wasn't expecting me to run the five-hundred-yard dash right after my cast was removed."

"I'm still not sure—"

"Ben, I'll be fine. Please, quit worrying about me."

"Okay. If you promise me you'll stay off that foot."

"You've got a deal. My last few laps around this room have made a believer out of me."

After he'd taken his seat, Susan braved another lame smile. "Look, Ben, I'm sorry. I had no right to lash out at you just now. I guess the pain of losing Dad is still there inside me, and sometimes it spills back to the surface. It has nothing to do with you, not really." Before Ben could comment, she continued with a telltale flutter in her voice, "And I suppose I came here today out of curiosity as well as for any other reason."

"Curiosity?"

She glanced away and muttered, "You made quite an impression on me when I was eight."

"Oh, did I?"

"You did." Catching his amused expression, she continued, "You had a haunted look—sort of like the heroes in the gothic novels I was reading at the time."

Ben chuckled. "Gothic novels? Isn't that somewhat precocious for an eight-year-old?"

Susan shrugged. "I always was a voracious reader. And gothic romances were all Aunt Florence kept in the house."

He chuckled. Then abruptly, his expression became serious, his eyes pensive. "Susan . . ."

"Yes?"

"I just want you to know that I did want to see you and Jamie again over the years. I wanted it quite badly."

"But?"

He sighed heavily. "We'll talk about it later on, I promise. But for now—Sue, please don't run off, not after all this time.

I really do want to become reacquainted with you. Won't you stay and have dinner with me?"

She eyed him quizzically. "What about you? It's Saturday night and you must have plans."

He shook his head. "Only a business meeting that got concluded early." He reached out and touched her hand. "Please stay?"

The warmth of Ben's hand on hers tipped the scale, convincing her that he really was being sincere, not just polite. She nodded. "Okay, I'd like that. But just for dinner."

"Fine." Ben was smiling as he stood and walked over to the kitchen phone. "I'll just order a few things from the market." He punched out a number, then winked at her. "You know, I'm glad you're here, Susan Nowotny."

"I'm glad I'm here, too," she whispered back.

3

WITHIN HALF AN HOUR, a boy from Simon David market appeared with the items Ben had ordered—wine and ingredients for dinner, as well as cat food, cat litter and disposable litter boxes. Though Susan protested, Ben insisted on cooking dinner for her. After much persuasion, he did let her help, and they fell into a companionable silence as she chopped vegetables at the table and he dipped steak in dry mustard and marinated it in brandy.

As Ben worked, his eyes kept straying to Susan. She'd stunned him when she'd burst in on him earlier, after all these years. When he'd last seen her, she'd been a child—thin, lost and vulnerable. Now she was all grown up, yet she'd managed to retain the innocent vulnerability that was just as endearing today as it had been almost twenty years ago.

More endearing, in fact. He groaned mentally as he recalled the moment when she'd fallen into his lap. She'd felt damn good there, jeans and all. Susan had matured well, he realized. She was now very beautiful, even exotic looking, with those large dark eyes and that intriguing little cleft in her chin.

Steady boy, he cautioned himself. He'd best remember who this girl was. Again Ben was slammed by guilt—the guilt he'd felt over Jim Nowotny's death and that had haunted him for so long. That same remorse made him feel very protective toward Susan now, and made him resolve to help her solve her problems. But he also knew the last thing he needed to do was to start thinking romantically about his old friend's daughter.

He scowled. Susan's situation did bother him. He realized she must have had a very compelling reason to start running today and seek out his help—and all his instincts told him her motivation had to do with much more than the passes supposedly made by her brother's friends. He strongly suspected she wasn't telling him the entire truth—another reason to keep things from becoming too heavy between them.

He glanced over at her again, and when she smiled back at him shyly, he reeled at the unexpected wave of tender protectiveness her lovely smile brought rushing. He tore his gaze away from hers and threw the steak into the frying pan.

When everything was almost ready, Susan excused herself to go wash up. A few moments later, after setting everything out in the dining room, Ben found her in the living room standing near the glass wall, gazing out at the view. By now, night had fallen, and a thousand lights had winked to life in the dramatic city skyline.

"Everything's ready, Sue," he told her as he approached.

She didn't turn, but stood staring out as if mesmerized. "Oh, Ben, the view is breathtaking!" she exclaimed in a reverent voice. "You must love living here!"

Observing her, Ben fought an almost overwhelming desire to go place his hands on her shoulders. Instead, he cleared his throat and repeated, "Dinner's ready."

She turned to him and smiled. "Oh, sorry. I forgot that you see this every day. It can't mean the same thing to you, can it?"

Smiling back, Ben turned to stare out at the skyline and realized with an alarming sense of awe that the view no longer appeared tarnished, not with Susan here.

Susan was quite impressed by the dinner Ben had prepared—steak Diane, baked potatoes and a marvelous Caesar salad he had whipped up with the efficiency of a master chef. As the two of them ate by candlelight and sampled a hearty red wine, she studied him sitting across from her, and found she felt much more comfortable with him now. Earlier he'd set a more casual tone by removing his jacket and tie, by rolling up his sleeves and unbuttoning the top button on his shirt. A dark lock had even come loose from his immaculately groomed hair, and now fell across his forehead, lending him a startling sensuality. He seemed a little more human now—and so much more appealing!

At first they made small talk about the food, then Ben questioned Susan regarding the past nineteen years. She filled him in on her life—how she'd graduated from Arlington State with a degree in computer science, how she'd been employed at Computronics for the past six years and had worked herself up from programmer to systems analyst.

"So you're a systems analyst at Computronics. I'm impressed," Ben said when she finished. "As a matter of fact, I'm a good friend of George Ellington, who also works there."

"Oh, you know Mr. Ellington?" Susan asked, rather taken aback. "He's head of personnel—the person who hired me, in fact."

Ben nodded, then added thoughtfully, "You know, Sue, we always need good computer people at the bank, where I work. Would you be interested in—"

"Thanks, Ben, but I'm really quite happy with my job," she put in stiffly.

He smiled. "So—tell me about Jamie, then."

"What about him?" Susan asked guardedly.

"What's he doing these days? Let's see, he'd be about twenty—um—"

"Four," Susan finished. "Well, after high school, Jamie was in the Army for a while." She paused, unwilling to tell Ben that Jamie had been dishonorably discharged for stealing a watch from the Post Exchange to pay off his gambling markers. "And now, he's working as a salesman at a sporting goods store."

"I see."

"What about you, Ben?" Susan asked, eager to change the subject. "What have you been doing all these years?"

"Well, after I got out of the Army, I was supposed to go to Cornell, to the School of Hotel Management. You see, my family owns a chain of hotels, and of course Dad wanted me to follow in his footsteps." He fingered his wineglass thoughtfully. "But Vietnam—did something to me."

"If you don't mind my asking, Ben, how did you end up in the Army, anyway? I mean, couldn't you have become exempted from service if you were planning to go on to college?"

He nodded, smiling at her ironically. "If you want to know the truth—and this sounds crazy in retrospect—I enlisted. I wanted to go to flight school, and I guess I lucked out, because at the time, the Army was desperate for helicopter pilots." He sighed, then continued, "And I suppose that at eighteen, I was caught up in the throes of severe rebellion against the future my parents had so neatly programmed for me."

"So you enlisted and got sent to Vietnam. And when you came home?"

He grinned self-deprecatingly. "When I got back, I rebelled even further by going to Harvard Business School instead of Cornell."

Susan chuckled.

"I know—I really made a strong statement, didn't I? Anyway, after getting my MBA, I returned to Dallas and got a job in banking, gradually working myself up to my present level."

"Which is president of Reunion Bank," Susan put in.

He raised an eyebrow at that. "You know?"

She shrugged. "Your name is mentioned in the newspapers a lot." Cutting her steak, she continued, "Well, I must say that I'm impressed, too—especially since you've achieved all your success on your own."

He shook his head as he set down his fork. "I wish I could say that is true, but I'm afraid your assessment of me is entirely too noble. The fact that I was an Adams of *the* Dallas Adamses definitely boosted my career. This is a class-conscious town, and from the moment I started working in the executive training program at a large downtown bank, I was hobnobbing with people I'd known all my life—friends of my parents."

"I see. So how do you and your parents get along today?"

"Oh—we're quite civil with each other." He shrugged. "We never have been exceptionally close. Actually, they're in Europe on an extended tour right now."

"At least you have them," Susan muttered.

Hearing the bitterness in her remark, Ben glanced at her intently, and for a moment they shared an anguished look. "I know, dear. That must have been so rough on you and Jamie—growing up without both your parents."

"We had Aunt Florence," Susan put in. "She always meant well—even if she was rather neurotic in raising us."

"Ah, yes, Aunt Florence and her gothic novels," Ben said with a kindly smile. He gestured at the table. "Well, Sue, shall I whip up some dessert? What would you say of crepes suzette, for instance?"

"Oh, no, I'm stuffed. The dinner was wonderful."

"So was the company," he replied. An awkward silence fell between them. "Coffee, then?" he suggested.

Folding her napkin, Susan shook her head. "Really, Ben, I must be going. It's been great, but Rumor and I have imposed on you long enough."

"Nonsense. I thought we had it settled that you're staying here for a day or two until we can find you a place of your own."

"You had it settled. I have to get back to my apartment."

He scowled. "And what if your brother's friends are still there?"

"I'm sure that by now, they've departed for greener pastures."

"And if they haven't?"

Susan sighed. "Ben, this is all academic. If they're still there, I'll cross that bridge when I come to it."

Ben adamantly shook his head. "Susan, that's no solution. I insist that you stay. Look, I have plenty of room, and I'm sure you'd enjoy the facilities here, the pool and sauna—"

Yet Susan was already standing. "Ben, thanks for everything, but I really do have to go."

Now he was standing, too. "Then at least let me drive you home."

"Thanks, but I'm sure I can get a taxi or—"

He shook a finger at her. "No, Susan. I must insist. It's dark outside, and there's no way I'm letting you go back to that apartment unless I can first check it out to make sure you'll be safe."

Susan sighed, realizing that Ben wasn't going to give on this point. And she did feel relieved to know that she wouldn't have to face her apartment alone. "Okay then. That's kind of you."

"It's my pleasure."

After helping Ben straighten up the kitchen, Susan gathered Rumor, who had been sleeping under the coffee table, while Ben grabbed his jacket and tie. They took the elevator down to the parking garage and climbed into his green Jaguar XJ6. Staring at the extravagant instrument panel as she settled herself into the low-slung leather seat, Susan had to admit to herself that traveling in Ben's luxurious sports car sure beat the heck out of the bus.

As they left the garage, he placed a tape in the deck. The collection of operatic themes surging from the sound system did marvelous things for her. But Ben's presence excited her even more, she had to admit. He just looked so handsome, male and solid sitting next to her in the darkness, his shoulders so broad and straight, his trousers pulling at his long muscular legs. Of course he wasn't really her type, she mused; she wasn't generally attracted to ultra-sophisticated, high-charged men. Indeed, after viewing his glitzy, impeccable world, she hated the thought of his seeing her shabby little apartment.

Nevertheless, Ben had been very kind and helpful toward her, for reasons she wasn't really sure of. But she was glad she'd made a stand about not staying over at his penthouse—she'd already decided it would be best not to become too deeply involved with him. The Ben Adams she'd met today was no longer the haunted shell of a boy she'd known previously; indeed, she had a strong feeling that this urbane banker would not respond sympathetically to her messed-up life.

Susan directed Ben to the rather run-down apartment complex off Mockingbird Lane where she and Jamie lived. He parked his car under a streetlight and helped her get out of the car with her cat. No one was in sight as they approached her place. But Susan got a sick feeling in the pit of her stomach as she noticed the door ahead of them was wide open.

Ben took her arm, restraining her. "Wait right here, Sue. I'm going in first."

She nodded, standing back as Ben proceeded inside. At once, yellow light spilled from the doorway. "My God!" she heard him exclaim.

Susan rushed inside, dropping Rumor, and saw what Ben was so shocked about. The apartment had been ransacked. Chairs and bookshelves had been overturned, drawers pulled out and their contents scattered. Cushions had been yanked off the chairs, a lamp overturned onto the couch, its shade askew. Susan realized that the thugs who had been chasing her had decided to look for money or valuables inside the apartment—with a vengeance. Of course they hadn't found anything. Jamie had hocked their TV and stereo long ago. Staring at the wholesale disaster Jamie had wreaked in their lives, Susan felt a momentary blinding anger toward her brother.

"Susan, what on earth—" Ben was saying, shaking his head as he turned to shut the door.

Susan gritted her teeth. "I just want you to know, Ben, that this isn't the way I usually keep house," she quipped, trying to cover her own humiliation and anger.

He still looked stunned. "Who could have done this?"

"I don't know—maybe Jamie's friends."

Ben's features whitened with anger. "My God, what kind of maniacs has your brother associated himself with? And what did they want from you earlier today? To think that they could have hurt you—"

"Look, Ben, I'm fine, and Jamie's friends are really harmless types—"

"Harmless types?" Ben's hand slashed the air. "How can you call this kind of violent and destructive behavior harmless?"

Susan bit her lip, feeling miserable in her attempt to cover up for Jamie. Lamely she said, "Well, maybe Jamie's friends had too much beer and trashed out the place a little."

"A little?" Shaking his head grimly, Ben strode toward the hallway. "Wait here a minute," he called over his shoulder.

"What are you doing?"

"Checking out the bedrooms," came his muted reply.

Susan waited tensely while Ben checked out the rest of the apartment. She didn't really expect him to find anyone there—certainly not Jamie, since her brother would doubtless be hiding out somewhere until things cooled down more.

Within a minute, Ben returned. "The bedrooms are also trashed," he informed her, "but there's no one around."

She watched him cross toward the desk. "Now what are you doing?"

"Calling the police, of course."

Alarmed, Susan hobbled to his side and grabbed the receiver from his hand. "No, Ben, please don't." As he frowned at her, she went on persuasively, "Look, whoever did this— well, they're gone now, and the place looks a lot worse than it really is. It's not like they slashed up the furniture or anything. Just go on home, Ben, and I'll get it all cleaned up in no time at all."

Ben looked incredulous, staring at Susan speechlessly for a moment. Then he began shaking his head almost violently. "No, Susan. After seeing this disaster, there's no way I'm letting you stay here alone." He pointed across the room. "Besides, they broke the lock on your door."

Biting her lip, Susan limped over to the door. Ben was right—the lock on the knob was shattered. She tried the inside safety bolt, feeling relieved when she discovered that it was still intact. "The night latch is still working," she called to Ben. "I'll be okay."

His reply was a short, derisive laugh. "That lock won't stop those maniacs if they really want to get back in. Pack a bag and you're coming home with me."

Turning and crossing back to Ben's side, Susan frowned at him as she balled her hands on her hips. "Now, wait just a minute—"

He shook a finger at her. "No, you wait. Anyone capable of doing this is also capable of—well, I don't even want to think of what they're capable of doing to you."

Susan sighed. She couldn't think of a rebuttal there.

In the meantime, he was picking up the phone again. "And I *am* calling the police, Susan. At the very least, I'm sure you've had some valuables stolen."

"No, Jamie and I didn't own anything valuable. Except—" Suddenly, Susan turned white. "Oh, no!"

Looking equally alarmed, Ben set down the receiver. "Sue, what is it?"

But Susan was already limping off toward the kitchen. "Mother's rings!"

By the time Ben caught up with her, Susan was kneeling on the kitchen floor, rifling through the contents of a drawer. Watching her sift through the various gadgets, Ben said, "If your mother's rings were in that drawer, I'm sure they're gone now. Another reason to call the police."

"I'm not looking for her rings here," Susan muttered as she rattled through the junk. "I'm looking for a screwdriver."

"Mind telling me what your mother's rings have to do with a screwdriver?"

"Sure. I need the screwdriver to loosen the air vent. That's where her rings are hidden."

"Women," Ben said, shaking his head. Glancing overhead, he asked, "Which air vent?"

"The one right here in the kitchen. Now if you'll be a doll and bring me a chair, Ben, I'll just unscrew—"

"Oh, no. There's no way I'm letting you stand on a chair and unscrew an air vent—not with your foot."

Susan stood with the screwdriver in her hand. "I wasn't planning to unscrew the air vent with my foot, Ben," she informed him teasingly.

"Nevertheless, I'll do it for you."

Standing on a chair, he unscrewed the vent cover and pulled it off—along with a good six inches of cobwebs. Scowling as he handed the cover to her, he asked, "Don't you think you should wash this?"

Susan shrugged as she took the filthy piece of metal. "Sure, why not? A trashed apartment and an immaculate vent cover. That makes sense."

As she worked at the sink, he asked, "Now, where are the rings?"

"Just feel up inside the vent—to the left. They're taped there."

"My God, you have a Machiavellian mind, Sue."

"I have to around here," she muttered under her breath.

"Bingo," Ben said seconds later. Hopping down from the chair he glanced at the wedding set. "Wow," he said appreciatively.

For a moment, both of them stared at the beautiful one-and-a-half-carat marquis diamond, nestled on bands generously dotted with smaller stones. Then Ben placed the rings in Susan's hands. "Dad spent a bundle on these," she explained, staring down at the glittering stones. "He wanted me to have them after Mom . . . Anyway, the rings survived the plane crash, even though my mother didn't."

"Your mother was killed in a plane crash?" Ben asked in a shocked voice.

"Yes—didn't Dad tell you?"

"Well, I knew that Jim was a widower, and that you kids were being raised by his sister back here in Dallas. But no, he never told me how his wife died. How tragic."

Susan expelled a painful sigh. "I'm afraid Mom's death wasn't just tragic—it was also quite scandalous."

He frowned. "In what way?"

Susan hesitated a moment before explaining. "Mom was secretary to the director of a large county hospital here. And while Dad was in Vietnam on his first tour, Mom's boss was indicted for embezzlement."

"Good Lord," Ben said, shaking his head. "You know, I think I remember reading something about that—"

"It was a real mess," Susan concurred. "Anyway, the state senate held hearings, and Mom was subpoenaed to testify. She and her boss were flying down to Austin in his private plane, when it crashed during a storm. They were both killed."

"God, Sue, how awful."

"Of course, the local gossip columns had a field day," she went on bitterly. "You know, 'Wife conspires with larcenous boss while husband risks life in Vietnam.' That sort of thing. And it was strongly hinted that my mom was in collusion with her boss—well, in more ways than one."

"Bless your heart, Sue. I can't tell you how sorry I am," Ben told her earnestly. "If it makes you feel any better, I find it impossible to believe that a mother of yours was involved in anything underhanded at all."

Susan smiled at Ben, feeling warmed by his sincerity. "You know, I always felt that way, too. I honestly believe my mom was just an innocent pawn. I only wish she'd gotten a chance to vindicate herself."

"And your father? How did he feel about the scandal and—and everything?"

"I'm not sure," Susan answered with a frown. "He never discussed it with Jamie or me. He was only home for a few months after Mom's death, then he reenlisted in the Army. Before we knew it, he was off to Vietnam on his second tour, and—well, you know the rest, don't you?"

Ben nodded, as Susan's words again brought to mind his painful guilt over her father's death.

Glancing off to hide a sudden tear, she added, "I have a hunch, though—"

"Yes?"

She swallowed hard. "I just don't think Dad believed in Mom's innocence."

Ben touched her arm gently. "Sue, I'm so sorry."

She shrugged. "It's not your fault."

"You've got to understand that Vietnam—" he told her quietly, "well, a lot of guys got dumped by their wives or girlfriends while they were over there. I guess it did something to us all."

Susan nodded, braving a smile at him. "I suppose you're right."

Letting his hand fall to his side, he cleared his throat. "So, what do you want to do with the rings?"

She extended the wedding set toward him. "If you don't mind, would you put them back where they were?"

He laughed shortly. "You've got to be kidding, Sue. After what just happened to your apartment? Look, I have a safe back at my penthouse—"

"Thanks, but that won't be necessary," she interrupted quickly. She realized that leaving the rings in Ben's safe would establish a tie to him, and right now, she didn't want to form any unnecessary ties to him. "The guys who trashed the place, didn't find the rings, did they? No one knows I keep them up there—not even Jamie. If he did, he'd—" All at once Susan realized she'd gone too far, and clamped her mouth shut.

But Ben had already picked up on her meaning, stepping closer and scowling down at her. "If he found them, Jamie would do what, Susan?"

"Never mind."

"Never mind?" he repeated impatiently. "It looks like you and I are going to have a long, serious talk. In fact—"

But before Ben could finish his sentence, a loud crash sounded from the living room. Both of them jumped at the noise, then Ben drew a finger to his mouth to warn Susan to be silent. Leaning over, he picked up a butcher knife, then straightened to face her. "Wait here," he ordered in a tense whisper.

"Ben, that's a butcher knife!" she whispered back, her eyes huge.

"No lie. I didn't think it was a sugar scoop, Sue. Now wait here while I find out what's going on in the living room."

Susan held her breath as Ben tiptoed out of the room with the knife. Seconds later, he returned, looking relieved as he set the knife on the counter. "It was only Rumor. He knocked the lamp off the couch."

"Oh, good. I'm glad it wasn't—"

"Right." Distractedly, Ben ran a hand through his hair. "Look, Susan, we've got to get you out of here." He took her mother's rings from her hand. "I'll replace these while you go pack a bag."

"But, Ben—"

"Please don't argue, Sue," he said as hopped back up on the chair. "It couldn't be more obvious that you're not safe here. And I'm not leaving without you."

That remark won a grudging smile from Susan as she handed Ben the vent cover and screwdriver. "You really want me to stay with you?"

"Didn't I just say that I'm not leaving without you?"

His vehemence gave her pause, especially as she stared up the hard masculine length of him. "Um, Ben, you wouldn't take advantage of a lame lady, would you?" she asked him with a crooked smile.

He winked down at her. "Of course not, Susan. I'll definitely wait until you're able-bodied."

She chuckled and waved him off. Suddenly she was tired of fighting him. And while she hated the thought of imposing on him, she found she really was frightened at the prospect of staying here alone. He was right, she realized. "Okay, Ben, you've got me convinced. I'll stay with you, but only for a day or two."

"Great," came his muffled reply.

Susan went off to her bedroom, gasping as she viewed the disaster there. Determinedly she grabbed a bag and began sifting through the havoc, packing a few necessities. Remembering Ben's mentioning the pool at his building, she included her bikini.

When she rejoined Ben in the living room a few moments later, he was setting down a plant he'd watered. "By the way, where has your brother been while all of this was going on?" he asked her.

She shrugged, realizing that Ben was becoming very suspicious—and with cause. "Oh, it's Saturday night. He always stays out late. You know how it is with young bachelors."

Ben didn't comment, frowning as he crossed over to take her bag.

She glanced at Rumor on the couch. "Um, Ben, what about—"

"You'll want to bring him with us, of course," Ben said forbearingly.

Susan bit her lip. "You don't mind?"

He raised an eyebrow at her. "Sue, no offense, but I wouldn't leave an alley cat here alone. Not even one called Rumor."

"Right."

As she picked Rumor up from the couch, Ben crossed to the desk and picked up the wilted Oriental bush. "We'll want to bring along this ming aralia, too."

"Oh, is that what that is?" Susan asked guiltily.

"Obviously it doesn't stand a chance here."

She stared at him lamely. "Sorry."

Susan avoided Ben's eye as they left the apartment together. Never before had she felt guilty of cruelty to plants. Then outside, she snapped her fingers and said, "Oh, I'll have to get my car."

He turned to her, astonished. "You have a car?"

"Well, yes. I have to get to work, you know."

"Then why didn't you take your car when you left today?"

Susan felt color rising in her face, and was grateful for the cover of darkness. Nothing got past this man, she realized. "Well, when I left today, I ran toward Mockingbird Lane, and the bus just happened to come along at that moment and—I just happened to board it."

"In other words, you were in such a hurry that you didn't even have time to go to your car." Abruptly Ben turned and stepped in front of her. "What did those guys try to do to you?" he asked angrily.

"Nothing, really—"

"Nothing, hell." Even in the darkness, she could tell that Ben's eyes were blazing, and the tension in his body and features was very intimidating. "They tried to rape you, didn't they, Susan? And why didn't you want me to call the police?"

"Please, Ben, it was nothing like that."

"Hah!"

He was forestalled from questioning her further as she sidestepped him and continued on toward her car. Cursing under his breath, he followed her.

But when they arrived in the parking lot, Susan uttered a cry of abject misery. All four of the tires on her car had been slashed. "Oh, damn!" she cried as Ben joined her next to her rather beat-up subcompact.

"Sore losers, weren't they?" Ben asked grimly.

"Oh, hell, how am I going to get to work now?"

"Well, there's no sense worrying about it tonight. Tomorrow I'll buy you some new tires."

She turned to him, vehemently shaking her head. "Oh no, there's no way I'd let you—"

"From what I've seen tonight, I'd say you're hardly in a financial position to buy new tires yourself, are you?"

That angered her, and she snapped back. "My, you're so generous, Mr Adams—and so tactful!"

"Of course," he continued, ignoring her flash of temper, "if you have insurance, that would cover the cost of new tires. But in order to file a claim, you'd have to notify the police, wouldn't you, Susan? And the last thing you want is to bring the police into this, right?"

They stared at each other in the charged silence, then Ben sighed in exasperation. "Come on. It's getting late."

As they started away, she found herself actually feeling fearful of Ben's mounting anger. Striding along next to her, he looked like a bomb ready to explode—not that she could blame him for that.

They actually spun gravel as the Jaguar left the parking lot, and once they were back out on Mockingbird Lane, Ben got straight to the point, glancing at her darkly as he shifted gears. "Want to tell me why you're lying, Sue?"

"L-lying?"

"All that nonsense about your brother's friends making a pass at you. You're scared, damned scared. I could see it in your eyes every minute we were in your apartment. You and Jamie are in trouble up to your eyeballs, aren't you?"

"I—I don't know what you're talking about."

He laughed bitterly. "Oh, yes, you do. And from what I've seen of you—your character—I'd say your brother is almost certainly the culprit in this."

Susan exploded. "How dare you say such things about Jamie! You know nothing about him!"

"I've seen enough tonight to know that he's put his sister's life in danger and that he's off hiding somewhere while you take the heat."

Susan was rendered speechless for a moment, totally undone by Ben's incisive logic. Finally she sputtered, "Jamie's just—just kind of fallen in with a bad crowd, like I told you before. You know how it is with young men his age."

"No, I don't. When I was Jamie's age, I was already an adult, and had been for some time. Furthermore, how old are you, now, Susan—twenty-seven?"

"Yes," she ground out.

"And did you behave like this when you were twenty-four?"

Before she could say anything, he made up the answer for her. "No, you didn't. You were responsible and mature then, just as you're responsible and mature now. And covering for

Jamie. And lying to me. So don't give me that crap about Jamie falling in with a bad crowd. He's in big trouble, bad trouble. And somehow he's managed to reel you in, too."

Susan couldn't answer as Ben wheeled the car into the parking garage, and both of them were tensely silent in the elevator going up to his penthouse. Susan found herself turning away from the angry reproach in his eyes. Even Rumor sensed the tension, digging his claws into Susan's arm.

Inside the penthouse, Susan put Rumor down then walked over to the glass wall. When Ben said her name, she turned to meet his challenging gaze.

"Any time you want to tell me the truth, Susan," he said quietly.

She lifted her chin slightly. "Right now, Ben, I'm just tired."

A flicker of remorse crossed his blue eyes. "I imagine you are." He moved closer. "And you've been limping even worse as the evening has progressed. I'm sure we're going to have to take you to a doctor on Monday."

"Ben—"

"But for now, there's a Jacuzzi in my bathroom. Why don't you go have a long soak? That should relieve the pain in your foot somewhat. Afterward, you can have my bedroom for the night—or the guest room—whichever you'd prefer."

"I'd prefer the guest room, thank you," she replied stiffly. "But the Jacuzzi first does sound wonderful."

"Please, be my guest." He turned and picked up her bag. "Want me to take this to the bedroom for you?"

She limped over and took the bag from his hand, shaking her head. "I can manage, thanks."

As she started off for the hallway, he called after her, "First door on the right."

After Susan left the room, Ben went over to the bar and poured himself a Scotch, taking a long sip and loosening his tie. He had been rough on Susan on the way back from her apartment, and he felt guilty about this, especially considering the pain she'd been in. Yet he knew he'd been right to question her. She was in some trouble—some terrible trouble regarding her brother—and she was definitely lying to him.

She was also arousing much more than his concerned curiosity, he realized ruefully. His hand shook slightly as he remembered her staring at the ruined apartment, the bewilderment and vulnerability on her face, the rush of protectiveness he'd felt.

The almost overwhelming desire to pull her into his arms and comfort her.

He groaned and downed the rest of his Scotch. Yes, Susan Nowotny had matured into a very appealing woman.

Except for the fact that her life was a complete disaster.

Ben poured himself another drink. He realized that his tender, protective feelings toward Susan doubtless sprang from the guilt he felt over her father's death, since she just wasn't the type he was normally attracted to. Oh, no. He liked a woman who was sophisticated and in charge, right? Someone self-possessed who landed on her feet. A girl like Susan—with her open naiveté and fresh charm—wasn't safe from the likes of him, any more than she was safe from her brother's lecherous friends.

He frowned. If he was to help Susan, he would need to keep things platonic between them. She very much needed a friend, and he needed to assuage old guilts.

For now, he had to lighten things up between them and get her to trust him. He could then help her solve her problems and get on with his own life.

In lieu of an olive branch, he decided to take her a brandy. Ben half filled two snifters, then strode down the hallway to his bedroom door. Juggling the snifters in one hand, he knocked, then waited. No answer. He pressed his ear against the door. No sounds of water running in the bathroom beyond.

He knocked again, and when Susan still didn't answer, he opened the room and stepped inside.

Just as he entered, Susan limped out of the bathroom wearing only a large towel. Ben froze in his tracks. Lord, the girl was a siren, standing there all sleek, rosy and glowing! Huge brown eyes, staring at him with a sexy mixture of alarm and vulnerability—gorgeous body—full breasts and very shapely, long legs. The fresh-washed scent of her filled the room, igniting his senses. Staring at her, he felt a very familiar, alarming twinge that was anything but platonic.

"Ben!" she exclaimed, clutching the towel tightly to her body.

"Sorry," he said lamely, holding up the snifters. "Thought you might want a brandy. I knocked, but there was no answer."

"I was in the Jacuzzi, remember?"

He smiled crookedly, unable to take his eyes off her. "Feel better now?"

She nodded, but looked more like a scared kitten ready to spring off.

Ben set down the glasses on the dresser and cleared his throat. "How's the foot?"

"O-kay," she stammered.

"You were still limping when you came out of the bathroom."

"Well, yes."

"Maybe I'd better have a look."

Before Susan could protest, Ben strode over to her and knelt by her feet. Even as she gasped, he took her right foot gently in his hand. "It's this one, right?"

"Right."

"Well, it looks okay. No swelling."

"Ben, it's fine."

He began to massage her foot and glanced up at her. "How does that feel?"

Now she had to smile. "Good," she managed breathlessly, her heart hammering as she caught the tender light in Ben's eyes as he stared up at her. She was grateful that at least the towel covered her to mid-thigh; yet she still felt quite exposed and vulnerable standing before him.

Then he glanced downward and continued his massage, and she stifled an urge to moan aloud. Susan never would have dreamed that having her foot touched could feel so erotic, but she found Ben's massage was definitely titillating—slow, firm and deliberate. And treacherously endearing.

After a moment he stood, staring down into her eyes as he caught a heavy breath. A husky note crept into his voice as he murmured, "You have lovely feet, Sue."

She laughed to hide her embarrassment. "I can't remember anyone complimenting my feet before."

He eyed her up and down slowly. "Well, I must say your body presents more than enough delightful temptations to keep a man's eyes from straying—er, quite that low."

Susan blushed and spoke with rising nervousness. "Ben, don't you think you should—"

But before she could finish, he continued in a rush, "Your eyes are captivating, so dark and large. And as for your mouth—"

Susan was opening that very mouth when Ben ducked down his head and kissed her.

She moaned, finding it very intimidating—not to mention, very provocative—to be kissed by a man dressed in an impeccable suit, while she wore only a towel. And Ben knew just how to kiss, too, with very direct, no-nonsense pressure that soon had her kissing him back, despite her fears and misgivings. She whimpered down in her throat and he rested his hands lightly on her bare shoulders. When his tongue boldly stroked hers, she almost lost control of the towel and her emotions. She sensed he wanted to pull her close, but was holding back due to her current state of near-undress.

Then, just as abruptly, Ben released her and pulled back. "Damn," he muttered, shaking his head. "Sorry."

She eyed him confusedly as she caught a ragged breath. "What was that for?"

"Perhaps a kiss to make it better?" he suggested ruefully.

"You mean you're not ready to kiss my foot yet?" she couldn't resist quipping back.

Ben chuckled. "I don't think I'd better answer that right now," he said meaningfully. Then he nodded toward the drinks on the dresser. "Why don't you have both the brandies, Sue? I think I've had enough."

With an amazed smile, she watched him turn and leave. It wasn't until the door was closed that she realized how badly she was trembling.

LATER, WHEN THE penthouse was dark, Ben lay in his big, lonely bed. Susan was gone now, but her scent lingered everywhere—sweet, sexy and compelling. Remembering the sight of her in the towel, the feel of her soft lips on his, he felt his heart hammer. He'd been stunned by his own, passionate response to her. She had tasted so delicious, so soft, so vulnerable. Their kiss had almost snapped his control, and right now he hungered for her in a very basic way.

He could no longer deny it. He *was* feeling attracted to Susan Nowotny, for whatever reason. What a way to be feeling about Jim Nowotny's daughter!

The girl was just so different from himself, and had so many problems. Of course, he wanted to help her. But she was also the last woman with whom he needed to become heavily involved, and their differences went way beyond the fact that his life was in perfect order and hers was a mess, and that she was lying to him about Jamie.

For how could he tell Susan that he felt responsible for Jim Nowotny's death?

DOWN THE HALL, with Rumor purring at the foot of her bed, Susan couldn't sleep as she reviewed her crazy day, being chased by the goons, straight into Ben Adams's arms. Her response to Ben's startling, provocative kiss an hour earlier had left no doubt in her mind. She knew she could become very attracted to this virile, dynamic banker. The man kissed with a finesse that made his erotic foot massage come in a distant second. And, remembering the burning look in his eyes, the insistent heat of his mouth on hers, she suspected that the attraction could well be mutual.

She did like Ben Adams—his strength, his intelligence, his protectiveness. But he'd put her off with his aggressiveness tonight; particularly, with his questions and comments about Jamie. No one could come between Susan and her brother. She'd been defending him for a lifetime, and she wasn't about to stop now.

Yet what was she going to do about him? Jamie's life was out of control now, and consequently her life was out of control. She truly had no place to go—a demoralizing prospect at her age. Jamie's creditors were stalking him—stalking her—and they were getting mean. She had to do something to make her brother take responsibility for his own life.

Should she tell Ben the truth? She shook her head in the darkness. Judging from his comments in the car tonight, he'd likely blow his stack—and insist she cut her brother loose. And this she could never do. Jamie might be exasperating, but he was the only family she had.

And the fact that Ben had pretty much cut himself off from her and Jamie before still nagged at her, making her wonder why he was acting so Johnny-on-the-spot now.

She sighed unhappily into her pillow. Granted, Ben was doing everything he could to help her, and she was sorely tempted to take what he offered—to let him share her burdens. But she knew it wouldn't be right. Their worlds were too different, and too much stood between them.

No, she'd best stick by her guns, and return home right after the weekend, before she found it far too difficult to walk out Ben Adams's door.

4

THE NEXT MORNING, Susan awakened to the smell of bacon frying. She stretched, glancing around at the room where she had slept. Like the rest of Ben's penthouse, the guest room was decorated with ultra-modern, masculine furnishings—pale gray carpeting and matching drapes, handsome walnut contemporary furniture, and on the walls, black-and-white abstract paintings which complemented the geometric-patterned quilt on the bed. The effect was soothing and neutral but rather cold; Susan would have welcomed some warm splashes of color.

She yawned as she got out of bed. She had not rested well the previous night, even though her bed couldn't have been more comfortable. She supposed being around Ben Adams both fascinated and perturbed her, and she somehow knew she wouldn't truly feel comfortable until she returned home.

She dressed in white slacks, a casual blue shirt and sandals, then completed her toilette in the guest bathroom. Then she went out into the kitchen.

She paused just inside the kitchen doorway, staring at Ben across from her at the range. He wore khaki slacks and an aqua-and-white striped polo shirt, and he was industriously cooking omelets. He looked very handsome with the sun outlining his chiseled features and shining in his dark, thick hair. Susan found his expression of intense concentration especially endearing. Staring at him, she couldn't help but recall their intimacies the previous night, and her heart lurched at the memory. Her response to his kiss had been unsettling and potent. No wonder Ben Adams was considered one of this city's most prized catches—he was nothing if not a sexy, appealing man.

"Good morning, Ben," she said at last.

Setting down his spatula, he turned to smile at her, and once again she was struck by how blue and vibrant his eyes were. "Well, good morning, Sue. Sleep well?"

"Yes," she lied. She glanced at the range. "Look, you don't have to cook breakfast for me."

"My pleasure," he said, turning to flip the omelet he was preparing. "How's the foot today?"

"Much better, thanks."

"Good."

As Ben continued with his cooking, Susan glanced at the table, which was already festively set for two, with even a yellow rose in a vase. She found Ben's thoughtfulness tugging at her heartstrings. "May I help?"

He grinned as he lifted the omelet out of the pan onto a serving dish. "You can pour the orange juice," he said. Then, as Rumor suddenly bounded into the room with a wail of hunger, he added, "And you can feed your cat."

Moments later, the two were seated, having their breakfast of omelets, muffins, coffee and orange juice. "Ben, this omelet is divine," Susan said sincerely. "Let's see, you added bacon, cheese, mushrooms, peppers—"

"And a dash of Tabasco," he supplied.

"Well, the result is marvelous. And this coffee is wonderful, too. It's so rich."

"I ground the beans myself," he put in modestly. "It's the mocha mix from Neiman's."

At this, Susan resisted an urge to roll her eyes. Just to think of being able to afford to purchase one's coffee beans at a posh store like Neiman Marcus! She couldn't afford coffee beans, period; she was lucky to be able to buy the cheapest instant at the market. To Ben, she said at last, "You're quite an accomplished cook."

He shrugged. "My housekeeper isn't here all the time, and restaurants tend to become tiresome, especially when one is eating alone."

"Don't tell me that you—one of Big D's most eligible bachelors—eat alone?" Susan asked ruefully. "I find that hard to believe."

He stared at her with a frankness she found unnerving. "Actually, I eat alone a lot more than I'd care to admit."

Susan cleared her throat nervously as she returned her attention to the food. "I still say you're doing far too much for me."

"Not at all," he said with a warm smile. "Susan, why don't you spend the day with me?" he asked casually.

She dropped her fork. "But don't you have plans?"

He shook his head. "I have some loan portfolios to review this evening, but my day is free. The only thing I have to do is to pick up a painting at an art gallery in Highland Park." At her puzzled glance, he added, "The owner called yesterday to say the painting has arrived from New York, but since I was tied up with business all day then, he's opening up for me this morning so I can pick it up."

"I see," Susan murmured. "Ben, you really shouldn't feel obligated to plan your day around me—"

"But I want to plan my day around you," he interrupted, and their eyes locked for a meaningful moment. Embarrassed, Susan glanced away. "As I told you last night, Susan, I think we should become better acquainted. And today is the perfect opportunity."

"Well, okay," she conceded. After all, it was only one day, she rationalized to herself.

"And sometime today, I also want to buy you some new tires for your car," he continued casually.

Susan stared at him in rigid defiance. "Ben, no way. I'll take care of the tires myself tomorrow."

He sighed. "Then you'll let me drive you to work?"

"I can take a bus."

"You'll let me drive you to work?" he repeated, raising an eyebrow at her.

She expelled a heavy, exasperated breath. "Okay. But since you've prepared this wonderful breakfast, I must insist on cleaning up."

"You've got a deal," he said with a grin.

As Susan got up to take the dishes to the sink, Ben watched her. He was so glad that she'd consented to spend the day with him. He'd been afraid that he may have pushed her too much the previous night, and he'd decided that today he needed to back off a bit, get to know her better and let her build up some trust in him. Then, he hoped she would confide in him and he could help her resolve her situation.

She caught his stare now and smiled at him shyly, and he felt his heart hammer in response. Damn. She had the innocently seductive smile of an enchantress. And she looked so slender and lovely in her white slacks and blue shirt; the sun gleamed in her dark curly hair as she worked at the sink. He doubted he'd ever seen a woman with a face or body quite as perfect as hers. Indeed, every time he looked at Susan, he saw another facet to her beauty. Right now, it was the captivating heart-shaped indentation on top of her lovely, full mouth—a mouth he had claimed for his own for a reckless, wonderful moment last night.

Ben tore his gaze away from her with a groan. He hadn't taken a woman to bed in a while, and having Susan around was obviously enough temptation to make him notice that lack like a fire burning in the middle of his living room. He knew he'd best solve her problems quickly and then get her out of his life—for both their sakes.

FORTY-FIVE MINUTES LATER, Ben and Susan were in his Jaguar heading for Highland Park. The morning was mild and sunny; Ben had opened the sunroof, and a fresh, sweet-smelling breeze poured in. They moved down shady streets, past substantial, well-kept houses dating from the twenties and thirties.

Sitting next to Ben, Susan found she felt excited at the prospect of spending the day with him. He looked quite the debonair bachelor in his dark glasses, and he wore a crisp, enticing, woodsy male fragrance. Ben hadn't mentioned their shared kiss the previous night, and Susan appreciated that— as well as the fact that he hadn't pressured her again regarding her problems at home.

He was dressed more casually today. But as she stared at the gold watch on his wrist—a watch she was certain must be valued in five figures—she was immediately reminded of the differences in their life-styles. And just to think that the owner of the Highland Park gallery was opening his shop on a Sunday morning strictly for Ben Adams's convenience! Remembering the Picasso line drawing over Ben's fireplace, the striking contemporary paintings all over his penthouse, she shook her head ruefully. He must regularly spend a fortune at the gallery.

Moments later they pulled into the shopping center, which was a quaint collection of shops with tiled roofs, stucco facades and green canvas awnings. The stores were arranged in a quadrangle among trees and Victorian street lamps.

Ben parked his Jaguar in front of Courtland's Gallery, whose facade of leaded glass panels gave the establishment an old-English flavor. Ben helped Susan out of the car, then they approached the heavy oaken door. He knocked, and as they awaited a response, he turned to her with a smile. "You're not limping as badly today, Susan. Your foot must be better."

"It really is, Ben."

"I still say it wouldn't hurt to take you to a doctor tomorrow. Better safe than sorry."

Susan was about to say that she couldn't afford to see a doctor for such an inconsequential reason, but then they both turned as the heavy door swung open, and a beautiful woman in a designer suit greeted them. "Well, hello there, you two. Come right in."

Susan noted that Ben looked taken aback as he stared at their hostess—a blond, heavily bejeweled woman who looked to be in her late twenties. "Why, Cynthia," he said as he ushered Susan inside. "This is a surprise. When I spoke with your father yesterday, I was given the impression that he'd be meeting me personally this morning."

"Oh, Dad wanted to go on to church with Mother, so I volunteered to pinch-hit," Cynthia told him sweetly.

Ben coughed. "I see. How are you doing, Cynthia?"

"Not as well as I could be, Ben," she replied pointedly. Glancing at Susan, she added, "Well, darling, are you acquiring more than art these days?"

Ben turned apologetically to Susan. "Oh, sorry. Susan, this is an old friend of mine, Cynthia Courtland. Cynthia, this is Susan Nowotny."

"How do you do?" Susan asked awkwardly, extending her hand. As the two women shook hands, Susan noted Cynthia's impeccable manicure, the fingers dotted with rings and a gold watch whose crown was encircled by diamonds. Cynthia wore a heavy perfume that Susan found almost sickeningly sweet. As she glanced upward, she caught the coldly assessing gleam in the other woman's blue eyes. Quickly, she withdrew her hand. This woman had to have been involved with Ben before. There was no doubt in her mind there.

By now, Cynthia had turned back to him. "Well, I must say, Ben, your taste seems to be running to the exotic." She flashed Susan a brittle smile. "Your friend is quite striking."

Ben raised an admonishing brow at Cynthia. "Could you show me the painting, please!"

She slanted him a pouting look. "Then I take it you're not going to tell me more about your little friend?"

Even as Susan was gritting her teeth at being spoken of like some inanimate object, Ben replied dryly to their hostess, "Indeed, I'm not."

"You can't blame a girl for being curious, can you, darling?" Cynthia teased him. As he scowled back at her, she added, "Very well. If you must insist on pursuing such mundane matters as business, the painting's over there by the desk."

As Cynthia started to lead Ben off, he reached for Susan's hand. But she hung back. "Think I'll just look around the gallery for a minute," she told him.

"Okay, Sue," he replied, though he was frowning.

In a jangle of jewelry, Cynthia led Ben off. Susan strolled about the gallery, staring at the many fine paintings, which ranged from abstract to traditional to impressionistic, as Ben concluded his business with Cynthia at an antique desk toward the back. She heard Ben exclaim over the oil painting—another black-and-white, geometric design, and several times, she heard Cynthia laugh. She turned once and observed Cynthia touching Ben's arm as she leaned intimately toward him. Now Cynthia was brushing a bit of lint from Ben's sleeve—an imaginary bit of lint, Susan was certain, since she couldn't imagine Ben Adams with a speck of dust anywhere on his body. Then she watched Cynthia wink at Ben as she made out the sales slip. Susan gritted her teeth. There was something irritatingly cloying about Cynthia Courtland.

Moments later, the two rejoined Susan, Ben with the wrapped painting in hand. "You two come back soon, now," Cynthia told them smilingly as she led them to the door. But her eyes lingered on Susan for another cool, meaningful moment before she let them out.

Once they were back in Ben's car, he asked, "Why did you desert me in there, Sue?"

"Desert you?" she repeated with an amazed laugh.

"Yes. I would have welcomed a bit of a buffering influence around Cynthia."

"Would you?" Susan asked with feigned astonishment. "You mean a big, healthy hunk like you needs protection from the fairer sex? Actually, Ben, I thought you might want a few moments alone with Cynthia. I rather suspected the two of you have a thing going."

He glanced at her darkly. "As a matter of fact, we did. But we don't anymore."

"Really?" she asked with a laugh.

He sighed with annoyance. "Susan, I suspect Cynthia only came down to the shop this morning to embarrass me—and she did. I broke up with her long ago, but evidently, she doesn't see things quite the same way."

"Well, I can't really blame her there," Susan said. "She does seem perfect for you, Ben—blond, beautiful, sophisticated, not to mention rich—"

"Do you think I judge women by exterior trappings alone?" he asked irritably.

She shrugged. "It's nothing to me how you judge women, Ben."

"Really?" he shot back. "Even after last night?"

They both knew at once what he was referring to, and it made Susan's face flame. She turned to stare out the window. "You just didn't want to kiss my foot," she mumbled at last, trying to cover her embarrassment with a show of humor.

Ben chuckled and returned his attention to the driving. But he hoped Susan hadn't noticed that his hands were trembling on the steering wheel. Damn Cynthia Courtland for doing her little number on him just now. If she'd wanted to turn the screws a bit regarding their failed love affair, she'd certainly succeeded. And she couldn't have chosen a worse time, when he'd brought Susan along.

Wait a minute, he cautioned himself. Why was he feeling so angry? Why should it bother him for Susan to meet one of his old girlfriends? And why on earth had he brought up the subject of their kiss last night—the very last thing he intended to do today? He realized that he wasn't even sure of his own motives anymore, not where Susan was concerned. But at the moment, he did dearly wish that Cynthia Courtland had never gotten out of bed this morning.

Susan, too, felt bemused as she continued to stare out the window. Now that she'd seen one of Ben's old flames, she knew what type of woman he normally pursued. Someone rich, glamorous, sophisticated. Totally unlike herself.

So why should it matter to her? Ben was but an old family friend helping her out in a pinch.

Nevertheless, she felt perturbed. And what disturbed her the most was the memory of what she'd felt back at the gallery—when she'd wanted to march across the room and pull Cynthia Courtland's hands off Ben.

THEY DROPPED the painting off at Ben's penthouse, then drove downtown to the West End Market district, an area of restored shops and restaurants that Susan had visited several times before on dates. The earlier tension between them evaporated as they were consumed by the mood of fun that pervaded the district.

They had a casual lunch at the Markethouse, an old brownstone building that had been restored into a shopping mall. Susan was pleasantly surprised that the president of Reunion Bank was actually having a hamburger and French fries for Sunday lunch. They even had a fight over the last French fry, until Susan perversely drenched it in ketchup.

Afterward they meandered through the various shops, which sold everything from stationery, candles and dolls, to bonsai plants and Creole foods. As they passed a chuck wagon jewelry cart, Ben caught Susan staring at a strand of blue-and-green crystal beads. On an impulse, he drew out his wallet, and before she could protest, he had bought the necklace from the smiling attendant.

"Ben, no," Susan protested, as he placed the beads in her hand. Glancing at the price tag, she gasped. "These cost fifty dollars."

He laughed. "You're easy to please."

"Ben—"

He took the necklace from her hand, removed the price tag, then placed the long strand around her neck. "You'd better stop protesting, Sue, or I'll buy you another one. Look, the beads go perfectly with your blouse."

As he led her off to the escalator, Ben watched Susan finger the beads, then glance at him shyly. She couldn't quite conceal a delighted smile. He realized that buying her the necklace had thrilled him. The women he usually dated expected baubles far more costly, and they never protested the gifts he bought them. There was something guileless about Susan that really drew him to her.

Later, as they left downtown, Ben asked Susan what she would like to do with their afternoon, and she suggested they go for a walk somewhere. He drove them out to White Rock Lake. There, they walked near the water, watching the colorful small sailboats bob about on the lake. They could hear children laughing at the recreation area behind them; a mild breeze blew across them as they strolled beneath the trees.

"I noticed that the picture you bought today was quite a striking abstract," Susan remarked. "You must really be into modern art, from all the paintings I've seen at your penthouse."

He shrugged. "Actually, my mother got me started when she gave me my Picasso as a housewarming present. And of course, she sent her decorator out to ensure the proper setting for her masterpiece—thus, the neutral color scheme at my penthouse. Actually, most of the art I possess I've acquired mainly as an investment. Someday, I may sell off my entire collection and start over."

"With what?" Susan asked, her curiosity piqued.

"I'm not sure. Perhaps something more traditional." He frowned for a moment. "Actually," he pondered aloud, "if you want to know the truth, something about my entire penthouse bothers me. It seems—"

"Impersonal?" she suggested.

He snapped his fingers. "Yes, that's it."

"Of course, it's quite beautiful," Susan hastily put in, hoping she hadn't offended him. "But it seems to need—"

He paused, touching her arm. "What do you think it needs, Sue?"

"Maybe some color?"

He chuckled as they started off again. "Perhaps I should get you to jot down your ideas on redecoration." He nodded toward the string of beads around her neck. "You do seem to have quite a flair for color yourself."

She turned away to stare at the water, feeling suddenly ill at ease. "It takes no particular talent to spot a pretty necklace at a jewelry stand."

He frowned. "You minded that I bought you the necklace, didn't you?"

"Well, actually, I did."

"Susan, it was only fifty dollars."

She glanced at him with sudden resentment. "Well, maybe fifty dollars doesn't mean the same thing to you that it does to me."

"Do you want me to apologize because I have money?" he asked patiently.

"No, of course not. I'm just saying that maybe I don't have the luxury of spending fifty dollars on a whim."

"I knew the necklace would please you," he pointed out, "so it wasn't just a whim. Look, would it make you feel better if I take us out to eat at a soup kitchen tonight?"

She laughed. "You wouldn't know one if you saw one."

"Would you know one if you saw one?" he teased.

"Actually, I wouldn't."

"So there," he said.

Staring down at the necklace again, Susan had to smile. "You know, I never did thank you," she admitted shyly.

"That's right, you didn't," he concurred agreeably.

She met his amused gaze. "Thank you," she said.

"You're welcome," he said.

They strolled along in companionable silence for a moment, then Ben murmured, "I'm glad you suggested we come out here. I haven't taken a walk like this in quite a while."

She glanced at him and smiled. "Well, you certainly look as if you get enough exercise."

"I do. But generally not walking through the park. Mostly I swim or jog, or use the exercise room back at my building."

"You probably need all that with your job."

He nodded. "There's a lot of pressure connected with my position. Sometimes I just have to get away. I go skiing in Vail fairly often. In fact, I have a condo there. Do you ski, Sue?"

Susan suddenly began to feel uncomfortable at this new reminder of the differences in hers and Ben's life-styles. "Only on water."

"Really?" he asked. "Well, if you can water-ski, I'm sure I could teach you to snow ski, too."

Susan became very quiet. She didn't know how to interpret Ben's last remark. He seemed to be hinting of a future between them, when they really had so little in common. Meeting Cynthia Courtland had certainly confirmed this for her.

After a moment, Ben reached out and took Susan's hand, tugging her to a halt. He stared at her earnestly. "You know,

Susan, I'd like for us to continue to be friends after this weekend."

"Why?" she asked.

"Why? I'd think that would be obvious. I'm an old friend of your family's."

"Ben, no offense, but it occurred to me long ago that if you really wanted a relationship with me and Jamie, you wouldn't have just dropped out of our lives like you did. Of course I'm grateful that you're helping me out in this pinch. But don't feel that you have to take courtesy too far."

Susan started off again, and Ben followed her, scowling. "Courtesy?" he asked. "Do you think that's all there is between us?"

Susan didn't reply.

Ben started to pursue the matter, then clamped his mouth shut. In truth, he was afraid of where an argument might lead. Susan had hit a nerve with her comments, since he did feel confused regarding his own motives. He wasn't sure whether the attraction and protectiveness he felt toward her was genuine, or whether it was guilt—a misguided fatherly instinct due to what had happened to her own father in Vietnam.

It was late afternoon by the time they arrived back at his penthouse. Going up in the elevator, he said, "I thought we'd go to Highland Park Cafeteria for dinner. But if you're not starving yet, why don't we go for a swim first?"

"Sure, that would be great, Ben."

Ten minutes later, Ben was standing in his living room, in his swim trunks with towel in hand, when he watched Susan step into the room in her bikini. The sight of her practically nude made his heart crash in his chest, and he was alarmed to feel a certain part of his anatomy spring up eagerly to greet her. He hastily shifted his towel.

His eyes, however, had a will of their own. Irresistibly, he roved his gaze over her bare, curvy legs, her smooth, flat stomach, her rounded breasts. Her blue bikini was quite skimpy and left little to the imagination. The bottom was composed of two strips of cloth held together by a wooden ring on each hip, while the top was comprised mostly of a teasing ruffle that barely covered her breasts.

At last, Ben emitted a low wolf whistle. "I'm not sure I should turn you loose in that."

She laughed. "It's only a swimsuit, Ben."

"It's not the swimsuit but what you've put into it," he said ruefully.

Susan eyed Ben in turn. He was hard-muscled, lean and tan, with a masculine expanse of hair covering his chest and tapering down to his slim waist. Glancing lower, she wondered why he was holding his towel against him in that odd way. Then, as realization dawned, she blushed and hastily drew her eyes away from dangerous territory. "I could pretty much say the same thing about you," she said unsteadily.

The two were staring at each other tensely when the phone rang. "Adams here," Ben answered impatiently. Then after a moment, he said, "Yes, yes, I remember. I thought he was fully committed to us, but I guess we'll have to try to get him back in the fold. Hey, hold on a minute, will you, Mike?" Ben placed his hand over the receiver and flashed Susan an apologetic smile. "Why don't you go on down to the pool, Sue. I'm afraid this will take a few minutes."

"Are you sure?"

"I'll come down just as quickly as I can."

Susan went down in the elevator and left the building through the side door. As she approached the gleaming pool, she found it deserted, except for a blond, thirtyish-looking man who was sunbathing on a chaise off to one side.

He greeted Susan with a whistle, whipping off his dark glasses and springing to his feet. "Well, hello, hello."

"Hi," she said stiffly, putting her towel down on a chair.

He came over and held out his hand as he studied her appreciatively. "You must be new around here. I'm Stanley Marchant."

Susan politely shook his hand. "Susan Nowotny."

"You just move in?"

She shook her head. "I'm staying with a friend."

"Lucky friend," he said, giving her another meaningful once-over.

Susan smiled to herself. She'd met many a man like Stanley; he seemed a typical flirt. "Actually, Ben should be joining me any minute," she added pointedly.

"Ben? Do you mean Ben Adams?"

"Yes. Do you know him?"

"Do I?" Stanley grinned broadly. "What do you want with a stodgy old banker like Ben? Now if you *really* want to have some fun—"

"You're just the man for the job, right?" Susan put in dryly.

He laughed. "Well, if you get bored with Ben, I'm in 18 D. Don't forget."

"Thanks for the offer," Susan said smoothly. "But for now, I really would like to swim."

"Oh, then I must show you around the pool," he said with an engaging grin. "There are some treacherous undercurrents down at the deep end."

"And woman-eating sharks, too, right?" Susan quipped back.

When Ben approached the pool fifteen minutes later, he at once spotted Susan down at the deep end, laughing as she tossed a beach ball at Stanley Marchant. He cursed under his breath. Stanley was an acquaintance and quite a womanizer. Ben didn't like him, and at the moment, he hated the idea of him flirting with Susan. Seeing the two of them together made him feel a rush of purely male possessiveness.

Putting down his towel, Ben hurried down to the deep end and dove in.

"Hi, Ben," Susan said as he emerged beside her, shaking water out of his eyes.

"Well, hello, Adams," Stanley called out with a grin, flashing his white teeth. "I was just becoming acquainted with your lovely houseguest."

I'll just bet you were, Ben thought to himself. "That's quite fine of you, Stan, but as you can see, I'm here to take over now," he said crisply.

Stanley whistled. "Don't tell me I was intruding on your territory, Adams?"

Ben's glower was ample reply.

Stanley held up a hand. "Okay, Adams, I get the message. No offense, I just wanted to show Susan the pool." He turned to wink at her. "Nice meeting you, Sue. And if you need any more help getting acclimated, just remember—18 D."

"How could I forget?" Susan called out cheerfully.

After Stanley left, Susan swam to the side of the pool and Ben joined her there. "I'd advise you to stay away from Stanley Marchant," he told her with a scowl.

"Oh, would you?" Susan replied defensively.

"He's a real jerk," Ben continued. "He's been renting a condo on the eighteenth floor for about a year now. During that time, he's been through a long string of women, wild parties, you name it. One time, he was bringing one woman into his apartment when another came out. She'd come by to water his plants or something. Anyway, there was a cat fight out in the hallway that the police ended up having to break up. Stanley almost got evicted that time. But somehow, he managed to placate the owners of the condo."

Susan laughed. "He seems like a fairly harmless flirt to me." As Ben raised an eyebrow at her, she added, "Look, all he was doing was telling me about the pool, showing me the deep end and all—"

Ben harrumphed. "Oh, was he? I'm sure there's a great deal more he'd like to show you."

"Ben, I can take care of myself," she put in heatedly.

"Really? Is that why you arrived desperate on my doorstep last night?"

Susan's lovely eyes flashed with anger, then abruptly she swam off. Ben cursed under his breath. His goal for the day was to become better friends with Susan, to get her to trust him more, and he was certainly doing a bang-up job so far. He couldn't seem to keep his foot out of his mouth, first by mentioning their kiss last night, and now, by making a pointed crack about her problems.

Yet the truth was, after seeing her with Stanley, what he really wanted to do was to draw that lovely, slim body next to his and kiss those lush, heart-shaped lips again. . . .

He groaned. What was wrong with him? How easily he seemed to forget that he was supposed to help Jim Nowotny's daughter, not seduce her. Now she was mad at him, and justifiably so. It was high time to lighten things up between them.

Ben chased Susan toward the shallow end of the pool, caught her by the ankle and dunked her. She came up spitting and fighting and he laughed his delight. After that, the atmosphere was playful between them as they tossed the ball and swam laps together. At one point, he surfaced next to her in a corner of the pool. His body rubbed the length of hers, and the sensation was stunningly erotic. Staring down into Susan's vibrant brown eyes, Ben suddenly felt as if he were drowning.

Later, he watched her climb out of the pool, the water sluicing down her gorgeous, slim body. As she leaned over to pick up her towel, he was surprised he didn't sink through the bottom of the pool. She had the cutest behind he'd ever seen on a woman, and she was beautifully tanned and glowing.

Lord, he was getting in deep, deep trouble.

AN HOUR LATER, Ben and Susan sat at Highland Park Cafeteria, having dinner. He had changed into slacks and a sport shirt; she wore a skirt and blouse and the beads he'd earlier bought her. Seeing the string around her neck, Ben was secretly thrilled. And he couldn't shake off the provocative memory of Susan's lovely body pressed so close to his in the pool.

Susan, too, was remembering their swim. The moment when Ben had surfaced next to her had been even more disquieting than the moment earlier today when he'd bought her the necklace. She hadn't wanted to risk hurting his feelings by not wearing the beads tonight, even though it still bothered her that he'd spent the money on her. Ben was a baffling man in so many ways—he'd dropped out of her life for nineteen years, and yet now he seemed to really enjoy having her around. She sensed that something was building between them in a more private way. Yet she still believed they were the wrong two people to become involved. She certainly didn't want to saddle Ben with her chaotic life. Far better that he stick with his own kind—someone like the sophisticated Cynthia Courtland.

"Susan, have you thought of what you'll do tomorrow?" Ben asked as he cut his fish.

She set down her iced tea. "I'm returning home, Ben."

"Why rush off? You know I have plenty of room—"

"But that's not the issue. I have my own apartment waiting for me, and right now, it needs a lot of attention."

"Susan, we'll take care of that later. Won't you please reconsider—"

"Well, hello, Ben," a new voice chimed in.

Both of them turned at the sound of the cultured feminine voice. Susan glanced up to see a striking middle-aged woman hovering over them, a dinner tray in hand. She had beautifully coiffed red hair, wore heavy makeup and jewelry and an elegant silk designer dress. Susan wasn't particularly surprised that the woman had stopped by their table, since she and Ben had turned a number of heads as they walked from the serving line, and he'd already said hello to several acquaintances. Evidently in the circles Ben ran in, this cafeteria was the place to have dinner on a Sunday evening.

"Hello, Sybil," Ben was saying politely, putting down his napkin and preparing to stand.

"No, dear, don't get up," Sybil admonished. "I was just wondering if you'd introduce me to your delightful little friend here." She flashed Susan a brittle smile.

"Sybil, this is Susan Nowotny," Ben said dutifully. "Susan, meet Sybil Sayers."

"How do you do?" Susan said, taking the heavily beringed hand Sybil had extended. The woman's handshake was limp and cold, and Susan instinctively distrusted her.

"Charmed, I'm sure," Sybil said as she removed her hand. "You know, my dear, you really are quite fortunate," she went on sweetly.

"Oh?" Susan muttered, taken aback.

"Ah, yes, I was chatting with Cynthia Courtland earlier today, and she informed me that you were with Ben this morning, as well." Winking at Ben, she added, "Most women who get their hooks into Ben Adams don't last quite that long. You just love to play the field, don't you, darling?" She didn't give him a chance to reply, and turned to Susan instead. "Of course, I must say that you're rather different from Ben's usual fare, my dear." She glanced pointedly at Susan's clothing and jewelry. "Why, what darling beads you're wearing. Glass, aren't they?"

As Susan glanced, embarrassed, from Sybil to Ben, he cleared his throat and said dryly, "Don't let us keep you, Sybil."

She laughed, a forced, empty sound. "Very well, darlings, I can take a hint. By the way, are your parents still in Europe, Ben?"

"Still in Europe," he replied tersely.

"Well, ta ta, then," Sybil said, strolling off.

As soon as the woman was out of earshot, Ben sighed and glanced at Susan contritely. "Susan, I'm sorry about that."

"Who was that woman?"

"Sybil Sayers, our local society snoop."

"Oh, yes. I thought her name sounded familiar. I believe I've seen her column before."

"She's a witch," Ben gritted out.

Susan bit her lip. "I wonder if she heard you asking me to stay over at your penthouse."

"I could really give a damn what she heard." Irritably, he added, "I think Cynthia Courtland sicked her on us."

"You're kidding!"

"I'm afraid not. I'm sure that after Cynthia saw us together this morning, she went dashing off to call Sybil. The two of them are very tight. Anyway, Sybil knows I always have Sunday supper here, and—"

"I see," Susan murmured. "Cynthia must have been quite a sore loser, then. And according to Miss Sayers, there are a number of others out there just like her." She continued sweetly, "Poor Ben. When you venture out in public, you must feel as if you're treading through a mine field."

Ben was scowling, but couldn't reply as a waitress stopped by to pour them both more coffee. After the woman left, Ben nodded toward Susan's untouched peach cobbler. "Aren't you going to have your dessert?"

She shook her head, her appetite suddenly gone. She pushed the dish toward him. "Here, you have it."

"What?" he exclaimed. "You mean we're not going to argue over it? You're not going to douse the cobbler with ketchup?"

Susan smiled, knowing Ben was trying to lighten the mood. "No, I'm not going to argue."

Yet Ben was frowning as he began to eat the cobbler. Susan, too, found it difficult to maintain a pleasant facade as Ben finished his meal. The encounter with Sybil Sayers had thoroughly rattled her, and all at once she couldn't wait to get out of the cafeteria.

Once they were back at Ben's penthouse, Susan went over to the glass wall in the living room to watch the sunset over the city. After setting down his keys, Ben went over to join her. He stood behind her, resting a hand lightly on her shoulder. He stared down at her face. Her large eyes were focused straight ahead, her jaw clenched with pride. She looked so lovely, so feminine and fragile. Knowing that she was planning to leave tomorrow made him feel strangely blue. And he was certain the unwanted encounter with Sybil Sayers hadn't helped matters at all.

After a moment, he cleared his throat. "Susan, about what happened in the cafeteria. Again, I'm sorry if it upset you."

Susan shrugged. "That woman was rather nosy and brash, but that was hardly your fault, Ben. With your position in the community, I'm sure there's no avoiding people like her."

"Regarding my—past conquests . . . Susan, there's a lot of social life connected with my position at the bank. What I mean is—I just want you to know that I don't sleep with every debutante in this town."

She turned sharply to face him. "It's nothing to me who you sleep with, Ben."

"Is that so?" he snapped, suddenly angered. He knew it shouldn't matter to him what Susan thought about his love life—yet it did matter. And he was getting damned tired of hearing her deny that there was any spark of feeling between them.

Ben was broodingly silent for a moment, then asked, "Susan, did you notice that everyone who saw us together today assumed that we have a thing going?"

She moved away from him, unnerved by the direction the conversation was taking. "I noticed," she replied ruefully. "I suppose that was a logical, if erroneous, conclusion for people to reach. After all, we're both single."

"I think there's more to it than that."

"Oh?" she inquired, a telltale flutter in her voice.

"I think everyone was picking up on something that's building between us."

She turned, daring to meet his challenging gaze. "Perhaps you're bringing up a valid point there, Ben. We are two mature, available adults of the opposite sex. And that's why my continuing to stay here with you might lead to something—unwise."

"Unwise?" he repeated cynically. "You know, Susan, I really love your uncanny ability to sum up our relationship in a word or two. This afternoon, you reduced it all to courtesy, right? And now it's, what? Lust?"

Susan was quiet for a long moment. Then her eyes flashed accusingly to his. "Ben, we don't have a relationship," she said.

That's when something snapped in Ben. "So we don't have a relationship?" he asked angrily, moving toward her. "What am I, then, Susan? Just some brief, convenient layover in your life?"

She gestured miserably. "Ben, you're being unfair—"

"Am I? Then why don't you tell me this is just lust."

And Ben caught Susan in his arms and brought his mouth down on hers. Susan reeled, and a split second later, she clung to him. She realized that, as much as she'd fought her own feelings, she'd been waiting for this moment all day, that every minute they'd spent together had built toward this inevitability. And she knew she'd hurt Ben with her heedless words just now, and suddenly she ached to make amends. She pressed her lips eagerly into his, opening her mouth to his passionate possession. He tightened his grip and thrust his tongue into her mouth in slow, erotic circles. Susan went weak with longing, running her fingers over the smooth, solid muscles of Ben's back. She could feel his arousal pressing into her pelvis, and all at once she ached to feel that wonderful hardness deep inside her.

They were both breathing raggedly when his lips moved to her cheek. "Well?" he demanded.

"Okay," she conceded quietly. "We both know there's more to it than that."

"That's better." He caught her face in his hands and looked down into her eyes. "You know, I could get used to having you around, Susan."

"But you mustn't," she whispered achingly.

He continued to stare at her intently. "Why? Because then you'd have to level with me about what's really going on in your life?"

With supreme effort, Susan managed to pull away. She walked over to the glass wall, taking a deep breath. "And what about you, Ben?" she challenged, at last. "If I stayed, wouldn't you have to tell me what really happened between you and Dad in Vietnam?"

Susan turned, watching Ben go pale. "Something happened, didn't it?" she continued aggressively, stepping forward. "And it's the reason you stayed away for nineteen years—and maybe even the reason you're so interested in me now."

Ben whistled low under his breath, shaking his head. "You're very perceptive, Susan," he said ironically. "I suppose we both have our private demons to wrestle. But how can you think I'm interested in you only because of your father?"

She shrugged. "There must be a reason, Ben. Otherwise, we're just too different."

Ben sighed, drawing a hand through his hair. "Susan, I know you're confused right now. And I'm not sure what any of this means, either. But please don't leave tomorrow. Let me help you—"

"Ben, I have to go," she cut in shakily. Turning from the look of disappointment in his eyes, she added, "Look, don't you have some papers to review this evening? I do have a few things to rinse out in the bathroom, so if you'll excuse me..."

Ben scowled as he watched her walk out of the room.

Ten minutes later, Susan was in a sober mood as she washed her underwear and swimsuit in the bathroom sink. She realized that the prospect of walking out of Ben Adams's life tomorrow saddened her. Their time together today had made her hunger to have much more with him. And Ben's kiss a moment ago had elicited a powerful response in her, a response that wasn't just physical.

It had been a beautiful, fairy-tale weekend. Ben Adams was a fascinating man, the kind of man she could easily fall in love with. But their brief run-in with Sybil Sayers tonight had brought reality crashing in on her. She realized that with Ben's high-powered position in the community, he very much lived his life in a goldfish bowl. And the last thing he needed was to become involved with a woman like her, with her scandalous family background. Even a friendship between them could hurt his standing in the community, she feared. Ben obviously needed to stick with women more like the socially prominent Cynthia Courtland.

And she strongly suspected that Ben was helping her for the wrong reason, mainly because of his former friendship with her dad. What had really happened between the two men in Vietnam, she might never know.

But one thing was for certain—she needed to get away from Ben Adams before she became too deeply involved and before she made his life as much of a mess as her own was.

In the living room, Ben stood alone watching the sunset. The mere fact that Susan was out of the room was a blatant reminder that tomorrow, she'd be out of his life entirely.

He knew she was the wrong woman for him, totally different from the type he was usually attracted to. The fact that she was Jim Nowotny's daughter still nagged at him, too—his guilt, his uncertainty regarding his own motives, his reluctance to tell her the truth regarding Jim's death. Susan was already suspicious. Her comments at the park and just now had left no doubt. Yet could he risk diminishing himself in her eyes by telling her what had really happened nineteen years ago?

For, through it all, Susan had fascinated him. He'd never known anyone quite like her before. She was so fresh and unspoiled. He usually took dates to concerts or benefits, yet today he'd found the simple activities with her delightful. He grinned as he remembered their battle over the French fry, their walk through the park, their playful and oh-so-sexy moments in the pool. Her joy over the inexpensive necklace he bought her made him want to shower her with far costlier jewels. By contrast, the women he had dated before seemed brittle and pretentious.

And kissing Susan just now . . . By damn, if she thought there was nothing but lust between them, he had a thing or two to teach her.

He sighed. She still wasn't willing to confide in him. She still was determined to pull away.

She was the wrong woman for him. And she was slipping through his fingers.

5

THE NEXT MORNING, Ben was up early preparing breakfast for himself and Susan. Rumor bounded into the kitchen to join him, rubbing against Ben's leg and meowing. Ben chuckled at the sight; Rumor had been acting warmer toward him ever since he had fed the cat that steak Saturday night. Now, Ben fed Rumor a raw egg, followed by half a can of tuna. Rumor devoured his repast then sprawled himself at Ben's feet, purring and occasionally batting at Ben's slippers.

Once the orange juice, Belgian waffles and bacon were prepared, Ben left the kitchen and went hunting for Susan. So far this morning, he'd heard no sounds of her stirring. He rapped gently on her bedroom door, and when she didn't answer, he opened it and stepped inside.

The sight of Susan on the bed seared him. She lay sprawled on her stomach on top of the covers; she was wearing a short, candy-striped nightshirt. She was a hot splash of pure temptation in the cool, neutral room. The draperies were open, and the light drifting through the sheer panels outlined her golden, supple form. Her dark hair was sexily disheveled, her long eyelashes resting against her smooth cheeks. One shapely leg was drawn up toward her middle, her indolent, sexy pose twisting the nightshirt up over her bottom. Her bikini panties had also ridden high over her hips, and the effect couldn't have been more provocative. Try though he did, Ben couldn't take his eyes off her delightful derriere, crisscrossed by strips of sizzling, lacy pink. He felt a painful twinge of arousal.

She's in the wrong bed, was his first thought. Then he groaned to himself, feeling like a voyeur. "Susan?" he whispered.

When she didn't stir, he walked over and gently shook her shoulder. Then he backed off, as if touching her had burned him. He cleared his throat. "Susan? Time to get up."

At last Susan began to stir. She rubbed her eyes and turned to look up at Ben. He was wearing a thick, navy velour robe, and he looked very sexy with the heavy shadow of whiskers on his face. He was also staring at her with an intensity that made her stomach flutter.

"Oh, hi, Ben," she said sleepily. "What time is it?"

"Seven-fifteen," he replied. "Look, I didn't mean to barge in on you. But when I knocked, you didn't answer."

"That's okay," she said, stifling a yawn. "Actually, it's kind of hard to get me out of bed early in the morning."

"What man would want to?" he asked without thinking.

They stared at each other for a charged moment, then Ben glanced away and said in a rush, "Well, breakfast is ready, so any time you're ready—"

"You've cooked breakfast for me again?" she cut in with a laugh. "You know, Ben, you're spoiling me rotten. When I return home, I won't know what to do."

"Then don't return home," he said, with much more vehemence than he had intended.

Susan bit her lip. "Ben, do we have to start in again this early?"

He sighed. "I'll leave so you can dress."

"I'll just throw on a robe, then I'll join you," she said.

"Fine," he said.

An hour later, the atmosphere was strained between them as Ben drove Susan to work. Privately, both were preoccupied with the fact that she intended to return home that night.

Susan studied Ben across from her. Today he wore an impeccable blue pinstripe suit, a white shirt and dark maroon tie. He looked like the sophisticated, wealthy banker he was—and nothing like the casually dressed, engaging man who had eaten French fries with her yesterday, who had walked with her through the park and had dunked her in the pool. His bank president attire brought home for her the differences in their worlds and the painful fact that they were ill-suited. Yet still Ben looked ungodly sexy and handsome sitting next to her.

As he stopped the car at a light, he turned toward her. "I like your dress," he said with a kindly smile. "That Hawaiian print is so colorful."

Susan stared down at the bright print, which was a tropical blend of flowers in vivid turquoises, purples, pinks and greens. "Thanks. I made the dress myself."

"You made it yourself?" he asked, astonished. He couldn't recall ever dating a woman who had sewn before. "You did a beautiful job."

"I make most of my clothes," she added.

He turned his attention back to the road, accelerating the car. Frowning, he asked, "Did you make that bikini you wore yesterday?"

"As a matter of fact, I did."

"It was some sexy little number."

Susan shrugged, her chin coming up slightly. "I guess I like to feel sexy just like the next girl."

"Really?" he asked, an edge suddenly in his voice. "Who do you like to feel sexy for?"

For you, Susan was tempted to answer. But of course, she didn't. She turned away, nervously fingering one of her gold hoop earrings. The tension between them was thick as Ben pulled his Jaguar up to the curb in front of Computronics. Beyond them, the white brick building loomed, surrounded by neatly trimmed shrubbery. Half a dozen employees were hurrying toward the entrance.

Susan glanced at Ben, and both of their expressions were torn. "It was good of you to drive me to work, Ben," she said at last.

He removed his dark glasses, and she was stabbed with guilt as she caught the earnest look in his blue eyes. "Susan, won't you change your mind and stay with me a few more days?"

"Ben, we've been over this already. I need to get back home."

"Susan, your apartment is a wreck—"

"It's my home," she cut in heatedly.

"I know that. I'm just saying that it's hardly livable at this point. Why don't you stay with me a while longer, and then we can spend an hour or so each day getting your place back in shape—"

But Susan was adamantly shaking her head. "Ben, I can take care of it myself."

"And what if your brother's friends come around again?"

"I'll be careful." She glanced nervously at her watch. "Look, I've got to go."

He caught her wrist and stared at her intently. "Then at least let me drive you back to your apartment after work."

"Thanks, but I can catch a bus. Anyway, I'm going to try to get off early so I can get my car fixed. Then I'll come by your place and get my things—and Rumor."

Ben chuckled. "That's right—you didn't bring either of them along with you."

She bit her lip, color rising in her face. "Frankly, Ben, I didn't want to walk into work carrying either my suitcase, or my cat. But if you mind—I mean, about Rumor—"

"Of course not," he said, releasing her hand.

"I promise I will come by just as soon as I get new tires on my car." Awkwardly, she added, "Look, would it be a problem if I can't make it by till tomorrow? I'm not sure how late it'll be, finding new tires and getting them put on. But of course, there's Rumor to consider—"

"It won't be a problem," Ben cut in tersely.

"Are you sure? I mean, if I can't make it by tonight, I'll certainly swing by tomorrow during my lunch hour and pick up Rumor and my things. Didn't you say your housekeeper is usually there during the day?"

Ben sighed. "In other words, you don't want to come by when I'm there."

Susan lowered her eyes. "It might be better if I didn't. I just don't see any point in it, Ben."

"Don't you?" he asked with sudden bitterness. Abruptly, he caught her hand again and said, "Susan, please reconsider."

And he drew her closer across the console and kissed her. Only their lips touched, but the need flaring between them left Susan's heart racing. Ben's tongue pressed inside her mouth with insistent intimacy, and Susan found herself softening, kissing him back.

Her cheeks were hot when they moved apart. "Isn't that a reason to come back?" he asked her, staring at her in an intense, unnerving way.

Susan sighed. She hated to hurt Ben—he looked so sincere and concerned. At last she said sadly, "Actually, Ben, it's a reason not to come back. We both know it couldn't lead anywhere." Before he could protest, she added, "Thanks for everything," and quickly got out of the car.

Feeling abandoned, Ben watched Susan walk toward the door of Computronics. This lovely girl who had abruptly landed in his life Saturday night was now just as abruptly walking away from him. He hadn't gotten her to open up regarding her problems, and he was quite worried that she could be returning to a dangerous situation at home. But he didn't just want to help Susan. He wanted her in his bed.

Seeing her in that sexy nightshirt earlier this morning had left no doubt in his mind there.

Yet the two of them were so different that he had doubts about their building anything permanent. And having a fling with Jim Nowotny's daughter was certainly out of the question. Perhaps she was right. Perhaps pursuing this attraction would be unwise.

Still, he couldn't take his eyes off her. She had arrived at the front door of Computronics now, where she was joined by another young woman—a cute, petite redhead. The other girl said something to Susan, then laughed and turned toward his car, waving to him gaily. Ben waved back.

But Susan didn't even turn around as she squared her shoulders and swept through the door. Ben cursed as he put his car in gear and pulled away from the curb.

"HEY, SUE, who was that dreamboat in the Jag?" Susan's friend, Gloria, asked as the two women stepped inside.

"He's an old friend of my family's," Susan replied awkwardly.

"An old friend, my foot," Gloria replied, elbowing Susan slyly. "I saw that torrid kiss the two of you exchanged before he let you out of the car."

"I come from an affectionate family," Susan put in lamely.

Gloria hooted with laughter. "What about your old friend? Is he the affectionate type, too?"

Normally, Susan would have enjoyed the ribbing with her friend. But today, she could only throw Gloria a resentful glance as she turned away toward the door to her office. Instead of laughing, she felt like going to the ladies room and crying her eyes out.

Ben had been right, she realized. She didn't want to go by his penthouse again while he was there. If she did, she might never leave.

AT THREE that afternoon, Ben sat in his posh office on the third floor of a downtown building. A huge stack of paperwork rested before him on his massive desk, but he'd had trouble concentrating on business all day.

He'd been consumed with thoughts of Susan, and for the dozenth time, he marveled at this reality. Ben was usually able to maintain a comfortable level of detachment where women were concerned. He knew how to become involved, without having to put his emotions on the line. But Susan was different. With each smile, each sigh, each movement of her lovely body, she sent arrows flying into his heart.

Did he feel this way because she had resisted him? Susan had held herself apart from him—yet at the same time, he'd never met a woman quite as warm, vulnerable or genuine as she was.

And he'd never before felt like a knight in shining armor— not until Susan came along. . . .

A peremptory rap at his door interrupted his musings, and his secretary, Agnes Miller, stepped into the room. Agnes was an efficient, middle-aged type; she'd been Ben's right hand for several years now.

Agnes walked over to Ben's desk and set down a stack of portfolios. He groaned. "Are those the revised financial reports?"

She smiled. "Well, sir, you did say you wanted to start reviewing these. After all, the bank examiners are coming in three weeks."

Ben sighed. "And I've got all those participations to line up for Southbridge Manor. Reunion will be servicing the loan, but we'll need other banks to help with the financing."

"Do you want to start on the letters and calls today, sir?"

Ben rapped his pencil on the desktop. "Actually, I was hoping to leave early. Anything critical on the agenda for the rest of the afternoon?"

"Well, you have a meeting with three of our loan officers at four-thirty—"

"Will you cancel it, please, and set up something for early tomorrow morning?"

"Certainly, sir. Anything else?"

"Not today, thanks."

As Agnes started to leave, Ben remembered. "Oh, Agnes, by the way—"

She turned at the door. "Yes, sir?"

"Did you take care of that little project I gave you this morning?"

She smiled. "Yes, sir. The garage already called, and it's a *fait accompli*."

Ben grinned. "And did you call my internist?"

"Yes, sir. He recommended an orthopedic surgeon, and that appointment has been set up for Miss Nowotny for twelve-thirty tomorrow."

"Splendid. Agnes, what would I do without you?"

She rolled her eyes. "You'll be remembering all of this at my next review, I presume?"

Ben chuckled. "Of course."

After Agnes left, Ben stood and walked over to the window. He flexed his stiff shoulders and stared down at the busy streets of downtown Dallas. He knew exactly what he was going to do an hour from now—albeit, against his better judgment. He was going to get in his car, go to Susan's apartment, and try his damndest to convince her to come home with him.

6

AT FOUR THAT AFTERNOON, Susan caught a bus to her apartment off Mockingbird Lane. She was preoccupied and had much to do this evening, not the least of which was to find new tires for her car and get them put on. She prayed the tires would be available at a nearby store where she had a charge account.

She walked into the exact same chaos she and Ben had viewed Saturday night. The only difference was that Jamie was slouched on the couch, asleep, with headphones on. He wore a rumpled pair of slacks and an equally rumpled shirt.

Susan stared at her brother with some resentment. Jamie was a handsome young man—blond and blue-eyed, a boyish image of their father. But there the resemblance ended. Susan well remembered her dad as being neat, responsible and honest. Jamie was slovenly, irresponsible and all too often dishonest. Yet there was a helplessness about him that could be fatally endearing, Susan knew. Despite his exasperating behavior, she'd never completely given up on him.

"Jamie?" she asked. When he didn't respond, she walked over and shook him.

Jamie jerked awake, rubbed his eyes and removed his headphones. "Oh, hi, Susie." He glanced down at her leg. "How's the foot? I see you got your cast removed."

Susan shot him a withering look, but didn't comment. "How long have you been here?"

Jamie blinked at his watch. "About three hours, I guess."

"Three hours? Didn't you go to work today?"

Jamie avoided Susan's eye. "I lost my job, Sis."

"Oh, no." Susan collapsed on the couch next to him.

"I'm sorry," Jamie said sheepishly. Quickly, he added, "But it wasn't my fault."

"Nothing ever is," Susan muttered ruefully.

"You see, those idiots who have been hounding me for money came by the store, and my boss didn't take kindly to—"

Then Jamie stopped short at his sister's bitter laughter. "Those idiots have been hounding you for money because you owe them three thousand dollars! And furthermore, they came after *me* on Saturday."

Jamie sat stiffly upright, looking alarmed. "Oh, no, Susie. When I saw the apartment, I figured they'd been rifling through it for valuables. But—did they hurt you?"

Susan shot him an angry glance. "No, they only chased me practically into the ground. I'd just gotten my cast removed, and I'm stunned I was able to outrun them."

Jamie swallowed hard. "So where have you been since then?"

"With an old friend of Dad's. I stayed with him this weekend, since obviously I wasn't safe here."

"I'm sorry," Jamie said contritely. "Who is this old friend?"

"Do you remember Ben Adams?" she asked. As Jamie shook his head, she added, "No, I suppose you wouldn't. He was a close friend of Dad's in Vietnam. He came to see us several months after Dad got killed. But that was nineteen years ago, and you were only five."

Jamie nodded. "Are you going to be seeing this guy again?"

"No," Susan said in a low voice. "Though I thank God he was around this weekend to help me."

"Yeah," Jamie said, running a hand through his hair. An awkward silence stretched between them. "Aunt Florence called a few minutes ago to check up on us," he said finally. "She wanted to come over and bring us a casserole, but I talked her out of it."

"Thank heaven!" Susan declared. "She'd have a stroke if she saw this place." She threw Jamie an admonishing glance. "If you've been around three hours, you might at least have straightened things up a bit."

Again Jamie avoided Susan's eyes. "I'm tired, Sis."

Susan's jaw tightened. "Meaning you went to another all-night poker game?"

Jamie sighed miserably. "What can I say? I have to find some way to come up with the money to pay off my debts."

Susan was aghast. "Good Lord, Jamie! When are you going to realize that gambling is what got you in this predicament in the first place? It's insane of you to try to win the money to pay off your markers."

Not seeming to hear her, Jamie asked plaintively "Susie, do you think you could bail me out? Just one more time—"

Susan's laugh was deeply embittered. "Jamie, I'm totally busted financially, thanks to you. Not only that, but your gambling buddies slashed the tires on my car, and I'm not even sure I can pay to get them replaced."

"Oh, no, Sis. I'm so sorry." Jamie bit his lip, then added, "What about Mother's rings?"

"What about them?" Susan's voice was rising.

"Did the guys who trashed the place find them?"

"No."

"If only you'd let me hock them. Then I'd have a stake big enough to—"

"Jamie, we've been over this a thousand times," Susan cut in heatedly. "The rings are the only thing I have left of Mom, and I'm not letting you have them—"

"Susan, it's the only way—"

Then they both stopped talking as a sharp rap sounded at the door. Susan paled, fearing the thugs might have returned again. She quickly drew her index finger to her mouth, warning Jamie to be silent. Then she tiptoed to the door and stared through the peephole.

Ben was standing out on the stoop. Susan breathed a sigh of relief; then anxiety drifted in as she wondered if he'd overheard her arguing with Jamie. Hell, she didn't care right now. She opened the door and their eyes locked for a meaningful moment; he stood outlined in the fading light, so masterfully handsome in his dark suit. She felt filled with unaccountable joy that he'd come after her.

"Hi, Susan," he said at last.

"Hi, Ben, come on in," she replied stiffly.

Ben walked into the room and Jamie hastily stood. "You must be Ben Adams," he said, extending his hand. "Susan was just telling me about you."

"And you must be Jamie." Ben shook Jamie's hand and studied him with an assessing frown.

"I want to thank you for helping my sister out this weekend," Jamie added self-consciously.

Ben glanced at Susan. "She's most welcome."

Susan cleared her throat. "Ben, what are you doing here?"

"I just wanted to make sure you're okay." He glanced around at the disastrous room, then raised an eyebrow at her meaningfully.

"I'm fine, really," she replied. "I just haven't had a chance to tidy things up as yet."

Ben laughed ruefully, then said, "Susan, may I have a word with you outside?"

"Well, I suppose so—"

"Good." He took her purse from the coffee table and stuffed it in her hand. "Nice meeting you," he said to Jamie before tugging her outside.

Out on the walkway, she said nervously, "Well, Ben, you must keep banker's hours to be off so early—"

He laughed. "Not at all. I deliberately left early because I wanted to come get you."

"Come get me?" she repeated tremulously.

Abruptly he pulled her into his arms. Her heart pounded as he stared down into her eyes and whispered intensely, "Susan I tried to tell myself all day that it was for the best, your going home. But it was just no good. I couldn't get you out of my mind."

Before she could protest, Ben was kissing her, pressing his mouth insistently on hers and teasing her lips apart with his tongue. Susan whimpered and clung to him, opening her mouth wide and pressing her own tongue against his smooth teeth. She couldn't help her feelings, either. She was just so glad to see him again, so glad he'd come after her.

Afterward Ben caught her face in his hands and looked at her intently. "Susan, please come back to my penthouse. At least for a little while. We have to talk—and I still don't think you're safe here."

Susan hesitated. While she was delighted to see Ben, she still had doubts about becoming more involved with him. Reluctantly she pulled away. "Ben, I'll be fine. Besides, I have to get my car fixed tonight."

"Do you?" he asked with a smile.

"Yes. Then I promise I'll come by and get Rumor—"

"Why not come now?" he cut in, tugging her off again. "Ben!"

But he merely continued on with her in tow. Seconds later, they emerged in the parking lot, where she spotted Ben's car parked next to her own, which now sported four brand new tires! Ben's grin told her at once that he'd had the tires put on.

"Ben, you shouldn't have," she scolded.

"Now you have no excuse for not coming home with me," he pointed out. "I didn't want you spending your entire evening hunting down tires. So come along, now. Rumor misses you."

She balled her hands on her hips. "Ben, I'm going to repay you every dime you've spent on those tires."

"Good. We'll arrange a repayment schedule. You can drop a payment off each day—*in person.*"

Susan rolled her eyes. Ben's charm was both infectious and defeating. At last, she waved him off and said, "Okay, I'll follow you home. But only to pack and get my cat, and arrange that repayment schedule."

"Splendid." Grinning, he went off to his own car.

Susan was stunned at how elated she felt as she followed Ben home. Perhaps she was being foolish; yet Ben had so endeared himself to her by coming after her. And he'd had the tires put on her car. How was she ever going to repay him for everything he'd done?

She did feel an uneasy moment or two as she watched a battered yellow sports car move in behind her and follow her through traffic. She couldn't see who was driving the car through the darkly tinted windshield. A few blocks later, the car disappeared, to her relief.

When they arrived back at Ben's penthouse, Rumor bounded into Susan's arms. She sat down on the couch, petting him. "Hi, fella. Miss me?"

Ben went over to the bar and poured them both a white wine. He sat down next to Susan on the couch, handing her her glass. As she thanked him and began to sip her drink, Rumor bounded off.

"As soon as I drink this, I've got to pack, Ben," she told him. "I've imposed on you long enough, and I really need to get home and start attacking the mess."

He eyed her steadily. "Susan, when I was standing outside your door a while ago, I overheard part of your argument with Jamie."

"Oh," she muttered, taken aback.

Gently, he said, "Do you want to tell me what kind of trouble Jamie is in? Drugs? Alcohol? Gambling? What?"

Feeling highly disconcerted, Susan set down her wine, stood and walked over to the glass wall. "What makes you think Jamie is in trouble?" she asked with a telltale catch in her voice.

Ben laughed shortly as he set down his own glass, stood and walked over to join her. "Why else would he want to hock your mother's rings?"

Susan sighed heavily. "Look, Ben, this is my problem."

"Is it? Then why did you come to me for help the other day?"

She turned to him, bravely meeting his challenging gaze. "That was a mistake."

At once, she regretted her words, as she watched him scowl, watched an expression of hurt cross his eyes. She reached out to touch his arm, but he was already turning away. He picked up his wineglass from the coffee table, then walked over to the bar and poured himself another drink.

He was about to raise the filled glass when Susan placed her hand over his. "Ben, I'm sorry."

He turned and caught her roughly in his arms, holding her close to his hard, aroused body. He hooked one arm behind her neck, and was about to cover her mouth with his when she stretched on tiptoe and kissed him—a sweet, soft kiss that made her apology complete. He groaned and pressed his mouth into hers with deepening hunger. She kissed him back with a need that stunned her and made her pulses pound in her ears.

A moment later, he tucked her head under his chin, and she inhaled the exciting, comforting smell of him. She could hear the hard beating of his heart as he whispered, "Susan, I won't lie to you. I think you know how much I want you."

"Is that why you came after me?"

"Partly."

His fingers caught the tip of her chin, tilting her face toward his again. She went weak at the look of stark need in his eyes.

"We shouldn't," she whispered shakily.

"We shouldn't?" he repeated with a scowl, releasing her. "So you're not going to tell me where you stand on this?"

"I think I just showed you," she said ruefully. As he took an aggressive step toward her, she added, "Ben, I'd better go now."

"Why? Are you afraid of what might happen if you stay?"

She could barely meet his eye. "In all honesty, yes."

"Because I want to make love to you?" he asked.

She was surprised her knees still supported her. "Yes."

He moved closer, the intense gleam in his eyes mesmerizing her. "You know, it might be a beginning for us, Susan. It might break down some barriers between us."

She turned away, trembling. He watched her shoulders sag. "I can't agree," she said at last. "I just don't feel we have a basis for building anything beyond that."

He whistled. "Boy, when you go for a man's ego, you carry a machete."

She turned to him contritely. "I'm sorry, Ben. Look, I'd better go pack."

Exasperated, he demanded, "Damn it, Susan, why are you so determined to pull away from me?"

As soon as Ben saw the fear flashing in Susan's eyes, he knew he'd gone too far. She had that look of a kitten again—vulnerable, scared, ready to spring off. He held up a hand. "Okay, Susan. Look, I'm not going to press this *attraction* we're feeling. Just stay here, please."

She stared at him in anguish and confusion. "But why—"

"Hear me out. It would be one thing if you'd tell me what's going on. But I don't even know what you're facing, how bad things are. If you leave, I'll be worried sick about you and I won't get a wink of sleep."

Susan sighed. She hated the thought of being responsible for Ben's having a sleepless night. And somehow she knew he was fully prepared to argue with her until he wore her down. "Okay, Ben, I'll stay. But just for tonight." Hadn't she said those very words before? she asked herself ruefully. She seemed to have little self-control where Ben was concerned.

"Great," he said with a grin. "Why don't we . . ."

"Yes?"

Ben had been about to ask Susan out to the most expensive restaurant he knew, but somehow, he sensed this might put her off. "How 'bout some Mexican food?" he asked instead.

"Sounds wonderful."

THEY HAD A FUN TIME at On the Border downtown. Ben was charm personified as they ate fajitas and sipped margaritas. Susan enjoyed the festive atmosphere and welcomed a lightening of the tension between herself and Ben after their emotional scene back at his penthouse.

Ben had said he wanted her. Even now, the memory made her burn. At least he'd been honest. And so had she—as honest as she could be at this point.

But Susan still didn't understand why Ben Adams wanted to take on her life and all her problems. This man could have his pick of the finest Dallas womanhood had to offer. Had it all come down to that age-old sexual urge that sooner or later seemed to intrude on every relationship? Or was something else driving him?

Later, as they left the restaurant and walked toward Ben's car, he glanced at his watch and said, "Hey, it's only seven-thirty. If we hurry, we can catch a musical at Fair Park."

After an initial protest or two, Susan agreed.

At the auditorium in Fair Park, Ben strode up to the ticket counter and bought the most expensive tickets still available; since it was a weeknight, they were able to get good seats for *The Unsinkable Molly Brown.* As they waited in the fifth row for the performance to begin, Ben took Susan's hand and said casually, "By the way, I made a appointment for you to see an orthopedic surgeon tomorrow regarding your foot. It's at twelve-thirty, and, of course, it's on me."

"Ben!" Susan said irately.

"You had mentioned planning to come by my penthouse tomorrow at noon, anyway," Ben continued evenly, "so I assumed you were free then."

Susan sighed in exasperation. "You've had everything planned, haven't you? Including my staying over at your penthouse tonight."

"Susan, whether you agreed to stay with me or not, I was determined that you see a doctor tomorrow."

"Ben, for the hundredth time, *my foot is fine.*"

"You still limp a little at times, and that worries me," he continued unflappably, ignoring her flash of temper. He turned to give her one of those direct looks that she found so irresistible. "You don't want me to worry, do you, Susan?"

Susan mumbled something very unladylike, before she said, "You know, Ben Adams, you're a martinet."

He chuckled. "How do you think I got to be a bank president?"

"And have all the women you've dated obeyed your orders unquestioningly?"

He considered that for a moment, then grinned. "Actually, they have."

"I'm not surprised," Susan muttered.

Ben laughed as the orchestra began the overture.

The performance was delightful—exhilarating, lively music, wonderful singing and dancing. Susan was soon caught up in the magic, utterly entranced. In her excitement, she reached for Ben's hand in the darkness, squeezing it. By the time she thought to pull away, he'd already entwined his fingers tightly through hers.

During the intermission, Ben and Susan had a glass of wine in the lobby. He frowned as he watched a couple of passing men stare at her pointedly. She had turned a number of male heads at the restaurant, too, he recalled irritably.

"I'm so glad you suggested this, Ben," she was saying. "Harve Presnell and Debbie Reynolds are wonderful. I just hope that when I'm her age, I'll be able to move like she does."

Ben smiled. "Oh, I'm sure you will."

Susan continued to rave over the musical, and listening to her, Ben was delighted. He was sure she didn't get to attend many performances such as this. She looked so adorable in her vibrant flowered dress, her dark eyes glowing animatedly as she spoke. Each place he took her seemed so new and special now, as he saw the world through her fresh, unspoiled eyes. He felt a surge of pride and joy that she was with him, that he'd managed to convince her to stay at his penthouse.

Then, as yet another passing man stared boldly at her, Ben felt a keen thrill of possessive pleasure.

It was after eleven by the time they returned to Ben's penthouse. "Would you like a cognac?" he asked in the living room.

Susan shook her head. "Thanks, but if I drink it, I doubt I'll make it down the hall to bed." She stifled a yawn, then smiled at him brightly. "The evening was great fun, Ben. Thanks for everything."

"You're most welcome," he replied, again delighting in her unabashed pleasure. "But before you go to bed—"

"Yes?"

Ben stared at Susan intently. She was a delicious splash of temptation standing across from him, her brown eyes so large, lovely and expectant. All night he'd tried to be rational—struggling between his desire for her and his guilt, and wondering if the two had to be mutually exclusive. Now, he feared he was about to abandon all that remained of his good judgment.

"How about a good-night kiss?" he whispered.

Susan's heart lurched as Ben moved determinedly toward her. The evening had been lighthearted and wonderful, but now the gleam in his eyes was anything but casual. Remembering the devastating sweetness of his kisses earlier, she didn't know if she wanted to run away or rush into his arms. The man was so damned appealing, and yet she couldn't get past the feeling that giving in to him would be a mistake.

"Why do you keep staring at me that way?" she asked at last, over the wild pounding of her heart.

He laughed dryly. "I think it would be obvious. You must be aware that you're extraordinarily beautiful, Susan."

She shrugged. "Well, I've always known I'm unusual."

"Try captivating," he said. "Are you—um—pursued a lot?"

She glanced at him suspiciously. "Is this a subtle reference to Stanley Marchant yesterday?"

"You turned a lot of male heads tonight, too."

She sighed. "Well, I suppose I've had my share of proposals, legitimate and otherwise."

Ben scowled at this.

"But I have found that most men are only after one thing," she went on, tilting her chin at him.

"Oh, are they?" His scowl deepened.

"Don't get me wrong. I'm not objecting to sex on principle." She looked at him straight in the eye. "I just feel it should mean something."

"It would with us," he said huskily.

"That's what every man says," she muttered.

Ben paused in his tracks, wondering about the bitterness that had suddenly crept into Susan's voice. Earlier tonight, he'd brought their attraction out into the open, and now she seemed to be challenging the legitimacy of his feelings. "It's not that way with every man," he told her patiently. "For instance, think about good old Johnny Brown."

"What about him?"

"The instant he laid eyes on Molly, he knew she was the one for him."

"Things were much less complicated then," she said with bravado.

"They can be uncomplicated now," he said, closing in and taking her in his arms. She squirmed and caught a sharp little breath, and he smiled to himself. As much as she denied it, he knew she wanted him, too. The flush on her cheeks and the way her lips were softly parted gave her away. Meaningfully he said, "Of course, Molly put up quite a fight—"

"Is that what this is about for you?" she cut in. "The thrill of pursuit? Not many women fight you, do they, Ben?"

He smiled slowly. "No, not many women do. Now, about that good-night kiss—"

As he ducked toward her, she pushed against his chest and said breathlessly, "Ben, I thought you said you weren't going to push this attraction."

"Maybe I lied," he said.

Yet instead of claiming her passionately, Ben opted for more subtle tactics. He leaned over and planted soft kisses on Susan's forehead, her nose, her ear, her chin. Her breathing quickened, and he delighted to the soft, sexy sound. He noted that her lower lip was trembling, and the sweet evidence of her vulnerability made his loins twinge in painful readiness. Irresistibly, he ran his tongue over that sensual underlip, and Susan gasped in pleasure. With an incoherent cry, she caught his face in her hands and brought his mouth down hard on hers. He kissed her back with enervating tenderness, stroking his fingertips gently across her breasts. She tottered, weak-kneed, and he caught her closer, splaying his fingers across her bottom to moor her tightly to him.

After a moment, they paused to catch their breath. Ben's lips moved to Susan's hair and he inhaled the sweet, warm apple scent of her shampoo. "Susan, why did you speak so bitterly just now? Has someone hurt you?"

"Maybe," she said noncommittally.

"I want you to know something. I didn't lie—I'd never try to force anything on you."

"I know that, Ben," she said quietly, pressing her face against his shirtfront. "And I guess that's why I stayed. I feel safe here."

He drew back and cupped her face with his hands. His eyes were lit with joy. "Do you? Then that's a beginning, isn't it, darling?"

She bit her lip. "It might be," she acknowledged at last.

He brushed a wisp of her hair from her eyes. "Susan, when are you going to tell me the truth about what's going on in your life? You know you can trust me?"

Susan felt torn. Ben was wonderful, but she still doubted how gallant he'd be if he knew the whole sordid truth about her problems.

When she didn't answer, he coaxed her again—awkwardly. "And you wanted to know about your father and me, what happened in Vietnam. I want to share with you, Susan. But it has to be a two-way street. Do you understand that?"

"Yes," she whispered. She couldn't blame him for wanting reciprocal honesty.

"Think about it, will you, darling?"

"Okay," she said. "Good night."

"Good night, Susan."

Susan went off to her room with miserably torn feelings. The evening had been delightful. Ben had endeared himself to her with his charm and solicitude. Not to mention, his sex appeal! Most tormenting of all was the fact that what she really wanted to do was to go down the hallway to his room and climb into bed with him. It had been so wonderful having him hold her earlier, being surrounded by his strength.

And she really did want to know the truth about the demon Ben was wrestling regarding Vietnam, and her father. She sensed he was ready to confide in her. Yet she knew that if she went to him now, she'd have to meet him halfway, by being honest about her own problems. Then he'd insist she cut Jamie loose. And this she could never do.

Besides, when Ben found out about Jamie, he'd surely realize how wrong they were for each other, and what a liability she could be to his career. As different as they were, they really had no basis for a future, anyway.

She was getting in far too deep with him, she knew. Yet she couldn't let it end.

THE NEXT MORNING, Susan was working on a program at her computer when Gloria Watkins stopped by her desk, tossing down a section from a local newspaper. "Well, hello, Miss Celebrity," she said slyly.

With a puzzled frown, Susan picked up the column. Toward the middle of the page, she read:

> At a popular cafeteria the other night, I ran into that darling bachelor-about-town, Reunion Bank's Ben Adams. Ben was having an intimate supper with latest heartthrob. Susan Nowotny is something of a mystery lady, it seems—she was certainly a nonentity before this reporter spotted her with the oh-so-eligible Mr. Adams. And our favorite banker is certainly keeping mum on the subject of Sue—although I did overhear Ben begging her to stay over at his penthouse. Hmmmmmm…how's that for a juicy tidbit? Romance is clearly in the air. Don't worry, darlings. Sybil will land you a scoop on this unlikely pair soon.

"Damn!" Susan muttered, tossing aside the column.

"I thought you'd be thrilled," Gloria said with a laugh.

"Hardly," Susan said ruefully. "I have no wish to embarrass Ben Adams. Like I told you, he's just a friend."

"Oh sure, Sue," Gloria said with a forbearing smile. "You arrive at work yesterday with your lips smoldering, and he's just a friend."

Susan could hear Gloria laughing all the way out the door.

Following the dismaying incident, Susan found it hard to concentrate on work all day. She kept wondering how long it would be before Sybil Sayers—or someone else—dug up some real dirt on her family background. She knew now that she could really hurt Ben by continuing to stay with him, and this reaffirmed her feeling that she must return home. The treacherous emotions she'd felt while in his arms last night only added to her resolve. She was clearly playing with fire by continuing to stay with him.

That afternoon at four-thirty, she drove to Ben's penthouse. She hoped his housekeeper would still be there, so she could gather her things and Rumor before he arrived.

Yet as she parked her car in the garage, a sick feeling overcame her as a familiar, battered yellow sports car squealed to a halt next to her. Before she could even think to lock her door, a dark-clad, bearded man sprang out and threw open her own door. "Get out, lady. Now."

Susan's heart beat crazily as she recognized one of the three thugs who had confronted her last weekend. She realized with horror that they must have followed her here from her apartment yesterday afternoon, and that today, they had waited to catch her alone. She glanced about the garage frantically, but no one else was close by to help her.

"I said, get out!" the man barked, grabbing Susan's hand.

As he yanked her out of the seat, two more thugs emerged from the other vehicle. All three of them closed in on her, pinning her against her car. It was a horrifying repetition of Saturday afternoon.

"What do you want?" she asked the first man, struggling not to betray her fear.

He laughed bitterly. His fierce, bearded face hovered mere inches from hers, and the smell of his soured breath and smoky clothing nauseated her. "What the hell do you think we want? We want the three thousand dollars your scum of a brother still owes us."

"Look, as I've told you before, I just don't have it—"

"Don't give me that crap, lady!" the man in black snarled. "You've got plenty of dough, or you wouldn't be staying here." His dark eyes ogled her figure insultingly. "And from the looks of the guy you're staying with, I'd say you're earning it on your back, aren't you, Susie?" He tugged at a gold earring at her ear and continued in a sickeningly sweet voice, "That's what your brother calls you—Susie, right? Tell me, what does your new boyfriend call you?"

As the other two men laughed ribaldly, Susan protested, "Please, he's just a friend."

The hoodlum snorted with disdain and reached for his back pocket, pulling out a switchblade and flipping it open. Susan's eyes grew huge as he grinned and waved the knife in her face. Her heart was pounding so hard she feared it would burst in her chest.

Glancing at one of his friends, the bearded man said, "Hey Billie, I think we've been nice to this bitch long enough, don't you?"

Susan was utterly terrified, certain she was about to be sliced to ribbons. Then the sound of squealing tires momentarily distracted her and the thugs. Through the corner of her eye, she saw Ben's Jaguar lurch to a halt perpendicular to her own car. Seconds later, he sprang from the car, white-faced as he took in the scene in front of him.

"Ben!" she cried.

She tried to break away and run toward him, but the hoodlum was too fast for her, grabbing her around the neck and bringing his knife up to her throat. She didn't dare move as the man yelled to Ben, "Hold it right there, mister, or the bitch is dead!"

Ben froze in his tracks, swallowing hard; his eyes locked with Susan's for an anguished moment. To the hoodlum, he said calmly, "Please, let her go."

"Oh, yeah?" the man snarled back at Ben. "What's it worth to you, man?"

7

WITH HELPLESS HORROR, Ben stared at Susan, caught in the grip of a knife-wielding maniac. When he'd driven into the garage seconds earlier, he'd spotted her, pinned against her car by three menacing strangers. Now, seeing her with the knife at her throat, all he could think of was that he had to get her away from these men before they killed her. He must keep his wits about him; he mustn't provoke these lunatics.

"Please," he repeated with a calm he hardly felt, "just let her go."

"Not until she gives us the money," the man who held her retorted.

"What money?" Ben asked.

"Three thousand dollars."

"I see. And Susan owes you this money?"

"No—her brother does."

"Then why are you hassling her?"

The man shrugged. "She's paid off his gambling markers before."

Ben's gaze crossed Susan's for a charged, anguished moment. "Okay, then," he told the man. "Let her go and I'll give you the money."

The man grinned. "Sure. Hand over the cash and she's all yours."

"Look, I don't have that much on me," Ben said, fearing he was about to lose his patience and try something very foolish. "I can give you a check—"

But the cynical laughter of all three men cut Ben's words short. "Forget it, man," one of them snapped.

Ben struggled to steady himself, staring at Susan's dark, terrified eyes, the knife at her throat that could end her lovely life in a split second. The man who held her appeared more and more nervous as the seconds ticked by. Ben's heart crashed in his chest, and desperation rose like bile in his throat. What would he do if he couldn't persuade these animals to let her go?

"Can you please lower that knife and we'll arrange something?" he pleaded.

The hoodlum shook his head. "Not until you say something we want to hear, man."

Ben held up a hand. "Okay. I work at a local bank. Come by there tomorrow and I promise you'll be given the full amount—in cash."

The man snorted. "Come to your bank, eh, man? That sounds like a trap to me."

"No, it won't be, I promise," Ben said adamantly. "I swear to you, I'll give you the money. Do you know where Reunion Bank is?"

"Yeah," the hoodlum said.

"Come to the lobby at nine tomorrow morning and I'll meet you there—with the cash."

The man looked as if he were wavering. "What if we want another five hundred in interest?"

"You've got it. Just let her go."

The hoodlum glanced at his cronies. One of them shrugged, while the other nodded. He grudgingly lowered his knife, and Susan caught a shaky breath of relief. But the thug still didn't release her, digging his fingers into her forearm as he waved the knife threateningly toward Ben. "Look, man, if you dare double-cross us, I swear we'll find you—and her—and we'll—"

"I'm not going to double-cross you," Ben said with all the vehemence he could summon. "I just want you to leave her alone—understood?"

"Okay, you've got a deal. We'll be there tomorrow, and you damn well better have the cash."

The man shoved Susan toward Ben, then he and the others hopped in their car and drove off in a squeal of tires.

Susan fell into Ben's arms, sobbing. "Oh, Ben, thank God you came when you did!"

Yet he didn't reply, and his arms felt stiff about her. Taking her hand, he said gruffly, "Let's get you upstairs."

Once they were in the elevator, Susan dared a glance at Ben and realized he looked absolutely furious. He was still white-faced, his jaw clenched, his eyes blazing.

"Ben, I'm sorry," she said helplessly.

"Did he hurt you?" he asked angrily.

"What?" she replied, taken aback.

"Did that bastard cut you?"

Her fingers automatically slid to her neck. "No."

Ben turned away, blinking rapidly.

A second later, the elevator stopped on his floor. Ben was coldly silent as he ushered Susan into his penthouse. An Hispanic woman was in the living room running a vacuum cleaner. She turned it off and smiled at them. "Hello, sir. I was just about done."

"Hello, Mrs. Ramirez. Would you mind finishing up tomorrow?" Ben asked.

"No, not at all, sir," she replied. "I left dinner in the oven."

"Thanks, Mrs. Ramirez."

The woman put the vacuum cleaner away in a closet and left. Ben locked the door after her, then went straight to the bar, tugging off his tie. Not even glancing at Susan, he poured himself a stiff Scotch with no ice, downed it quickly, then poured another.

All this time, Susan stood helplessly watching him, watching his hand tremble on his glass, watching a muscle twitch in his strong jaw. At last she said, "Ben, I'm sorry—

I—uh—subjected you to that. I mean, you could have been hurt, or—"

He slammed his drink down on the bar and whirled on her. "*I* could have been hurt?" he repeated with a bitter, amazed laugh. "Do you realize that *you* could have been killed?"

And he walked off to the side of the room and stood there with his back to her, raking a hand through his hair. A moment later, he slammed his fist against the wall.

Watching him, Susan winced. She still felt horribly shaken up from the encounter in the garage. She needed Ben's comfort, but he obviously wasn't able to give it. Not that she could blame him.

Susan wiped a tear as she crossed over to the bar and picked up his discarded drink. She took a hearty gulp. Ben still stood across from her near the glass wall, the lines of his body rigid with repressed emotion. Her heart sank. She'd never wanted to hurt him this way. Now, she felt devastated by his anger. She realized that he'd come to mean a lot to her since last Saturday. She knew she'd hurt him terribly by not confiding in him, and she couldn't endure this painful alienation between them. . . .

Standing across from Susan, Ben tried to gain control of his raging feelings. He realized that not since he'd been a child had he been this close to breaking down.

When he'd seen Susan with a knife at her throat, he'd died a thousand deaths. He'd realized then how much she had come to mean to him in just a few short days. What he'd felt at that moment wasn't just guilt, far from it. Now, he was furious at her for not trusting him and for subjecting herself to a potentially lethal situation. And he was angry at himself, too, for getting this deeply involved with a woman who was obviously wrong for him.

It was all so ironic, he thought bitterly. For years, he'd been pursued by scores of available women; for years, his heart had been practically impervious to assault. Now, within mere days, this beautiful, maddening, elusive girl had crumbled all his well-laid defenses. Now he was falling in love with a woman whose life was in chaos—a woman who didn't trust him, who didn't even want him in her world. Perhaps this was some sort of divine retribution for all those hearts he'd toyed with over the years. Now, at last, he understood what it was like to have one's emotions out of control, to be on the losing end of a love affair. For at the moment, he felt that if he lost Susan, he would die.

Then he felt Susan's hand on his shoulder. He stiffened, and didn't dare turn.

"Ben—" she whispered from behind him.

"Susan, you shouldn't be touching me right now."

Ben's voice was full of hoarse warning, but Susan pressed on. "Ben, please don't be mad at me. God, I was so scared."

He turned to look at her, and when he saw the tears in her eyes, his resolve broke and he caught her close with a groan. "Susan, don't cry."

"But you're still mad at me—"

"Damn right, I'm angry. Angry enough to shake you, or—"

Then she staggered as his mouth caught hers with a hunger that took her breath away.

Ben's kiss was punishing in its intensity, and Susan was sobbing with joy as she kissed him back. At once, anger and fear became passion and need for them both. They clung to each other as their tongues collided with desperate hunger. Ben kissed Susan's cheek, her ears, her eyes, her nose, whispering, "Lord, I'm so glad you're all right, so damned relieved . . ." Then his lips drifted to the pulse on her throat. "If they'd shed one drop of your blood," he whispered in a frightening voice, "I would have killed those bastards. All three of them. I would have found a way."

"Ben, they didn't hurt me," Susan said breathlessly. "Just hold me, okay?"

Then she gasped as Ben tugged off her jacket. "I don't want to just hold you," he said thickly. His eyes blazed as he warned her. "I told you, Sue, you shouldn't be touching me right now. If you want out of this, you'd better say so now."

"I don't want out," she said achingly. Fighting tears again, she said, "I want you, Ben. I want us to be really close."

"Oh, Susan."

He groaned, and then his mouth was covering hers with long, drugging kisses. Soon, they found their way down the hallway to his bedroom. Just inside the door, they fell into each other's arms again, both feverish, both trembling with need. She pulled at his jacket, tugging it off him. He unbuttoned her blouse and undid the front closure of her bra, leaning over and teasing one taut nipple with his tongue. Susan gasped ecstatically and ran her hands through his thick, dark hair, and he opened his mouth wide, sucking the tip of her breast into his mouth. She cried out at the hot, wet pressure, the friction of his teeth against her sensitive flesh. A moment later, he repeated the ritual on her other breast, and she went weak with desire. Then he knelt in front of her, pressing his lips against her stomach as he unzipped her skirt. Her skirt rustled to the floor, followed by her half-slip.

Ben caught a ragged breath as he stared at Susan's sexy legs in her filmy stockings, her lovely, supple hips graced by a black lace garter belt and matching panties. "You're so feminine," he whispered, undoing her garters. "I just love that."

He slipped off her stockings and shoes, and she sank to her knees beside him, kissing him boldly as her breasts rubbed provocatively against his cotton shirt. He slipped his hands inside her panties, caressing her bare bottom and drawing her closer; she could feel gooseflesh breaking out everywhere he touched her. His hard readiness pressed against her pelvis, deepening the cutting need inside her. She unbuttoned his shirt and ran her hands over his bare chest, feeling his nipples harden beneath her fingertips. His own hands moved to her front, stroking her through her silky panties. She bucked, catching a wild, sharp breath; he pressed one hand tightly into the small of her back and eased down her panties and garter belt with the other.

"I want you so badly, Susan," he whispered intensely. "You've been driving me crazy for days. I want to get so deep inside you that you can't breathe."

"I want you, too," she whispered back. "Just that much."

He stood and pulled her to her feet. Her heart raced wildly as they crossed over to the bed together. She knew that when they came together, they would both explode, that it would be fierce and wild and very healing. She laid down and watched him remove the rest of his clothing. He was superbly muscular, tan, and hard, and she could barely breathe as she anticipated him filling her with his wonderful, straining arousal.

He sat down next to her, feasting his eyes on her. "You're so beautiful," he said reverently. "Your eyes are so deeply dilated, they're almost black, and your mouth is trembling—"

"For you," she whispered, hooking an arm about his neck and bringing his lips down to hers.

As Ben kissed her back, he slid his fingers down her body, over her taut nipples, past her smooth belly, and lower. She gasped as he felt her wet readiness, and then he thrust two fingers inside her, stretching and probing.

Susan moved wildly against Ben's hand and reached for his manhood, arousing him with bold, titillating strokes. He groaned and covered her body with his own, and the sensation was electrifying for them both. Susan loved the feel of Ben's coarse, hairy chest against her breasts, the crushing pressure of his muscled body on hers. Ben adored the feel of Susan beneath him—the softness of her breasts, the eagerness of hips, the promise of surrender in her dark eyes.

But as Ben's strong thighs nudged hers apart, as his manhood pressed low on her belly, she suddenly stiffened. "Ben, I haven't—I mean I'm not—"

"Do you want me to use something?" he asked, his eyes bright above hers.

"Yes."

Staring down into Susan's eyes, Ben found himself, for once, resisting the idea, not wanting anything to inhibit the intimacy. "If you got pregnant, I'd marry you," he whispered passionately, running his tongue over her mouth.

As Ben kissed her again, plunging his hot tongue deep into her mouth, Susan nearly lost sight of her good intentions. Finally, some vestige of common sense made her push him away and say breathlessly, "Ben, please."

He smiled. "Okay, darling." He fumbled with the nightstand, and she jumped as an ashtray went sailing off. "It's okay," he repeated. "Hold on a moment."

Susan crawled up next to him, watching him avidly and sinking her teeth into his shoulder. Her erotic ministrations played havoc with his dexterity. "Susan, damn it, if you want me to use this contraption, you're going to have to let me put it on."

Then she leaned over and her tongue made brazen contact with his right nipple, and with an agonized groan, he caught her about her slim waist and pulled her into his lap. She gasped as he penetrated in a single, deep stroke, possessing her so fully that she throbbed and ached about him—yet wondrously so.

"We just made it," he whispered roughly in her ear.

But then all levity died away, and there was only the sensation of flesh devouring flesh, of Ben's slow, endless deep thrusts, of Susan passionately arching to receive him. The room was so quiet, with only the rush of air from the vent overhead, and the sound of their labored breathing. Soon, even those sounds were drowned out as their mouths locked deeply and Ben's strokes reached a frenzied crescendo. Susan cried out, arching backward as she climaxed, then Ben pulled her back fast, holding her tightly to him as he took his own pleasure deep inside her.

8

LATER, A LIGHT RAIN began to fall. Lying in Ben's bed, Susan listened to the comforting sound while Ben was out of the room getting some wine.

When he walked back into the room carrying a tray with a bottle and glasses, Susan felt almost shy with him. He looked very sexy in his terry robe, which was tied loosely, revealing an enticing glimpse of his hair-roughened, muscular chest. There was a dark line of whiskers along his jaw, and his hair was still rumpled from where her fingers had wildly raked through it. Recalling their lovemaking, she couldn't believe the storm of desire that had consumed them. And, remembering how Ben had vowed to marry her if she got pregnant, she felt warm color suffuse her cheeks. Of course, he'd said those words while in the throes of passion, but somehow, she sensed that Ben Adams made few statements he didn't mean. This thought unsettled her as much as it set her senses to tingling.

Ben eyed her appreciatively as he set the tray down on the end table. "You look good in my T-shirt," he teased, bending over to give her a quick, possessive kiss.

As he straightened, she caught a sharp breath, then glanced down at the gray athletic shirt she wore. "Well, you weren't about to let me leave and get something of my own."

"No, I wasn't about to let you leave. Of course, I would have preferred that you wear nothing at all, but since you insisted on propriety, I wanted something of *mine* touching you." He handed her a filled glass of wine and sat down beside her, pouring himself a glassful. His cozy nearness and male scent filled her senses, reminding her again of their lovemaking earlier.

As Ben took a sip, he stared at her, his gaze more solemn. "You okay?"

"I'm fine."

He stroked the curve of her jaw with his fingertips. "You inspired me to make a pretty bold statement, Ms. Nowotny."

"I like bold statements, Mr. Adams."

He chuckled. "Do you?"

They were both quiet for a moment, enjoying their closeness as they listened to the rain spattering the rooftop. Then Ben said, "Sue, we need to talk."

Susan had been waiting for this. "Okay," she replied guardedly, sipping her wine.

He fixed her with a direct, piercing gaze. "First—I don't want you going anywhere. Not for a long time."

She bit her lip. "Ben—"

"Susan, you can't make love with me like you just did and then just walk out of my life."

She turned away, embarrassed.

"Sue?" he asked, touching her shoulder. "Are you already sorry?"

"No, I'm not sorry."

"Well, then?"

She turned to face him, her dark eyes reflecting her torn feelings. "Okay, I'll stick around, then. For a time. I really am drawn to you, Ben, but I'm just afraid there are a lot of road-blocks to our having—something permanent. We're so different."

"That's the next thing on my mind," he went on, staring at her earnestly. "We need to start communicating about a lot of things. We need to start breaking down some of those barriers."

She sighed, staring at her lap. "I guess you're right."

He took her hand. "Tell you what, Susan. I'll make a deal with you. I'll share something about myself if you'll share something about you."

"Okay," she said.

He took a long sip of his wine. "It's about your dad."

She nodded. "I knew there was some reason you dropped out of our lives for nineteen years."

He sighed. "Susan, that's not the way I wanted it to be. It's just that—"

"Yes?"

His anguished eyes met hers. "Vietnam as a very painful experience for me. And the most painful part had to do with your dad. I guess I stayed away from you and Jamie because I didn't want to be reminded."

"Go on," she said.

"You see, your father trained me when I first arrived in Nam, and more than once, Jim's wisdom saved my life. He had the maturity and judgment I lacked as a green pilot. Then, not long after I got my own helicopter, Jim and I both flew into a landing zone to pick up some wounded. We had two possible routes for leaving the LZ—to the east over Vietnam or to the west, over Laos. Jim radioed me that he was flying off to the west." Ben's fist was clenched on the sheet, and his voice was thick with emotion as he continued, "And, damn it, I didn't try to stop Jim, even though I had a funny feeling there were snipers out there. I had no proof, of course—it was just an intuition. So I didn't tell your father, I guess because I was still so green, and I couldn't believe that my judgment could have been better than his. Anyway, I took off to the east, Jim to the west. I made it, but Jim got shot down."

"Oh, Ben," Susan said, clutching his hand. "What hell it must have been for you to live with that."

"It has been that," he whispered.

"But you shouldn't feel guilty at all!" she put in vehemently. "My God, it's not like you knew someone was out there, it's just a feeling you had. Dad had the experience, just like you said, so it was just one of those things."

"I still feel I should have done something," he said grimly.

"Oh, Ben! What if you had done something, and Dad had gotten shot down anyway, on the way back to your base? You still would have blamed yourself."

He smiled at her. "Thanks for being so understanding."

Susan smiled back at him, wishing she could do more to comfort him. "I'm not just being understanding, Ben. It was a war, and those things happened."

They were quiet for a moment, holding hands and listening to the muffled sound of thunder. Then Ben said, "Okay, Susan, I've shared something about me. Now I want you to tell me about Jamie's gambling."

She sighed. "Where should I begin?"

"Well, when did it start?"

"When Jamie was a teenager. I've thought about it a lot, and I really think that the fact that we lost Mom and Dad when Jamie was still so young had a lot to do with his troubles. You see, my brother was the kind of kid who really needed a strong male role model, and Aunt Florence—well, she hardly fit the bill."

"I see."

"Anyway, Jamie's gambling began innocently enough, with some poker games with friends while he was in high school. But gradually, he got into it all—baseball lotteries, the horses, backroom casinos, you name it. He was dishonorably discharged from the Army because he got caught stealing a watch from the PX to cover his gambling debts. Since then, well, he's been into one scrape after another, and he hasn't been able to hold down a job."

Ben was frowning. "And you've bailed him out repeatedly, haven't you, Sue?"

"He's my brother," she put in defensively. "The only immediate family I have left. What would you expect me to do?"

Ben sighed. "You know, Sue, you're going to have to let him learn to stand on his own two feet."

Her jaw tightened. "Are you going to tell me it's him or you?"

"No, I wouldn't ask you to make a choice like that." He studied her carefully, his eyes narrowing. "Why? Have other men done so?"

She laughed ruefully. "You're very perceptive, Ben."

"I wondered why you spoke so bitterly about other men last night. Is that why you hesitated to tell me about Jamie's problems before?"

"Well, yes." She expelled a long breath. "Actually, I think Jamie's the main reason I haven't had a long-term relationship with any particular man. Most men don't respond sympathetically to his situation."

"Then it seems I have Jamie to thank in a certain sense." As Susan glanced at him confusedly, he stroked her mouth with his index finger and added huskily, "I don't want you to have a long-term relationship with any man—except me."

Ben leaned over and kissed her then; his heart hammered as he felt her lips softly trembling beneath his. He was tempted to pull her sweet, slim body beneath his and make love to her again, yet he knew too much still remained unsaid between them. Reluctantly he pulled away and looked down into her eyes. "Still, Sue, don't you think you should be a little more cautious where your brother is concerned? Look what happened today. Perhaps you should back away from him, at least for now."

Susan's brown eyes grew stormy. "Ben, he's my brother. And anyway, how can you even hint that I should cut Jamie loose, when you're planning to pay off his gambling markers? I don't want you to do that."

He shot her a look which she assumed was his best bank-president glare. "Susan, that's a point you'd best not argue with me, because you'll lose. I *will* pay off those hoodlums, not because of Jamie, but because subjecting you to that kind of danger again is totally out of the question. Is that understood?"

She bit her lip. "Now you're mad at me again."

He took her wineglass and his, and set them on the nightstand. "Come here," he said raggedly, pulling her into her lap.

Ben kissed her deeply, hungrily, caressing her bare thigh with his hand. "I'm not angry," he whispered against her mouth. "I simply refuse to let you get hurt."

Somehow, Susan found the strength to continue arguing. "But, Ben, it's just not right that you take on Jamie's debts. Do you think—"

"What?" he asked, scowling down at her.

Despite the hard thumping of her heart, she pressed on. "Well, you said you feel guilty over Dad's death. Maybe that's why you feel obligated to do all this."

He caught her face in his hands. His brow was deeply furrowed, his eyes gleaming fiercely as he said, "Susan, get something straight. I'm doing this because I *want* to. My God, do you think guilt is what I felt when I made love to you just now?"

"Well, no, but—"

Further discussion was sealed off by Ben's lips. Susan moaned and kissed him back. As much as she still had doubts about their relationship, Ben's possessiveness and protectiveness were so endearing.

After a moment, he pulled back to look down at her sternly. "There's one more item of unfinished business," he said ominously.

Susan's heart thudded. "Yes?"

He pressed his finger against her lips and said, "Susan, whatever your reason, you withheld some information from me that almost got you killed. Don't ever do that again."

"Okay," she said breathlessly. She looked up into his smoldering eyes and bit her lip. "You *are* still mad, aren't you?"

A hint of a smile tugged at his mouth. "Let's work on it," he whispered.

But even as he was leaning over to kiss her again, her stomach growled noisily, and they both backed off, laughing. "Poor baby," he teased, stroking his fingers across her smooth, flat belly. "All this exertion, and I haven't even fed you."

She curled her arms around his neck. "Oh, I can wait a while longer."

"But I doubt Mrs. Ramirez's chicken can," Ben put in with a grin. "I took a peek at it while I was in the kitchen, and I'd say it definitely looks stewed in its only juices."

Susan giggled. "Actually, Ben, my experience with chickens has not been good."

"Don't worry, I'll protect you," he put in gallantly, kissing the tip of her nose. "If you like, I'll hold you in my lap and spoon-feed you."

Susan rolled her eyes. "That won't be necessary," she said primly.

"Aw, shucks," he said.

Laughing, they got out of bed. Susan went off to her room to put on some shorts, while Ben dressed. She met him out in the kitchen; he, too, was wearing shorts and a T-shirt, and she feasted his eyes on his tall, muscular body. Just looking at his long sinewy legs, she couldn't help but recall the texture of his rough thighs against hers as he'd thrust into her. She felt a surge of longing again, and realized with awe and alarm how much he affected her. One look at him could turn her to jelly!

Since the rain had stopped, Ben suggested they eat on the small balcony adjoining the kitchen. He wiped off the small wrought iron table and chairs with a towel, while she set out the dishes and food. The view of the sunset over the Dallas skyline was fabulous, the air bracing and cool.

"Ben, this was a wonderful idea," Susan said eagerly, as they ate their chicken, asparagus, au gratin potatoes and salad. "Between the sunset and the rain, everything smells brand new and gleams like gold."

"I agree," he said reverently, staring at her. "You should see the glow in your eyes, the highlights in your hair."

She smirked at him. "I'm talking about the beautiful view."

"And I'm looking at it," he added solemnly.

They continued with their delightful banter as they finished the meal. Susan sensed they both needed this respite after their intense physical intimacy, their long heart-to-heart talk. Rumor came out to join them, and Susan fed him some bits of chicken. The cat was devouring the last of his feast, when abruptly he tensed and hissed, drawing up his back.

Susan glanced confusedly from Rumor to Ben. "What on earth—"

"Well, hello there, Mr. Adams," a stout female voice called out.

Ben and Susan turned to see an elderly woman standing on a balcony a few feet beyond them. The woman was tall and statuesque, sensibly dressed, and wore her gray hair in a comely bun. She held a measuring spoon in one hand, a box of plant food in the other, and was spooning the mixture into potted plants. At her feet—which were curiously clad in galoshes—was the cause of Rumor's current distress, a gorgeous silver Persian cat. The cat looked equally irate as it growled back at Rumor.

"Good evening, Miss Hennessey," Ben called back politely, as if oblivious to the battle lines being drawn between the two cats. "How are you doing?"

"Oh, just fine. Feeding my begonias. After the rain is always the best time, you know."

"Ah, yes, I must remember that," Ben replied with a benign smile as Rumor spat savagely at the other cat.

As Miss Hennessey's Persian emitted a particularly venomous hiss in return, the woman scolded, "Now, Priscilla, don't spit. It's so unladylike." She glanced at Susan and added, "Is he yours, my dear?"

"You mean the cat?" Susan asked, taken aback.

As Ben did his best to stifle a laugh, Miss Hennessey drew herself up stiffly and said, "Well, of course I meant the cat."

Susan smiled back at the woman sheepishly. "Yes, he's mine."

"Well, I'm afraid Pris is always rather snobby around these non-pedigreed types," Miss Hennessey put in archly. "You do understand, don't you, dear?" Before Susan could reply, she went on to Ben, "Well, Mr. Adams, I must run along. Priscilla and I didn't mean to intrude on your little tête-à-tête."

The woman squared her shoulders and reentered her apartment. Then the cat, tossing its nose disdainfully, followed suit.

As soon as Miss Hennessey was out of sight, Susan and Ben convulsed with laughter. "Who was that woman?" she asked.

"My neighbor from 22 B," Ben replied. "Miss Hennessey is an old maid—and an heiress. Her family owns one of the richest oil fields in west Texas."

Susan shook her head in amazement. "Do you realize that she was wearing galoshes, Ben? On her own balcony!"

He chuckled. "Well, it has been raining. Do you suppose the galoshes give her better traction?"

Susan's sides were splitting. "I wouldn't know. I've never worn them."

"I'm surprised she didn't put galoshes on the cat," Ben added, still chuckling. "Anyway, Miss Hennessey is a harmless enough sort, if something of a busybody."

The word busybody made Susan abruptly frown and set down her fork. Ben reached across the table and took her hand. "Sue, what is it? Did that old battle-ax upset you?"

"No. It's just that..." She drew a ragged breath, then asked, "Have you seen Sybil Sayers's column today?"

He scowled. "No."

"There was quite a tacky little paragraph about her run-in with us at the cafeteria."

Ben clenched his jaw. "To hell with her, then."

Susan stared at him earnestly. "Ben, I'm sorry if I've caused you any embarrassment."

He laughed shortly. "What are you talking about, Susan? It's not your fault that Sayers unsheathed her claws on us. If anything, I should apologize to you. I'm sure you didn't want that nosy snoop mentioning you in her column."

Susan grew silent, and Ben squeezed her hand. Suddenly he could feel her withdrawing from him. "Sue, you are going to stay with me, aren't you?"

"I said I would."

"Don't you think we should explore this, see where it leads?"

"I suppose so. But I still have my doubts."

"Then we need more time. You need to get to know my world, and I must get to know yours."

"Okay." But she avoided Ben's eye.

"Sue, what is it?" he asked exasperatedly. He squeezed her hand. "Come on. Tell me?"

She drew a heavy breath and looked him in the eye. "Okay, Ben. I won't lie to you. I'm no starry-eyed virgin. It's just that—I've never really been that close to a man before. I mean—I've never *lived* with a man before."

Ben grinned, pulling her out of her chair and into his lap. "I want you very close to me, Susan," he whispered tenderly, running his hand over her smooth, bare leg.

She shivered. "But I really don't know why you're so interested in me," she managed.

"Really? Even after this afternoon?"

Ben swooped down to kiss her, but Susan held him back breathlessly. "Ben, there's Miss Hennessey. Any minute, she's bound to reappear."

He winked at her. "Let's give her an eyeful, then."

But even as Ben kissed her, the wind whipped up, rattling the dishes. Laughing, the two of them got up, took everything back into the kitchen, put the food away and loaded the dishwasher.

As Susan was finishing up at the sink, Ben came up behind her, placing his hands on her waist and pressing his hot mouth against her cheek. She shuddered as he whispered, "So what do you want to do now, darling? Go out somewhere, or call it an early night?"

She turned in his arms. "Why don't we call it an early night?" As Ben grinned and caught her closer, she added, "But I think I'd like a bath first."

"Want your back scrubbed?" he asked wickedly.

Susan bit her lip. Ben's nearness played havoc on her senses, but she wasn't quite ready for that much intimacy as yet. "Perhaps another time?" she suggested gently.

"Okay," he said, surprising her with his acquiescence. "But I do insist on a rain check."

"Okay."

Susan had her bath in the guest bathroom, then went into her room to dress for bed. After a moment, she heard Ben's rap at her door. "Come in," she called.

He walked in wearing only pale blue pajama bottoms. His hair was damp and very sexy, curling around his forehead and the nape of his neck. Susan felt a delicious thrill of arousal, knowing that soon, they would be in each other's arms again.

"I decided to take a shower myself," he told her, looking her over in her nightshirt. "I even shaved." Then he whistled and added, "Damn, I love you in that candy-striped nightshirt."

She laughed. "I noticed the other morning."

"You noticed, huh? You look good enough to—"

"Yes?"

"Unwrap and lick," he said lecherously. He drew close to her, and she squealed as he grabbed a handful of the shirt and drew it up over her hips. "White panties this time, I see." He ran his index finger beneath the lacy band that rode high on one hip, and she shivered in pleasure. "They're sexy as hell, just like you."

Susan laughed as Ben drew her into his arms. She caught a sharp breath as he pressed his hand intimately into the small of her back.

"Sue, I've been wondering something," he said.

"Yes?" she asked.

Suddenly he looked very serious as he glanced around the room. "What are you doing in here?"

"Just dressing for bed," she said.

"Oh," he said, breathing a sigh of relief. He pressed his mouth against her ear. "Sleep with me tonight, darling?"

Susan hugged him tight, touched by his tender question. "It's nice to be asked."

He drew a deep, drugging lungful of her fresh, sweet scent. "I don't want to take you for granted, Sue. I mean, this afternoon was very intense, very spontaneous, very special. But if you need more time before—"

"I don't," she whispered, pulling back and staring up into his eyes. "I want to sleep with you, Ben. All night."

He muttered something and swung her up into his arms.

"Ben, you don't have to carry me to bed!"

"Believe me, at the moment, I do."

Susan laughed as he carried her off. She felt so needed, so cherished. She pressed her face against his warm chest, listening to the comforting sound of his heartbeat and drinking in the wonderful, clean smell of him. Seconds later, she landed on his soft bed. He stood above her for a moment, studying her with a sexy gleam in his eyes. Then he playfully picked up her right foot. "Now, about your saying that I didn't want to kiss your foot—"

"Yes?"

Ben was about to start nibbling on her toes, when he paused, suddenly serious. "Did you go see the doctor during lunch as planned?"

Susan rolled her eyes. "Yes, Ben. He took an X ray and told me exactly what I already knew—that my foot is fine, and the pain I've been feeling is due to severe stress on unused muscles. So there. I hope you're satisfied."

He chuckled. "Not yet."

Susan giggled as Ben began to nibble at her ticklish toes. She tried to wrestle herself away, but he held her fast and continued the torture. Then his warm lips moved up her foot, past her calf, her knee. Susan was breaking out in gooseflesh and moaning breathlessly by time his mouth reached her sensitive inner thigh. Then he abruptly stopped, grinning up at her.

"You stinker," she said with a mock pout. "You're nothing but a tease."

Susan caught Ben around the neck and brought his lips down on hers. They clung to each other, their tongues thrusting together, deeply and wildly. Ben raised her shirt and took her firm, bare breasts in his hand. He squeezed the tender globes gently, erotically, as he stared down at her.

"You're so beautiful," he whispered, "so firm and golden. Do you know you drove me crazy in the pool the other day?"

As he leaned over, nipping and tugging at one taut nipple with his teeth, she writhed in pleasure. "I figured I got to you then. You know, you're not bad in a swimsuit, either." She moved forward, running her hand wickedly down his body. "But you're better with it off."

"Why, you vixen. Prepare to be unwrapped—and licked."

Susan giggled ecstatically as Ben tugged off her nightshirt and wrestled her down. She gasped as he ran his tongue all over one breast, then the other, arousing her nipples to painful tautness. He moved lower, nuzzling her bare stomach with his mouth, and she moaned with pleasure. Then he shocked her by plunging his tongue into her belly button. She bucked, but he held her fast; then she relaxed and tangled her hands in his damp hair, enjoying the hot, titillating flick of his tongue.

"You've got the cutest little belly button," he said at last, glancing up at her with a devilish grin. "I could lick you all night."

"I..." Suddenly Susan was embarrassed. "No one ever did that before."

Ben chuckled. "You mean I got a virgin belly button? For that you get double treatment."

And he proceeded to torment her again, even as his hands boldly tugged off her panties. Susan breathed in short, sharp gasps as Ben parted her thighs, as his fingers again performed their wicked magic there. As his thumb flicked over her sensitive nub, her hips came up off the bed.

"Easy, darling," he whispered against her belly, pressing her down firmly into his hand. "It's okay."

"It's—much better than okay," Susan panted, and Ben laughed his delight.

Between the hot lapping of his tongue at her belly and the intimate press of his fingers, he soon had her in a breathless, painful state of arousal. After a moment, he glanced up at her, watching her reactions in fascination—her rapid breathing, the hot flush on her cheeks, the way she impatiently chewed her bottom lip.

"Susan, this afternoon, I hope I wasn't too passionate," he whispered. "I've never made love to a woman quite like that before."

"You mean I was your first frenzy?" she asked, between the waves of pleasure that slammed her.

"You were my first frenzy."

"Just think—a virgin frenzy and a virgin belly button," she gasped with a lopsided grin. But then the ecstasy grew too unbearable, and she could only moan and tug the sheets convulsively with pleasure.

When Ben finally withdrew his fingers, Susan lurched forward. She ran her tongue hungrily over his bare chest, his hard stomach, and plunged her hand inside his pajama bottoms, gripping his erection firmly. She delighted to his deep moan. He was so hard now, so distended, that she went weak at the thought of him inside her. As she stroked him boldly, he latched his mouth onto her neck and growled his satisfaction.

Moments later, she said breathlessly, "Um, Ben—"

"I know," he muttered. "Time to don my armor."

She giggled. "Well, you don't have to grumble so. Here, I'll help you this time."

Susan's fingers were remarkably nimble—her touch very erotic, as she drew the thin sheath over Ben's turgid manhood. When she drew her fingertips seductively lower, he groaned with agonized pleasure; her touch was like fire sizzling through his loins. Breathing heavily, he rolled her beneath him and surged quickly and deeply inside her. He thrilled to her sharp gasp, the mindless ecstasy in her dark eyes. Her nipples were hard little peaks, quivering beneath his chest, and her slim arms clung to his neck as if for dear life. Their hips thrust together in perfect rhythm. She felt warm and tight about him, the perfect sheath for his hard, driving need.

Susan arched to meet him, wrapping her legs around his waist to take him deeper. Her eager, trusting surrender drove him crazy. He slipped his hands beneath her and stretched the limits with slow, jolting thrusts. He nearly lost his mind as he watched her toss her head and whimper. He wanted to make it last forever, but knew he couldn't.

"Darling," he groaned, feeling himself slip away, "damn it, I can't—"

"Second frenzy," Susan somehow managed.

Then he became lost as his mouth took hers desperately, as he felt her sweet womanhood clenched about him, and felt himself explode.

9

THE NEXT FEW DAYS passed happily, with Susan and Ben getting to know each other better. While Susan still had grave doubts about a future for them, she couldn't bear the thought of leaving Ben. Sometimes she would call herself up short, ask herself what she thought she was doing—carrying on a torrid love affair with him, when she knew the two of them were not well-suited. Yet emotionally, she just couldn't make the break; she was sure she was falling in love with him.

Susan did feel good that she'd told Ben about Jamie's problems, and relieved that he hadn't tried to dictate to her regarding her brother, as other men had. She also felt glad that he had shared what happened between himself and her father in Vietnam. But she couldn't help but continue to wonder whether guilt might be spurring Ben's actions, at least in part, since she was so different from the type of women he would normally choose for himself. When they spent time together isolated and alone, everything was beautiful; yet Susan feared that they were living in a house of cards that might at any time collapse about them.

During this period, Susan didn't return home or call Jamie. She assumed that Ben had paid off her brother's gambling debts, although when she tried to ask him about this, his sole response was a steely glare that warned her not to pursue the matter. Susan knew that in staying away from home, she was avoiding her problems with Jamie, but her feelings were so torn she couldn't decide on a course of action regarding her brother.

Curiously, when help came, it was in the form of Ben. One morning at breakfast, he set down his coffee cup and said, "I know you don't talk about this much, Sue, but I sense that Jamie has really been on your mind."

She glanced up at him, astonished. "How did you know that?"

"Well, you get this faraway, preoccupied look on your face, and I always figure . . ." He cleared his throat and leaned toward her intently. "Sue, I don't mean to interfere, but I do have a good friend who is a therapist. Bill does a lot of work with compulsive gamblers and their families." Before Susan could protest, he went on, "Anyway, Bill and I met for drinks the other day, and he said he'd be delighted to talk with you about Jamie."

Susan's initial reaction was anger. "But you *really* don't want to interfere, do you Ben?"

He continued calmly, "Susan, you're dealing with a very difficult and serious situation as far as your brother is concerned. Don't you think you should at least find out some more information about compulsive gambling?"

She sighed. "I suppose you're right."

He reached into his breast pocket, then handed her a card across the table. "Call Bill today?"

Susan stared ruefully at the card, which read, William Newcomb, Psychiatrist. She breathed a heavy sigh. "My, you're so efficient, Ben."

"Susan?"

She glanced up at him, and felt guilty as she spotted the earnest, caring look in his eyes. "I'm sorry," she said contritely. She tucked the card into the pocket of her blouse. "Okay, Ben, I'll call him. Thanks."

Ben stood and pulled Susan to her feet. "Now come here and kiss me," he said tenderly. The crisp scent of his aftershave filled her senses as his lips moved slowly, thoroughly over hers. Afterward, he tucked her head under his chin and asked, "Still mad at me?"

Breathlessly, Susan shook her head. "How can I be mad at a man who kisses like that?"

At work, Susan dutifully called Bill Newcomb, hoping it would be a while before he could see her. However, the psychiatrist seemed delighted to hear from her, and insisted he could fit her in for a few minutes after work today.

When Susan arrived at the psychiatrist's downtown office at five-fifteen, his secretary had already left for the day, and Bill Newcomb himself greeted her and ushered her into his inner office. Newcomb was an affable, attractive man who appeared to be in his late thirties, and Susan liked him at once.

At first they got acquainted and spoke on general subjects. Newcomb explained that he and Ben belonged to the same country club, and had been tennis buddies for years. He seemed in no hurry to ask Susan about her problems, and she appreciated not being pushed.

Thus, when they'd exhausted the small talk, she felt confident enough to say, "Well, Ben tells me you do a lot of work with compulsive gamblers, Dr. Newcomb."

"Please call me Bill," he said with a smile. "And I do work a lot with gamblers—and their families."

Susan cleared her throat. "I suppose Ben told you I have a brother with a problem."

"Why don't you tell me about it, Susan."

Susan dove in, telling Newcomb all about Jamie's history and his current plight. She spoke of how she and Jamie had lost both parents, and how Aunt Florence had raised them. Then she admitted that she'd rescued Jamie from his scrapes and had tried everything she could to help him—all to no avail.

"I see," Bill murmured when she'd finished. "So why did you come here today, Susan?"

She smiled guiltily. "Mainly because Ben asked me to."

He chuckled. "That's honest. What do you feel you should be doing about your brother?"

She shook her head. "That's just it. I don't know. I mean, I get the feeling I'm not helping him, yet I'm not ready to—"

"Turn your back on him?"

"Yes. That's it, exactly." Susan gestured her frustration. "I guess one reason I've avoided getting professional help is that maybe I'm not ready to embrace the most obvious solution. I'm sure that to other people, I must seem like a fool, but I just can't cut Jamie loose."

He nodded. "Believe me, Susan, you're not a fool. Yours is a story I've heard many times before."

"It is?"

"You see, Susan, you must recognize that compulsive gambling is a disease, like alcoholism or drug addiction. Your brother really has no control over his own behavior. He may want to quit, but he'll only go back again and again."

Susan's face fell. "Then there's no hope?"

"I didn't say that. However, Jamie probably won't recover without some kind of help. And I'm afraid it's not the kind of help you've been giving him."

Susan bit her lip. "It's not?"

"Do you want me to continue?"

She sighed. "Yes."

"You see, an addict usually won't recover unless he's forced to take responsibility for is own actions. You've been indulging in what we call 'enabling' behavior—rescuing Jamie from his scrapes, and thus making it possible for him to continue gambling."

Susan laughed ruefully. "You don't mince words, do you?"

He leaned forward, lacing his fingers together on the desktop. "Susan, you must realize that the family of an addict is usually every bit as caught up in the emotions of the illness as is the addict himself. Your type of behavior is very typical of someone in your situation. Unfortunately, though, trying to rescue or change an addict rarely succeeds."

"So you're saying I should turn my back on Jamie?"

"No. Just don't rescue him. He'll never reach his bottom or become willing to seek help if there's always someone there to pull him back up. He needs more of a tough love approach."

"Tough love," Susan murmured. "I've heard that expression before. But isn't there anything I can do to help him?"

"Well, actually, we're increasingly recognizing intervention as an effective tool for treating addiction. If Jamie hits a really low point, that might be one viable approach. He might be more receptive to a suggestion for treatment then."

Susan was frowning. "I see."

He smiled kindly. "I know this is a lot to take in at once. Tell you what—I have some books I'd be delighted to lend you. They'll tell you all about compulsive gambling and its treatment. I also have some literature to give you on support groups that meet right here in the city."

Susan nodded. "I really appreciate it, Bill. You've given me much food for thought." She drew out her checkbook and added, "Since your secretary is not here, may I pay you for this session?"

He waved her off. "Heavens, no. As I told Ben, I'm delighted to chat with you about this. However, if you, or your brother, should decide you want to enter into long-term therapy, we can discuss financial arrangements then."

Susan took the books and literature, thanked Bill, and left. As she drove away, she mulled over the session. She knew the things Dr. Newcomb had said made sense, but could she really become that "tough" with her brother? She thought of the hoodlums in the parking garage with the knife, and shuddered. Could she leave Jamie at the mercy of creeps like that?

Yet what had Jamie done to her? It was a complicated issue, clouded by her love for him. But after seeing the psychiatrist, she did want to read the books he'd lent her and learn as much as she could about her brother's disease.

Susan stopped by her apartment to collect her mail and gather a few more things she needed. She was rather relieved to note that Jamie wasn't there. She had a lot of thinking to do before she faced him. But, glancing about at the still-chaotic room, she did vow to come back soon and start cleaning the place up; Ben had kept her too busy to do much about it, and she hated to continue leaving her apartment in such a state.

Half an hour later, Susan let herself in to Ben's penthouse with the key he'd given her days earlier. She found him sitting on the living-room couch, reading the paper. He was wearing a T-shirt and jeans. She'd never seen him in jeans before, and he looked damn sexy in them; she couldn't take her eyes off him as he hopped up and strode over to kiss her.

"How are you?" he asked.

She laughed, setting down her purse, briefcase and tote bag. "Hot."

He grinned down at her. "It's a scorcher outside." He glanced at his watch, then frowned. "You're rather late, my dear. Don't tell me you're already trying to step out on me?"

"Yes, as a matter of fact, I did meet a man after work." As his glower deepened, she added, "Your friend, Bill Newcomb."

Ben laughed. "For a minute there, you were flirting with wholesale jealous rage, lady." Stroking her cheek with his index finger, he added, "Did the session help?"

"Yes," she admitted. She glanced at the briefcase at her feet. "As a matter of fact, Bill lent me a wealth of reading material."

"Good. Well, shall we go out to eat tonight?"

Susan smiled, feeling relieved that Ben wasn't pressing her about the session with the psychiatrist. "What did you have in mind?"

"I thought I'd take you to my country club."

"Oh," she murmured, taken aback.

"Look, it's a great place," he assured her, "approved by the board of health and everything."

She laughed. "I'm sure it's fine."

He raised an eyebrow. "That didn't sound too sincere to me—"

"Well, after we ran into Sybil Sayers—"

"She doesn't belong," he hastily assured her.

"What about our darling Cynthia Courtland?"

Ben scowled. "She does. But I doubt we'll see her tonight. Anyway, why should we concern ourselves with her?"

Susan shrugged. "I guess I'm not the country club type."

"Come on. It's only dinner," he teased. Winking at her, he added, "You don't have to join until we're married."

"Ben!" As he grinned at her, she continued, "Really, I was hoping to just grab a sandwich with you, then spend the evening cleaning up my apartment. I stopped by there for a few minutes after my appointment, and that mess is really starting to get on my nerves."

He feigned a wounded look. "I can't believe you'd choose drudgery over spending the evening with me."

She rolled her eyes. "Oh, okay, I'll go. I don't know why I ever try to argue with you, anyway. But I want a bath first."

As she leaned over to pick up her things, he caught her hand. "How about that rain check?" he asked meaningfully.

Susan felt warm color suffuse her cheeks, felt her heart thrum wildly. She looked up at Ben, and went weak at the look of desire in his eyes. "I take it you want a bath, too?" she managed.

He caught her hips in his hands, hauling her close. His mouth was a mere hairbreadth away from hers, his breath hot on her lips as he whispered, "I think you know what I want, Susan."

Susan nodded, nestling her face against Ben's T-shirt. She knew what they both wanted. She throbbed everywhere Ben's hard, aroused body touched hers, and the male smell of him was a potent aphrodisiac. "Okay," she whispered.

"Great," he said, picking up her things.

In the bedroom, Ben put Susan's things down on the bed then rubbed his hands together gleefully. Giving her a mock leer, he said, "Well, my dear, shall I go run our bath?"

Susan cleared her throat. "Ben, could I have a few moments alone in the bathroom first?" Picking up her tote bag, she added awkwardly, "I mean, you seem to mind taking care of the—um—precautions, so while I was at my apartment, I picked up—"

"Yes?" he prodded with a fascinated smile.

"You know exactly what I'm talking about, you stinker." Before he could respond, she grabbed her bag and hurried into the bathroom.

As Susan undressed, she thought of how much she loved Ben's bathroom. The room was huge, with an enormous, raised marble tub at its center, a skylight above it. Imagining her and Ben in that tub, making love with the light streaming down, she felt an intense thrill of arousal. She glanced at the rest of the room. The vanity area took up half of one wall, and doors in each corner led to the shower, toilet and two large closets. Everywhere were mirrors—and the thought of the reflection she and Ben would create as they coupled was every bit as erotic as the anticipation of their physical intimacy.

Susan had removed her clothing and was unzipping her tote bag when the door opened behind her. "If you like, we can forego it altogether," Ben said.

Susan whirled, her face hot. "Ben!"

"Wow," he said, devouring her nakedness with slow, thorough eyes.

Susan stared back at him, just as mesmerized. He'd removed his T-shirt and had unsnapped his jeans, and the sight of the hard bulge straining against his zipper made her mouth go dry. Lord, he had never looked so sexy!

At last, she found her voice again. "Forego what? Taking a bath? Making love?"

He chuckled and drew closer. "Susan, I want you to know that I don't mind taking care of the birth control. It's just that with you, I'm willing to take more responsibility than that." As she turned away in embarrassment, he caught her chin in his hand and said earnestly, "I meant what I said the first time we made love."

"Oh." She swallowed hard. "You mean, when you said that you'd marry me if—"

"Yes." He drew her into his arms, and she caught a sharp breath as her breasts touched his hard, rough chest. "I've never felt quite this way about a woman before," he admitted, his voice suddenly low and raspy. "Before you came along, you wouldn't believe how careful I've been—"

"Oh, I believe you. One can't be to careful these days."

He took her face in his hands. "What I'm trying to say is that I wouldn't mind getting caught with you." As she tried to look away, he leaned over and kissed her quickly and possessively. His face hovered intimately above hers as he asked, "How about you, Susan? Would you want to get caught with me?"

"I . . ." She could barely breathe when he stared at her like this! "I don't know."

A troubled look crossed his eyes. "Susan, when you didn't come home on time, I thought you'd gone."

"Ben, I told you I'd hang around."

"Hang around?" he repeated ruefully. "That sounds like Rumor."

She shrugged. "Well, I guess my cat and I have a lot in common."

Yet Ben didn't look the least bit amused by her banter. "Susan, this isn't just an affair to me. Is it to you?"

Susan felt transfixed by his gaze, very much put on the spot. And equally aroused. "Well, no."

"I want this to be very long-term. I want this to be . . ."

Staring down into her eyes, Ben almost said "forever." He almost said, "for keeps." Yet somehow he knew Susan wasn't quite ready to hear those words as yet. Tucking her head beneath his chin, he whispered, "You arouse something primal in me, Susan. Something very basic. I look at you and I start thinking about homes, and children—"

"Ben, don't you think this is a little premature?"

He laughed. "I'm thirty-nine years old, Sue. How premature can that be?"

"Maybe you're just caught up in—" she paused, shuddering as he flicked his fingertips sensually across her taut nipple "—this."

"This?"

"You know what I mean, Ben."

"Oh, you mean our lovemaking? Actually, I would want a wife who enjoys sex with me. Frequent sex with me."

"Given your appetites, you'll need just such a wife."

"Have I just been insulted?" he asked self-righteously.

"Hardly," she breathed.

He chuckled and leaned over to nibble at the lobe of her ear. She shivered ecstatically as he wet her ear with his tongue and pressed his thumb into the underside of her breast.

"Don't you ever think about that kind of thing, Sue?" he whispered. "A home? A husband? What you'd like to have in the future?"

"Well, yes."

"Tell me what you think."

"I'd rather not."

"Come on, tell me."

"It's silly."

"*Tell me.*"

Susan's heart hammered as she stared up into his eyes. "Well, I am twenty-seven, and I'll admit that I've had—thoughts."

"Thoughts?"

"I think that sometimes, when a woman reaches a certain age—"

"Yes?"

"Well, sometimes when I go through the mall and see the young mothers with their babies, I want to cry." She buried her face against his chest. "So there, I've said it."

"Oh, darling," he whispered, stroking her hair, "that's the least silly thing I've ever heard."

Yet as much as Ben's nearness and tender words thrilled her, Susan remained troubled. Stroking her fingertips across his muscular, smooth back, she murmured, "Ben, there must be a thousand women in this town who would love to have your child."

"None of them are you, Susan."

"A lot of them are more suitable." With a rueful laugh, she added, "I mean, I've noticed that I'm not your usual type."

He chuckled, too, but then his eyes grew serious as he stared down at her. "Guess who's here with me now?" he asked, and kissed her, thrusting his tongue deep into her mouth.

Susan moaned, breathing hard as Ben withdrew his tongue from her mouth and flicked it slowly, sensuously down her throat. "You're not going to need a bath when I'm through," he said. "I'm going to lick all the salt off you."

Susan melted at his sexy words and erotic stroking. He insinuated a hand between their bodies and rubbed his palm boldly across the place that already throbbed so painfully for his touch.

Moments later, it took all Susan's willpower to push him away. "Ben, please, I must—"

"Yes, ma'am," he said, giving her a mock salute. "Go do your thing. I'll start the bath."

Susan grabbed her tote bag and ducked into the toilet. When she emerged from the adjacent room moments later, the air was steamy. Standing near the tub, Ben turned to look her over greedily. "I'm afraid the bath's not ready yet—but I am."

Ben strode forward, caught Susan to him and kissed her hungrily. Her tongue collided eagerly with his as her hands sought his jeans, tugging at his zipper. She freed his hard arousal and stroked him boldly. Both of them were struggling to breathe. Susan realized that the intimate discussion they'd had was all the foreplay either of them needed.

A moment later, Ben swung her around so her feet were braced on the first step to the bathtub, equalizing their heights. He gripped her about the waist and thrust into her deeply. She clung to him, loving the rough feel of his jeans against her soft thighs, the pressure and heat of him inside her. Ben's hard chest abraded her taut, tender nipples as he ground himself into her, and the sound of water rushing in the bathtub was an erotic accompaniment to their hungry coupling. Susan stretched upward, pressing her lips on Ben's and whispering soft, inarticulate pleas. His hands caught her buttocks, lifting her off the step. She cried out and wrapped her legs around his waist, clinging to him as they climaxed together.

Susan was limp when Ben carried her to the tub and set her down gently. He turned off the water, then stripped off his jeans and briefs and joined her, taking her in his arms and cradling her against him. She closed her eyes in ecstasy as the bubbles swirled around them. He ran his hand over her smooth breasts, her sleek belly and hips. His heart welled with tenderness as he looked down at her beautiful face, her dark lashes resting against her cheeks, her mouth pressed trustingly against his chest. He marvelled at how quickly this girl had realigned his values, had turned his entire life topsy-turvy.

There were women more suitable, she'd said. In an intellectual sense, he supposed he could see her point. But in this emotional moment, no woman seemed more perfect to Ben Adams than Susan was. There was still so much standing between them, and yet, they'd never seemed closer. If only this moment could be endless, he thought. If only he could hold her here forever.

She needed him, he knew; she just wasn't willing to acknowledge it as yet. He needed her, too. Having her in his life, sharing with her, had already lessened his painful guilt over Jim. And he hadn't even had to atone—for loving her was certainly no atonement.

"Susan," he whispered, nudging her gently.

He leaned over and kissed her, and she opened her eyes and smiled up at him.

They never made it to the country club.

10

THE FOLLOWING Monday morning, Ben was sitting in his downtown office, thinking of Susan. She was never out of his thoughts for long. He loved everything about her now—her honesty, her beauty, her unaffected charm. Since he'd been with her, he could actually feel himself changing, enjoying life as never before. He couldn't even remember the last time he'd really had fun with a woman, but he delighted in every moment with Sue. Every time he looked into her beautiful face and vibrant dark eyes, every time he held her in his arms, he found himself fantasizing about rings and weddings and having two or three little carbon copies of her toddling about the place.

Their time together had been wonderful, yet also very isolated. They'd spent the weekend going to movies and restaurants and lounging around the pool; they'd spent their evenings talking, playing chess or making love. He'd discovered how bright and quick she was, what a marvelous conversationalist she was. And what a passionate lover!

Yet on another level, Susan still eluded him. For ever since their run-ins with Cynthia Courtland and Sybil Sayers, Susan had resisted setting forth in his world again. And his career had social demands that she would have to learn to accept if they were to have a future together. Besides, he wanted to take her out, show her off to his friends. He was so proud that she was his.

He frowned. There was one particular obligation the he had avoided telling Susan about for several days now. The bank was cosponsoring an important benefit this weekend, and he wanted her to attend with him. He knew that she'd balk, especially when he told her that he was planning to buy her a gown to wear. Susan was very proud, and he feared he was about to tread all over that pride. But he wanted her out with him, experiencing his world. He wanted her to understand and accept what she'd be up against in the future, *their* future.

Not one to avoid issues for long, Ben took a deep, bracing breath, picked up the phone and dialed Susan's number at work.

SUSAN WAS FROWNING at her computer screen when the phone on her desk rang. "Susan Nowotny," she said rather irritably.

"Well, hello, darling."

She smiled. "Hi, Ben."

"You sound rather harried. Am I calling at a bad time?"

"No. It's just that I had this inventory program almost completed, then they decided to double the number of categories on me."

He chuckled. "Poor darling."

"So what are you up to, Ben?"

"Oh . . . wishing I were out of his damned office and in bed with you."

Susan chuckled. "That sounds just like you. My first obscene phone call of the day, too."

"It had better be your last," he quipped. More seriously, he continued, "I won't keep you for long. It's just that I've been meaning to ask you something for several days now."

"Oh? That sounds ominous."

"Not at all. You see, this weekend, the bank is cosponsoring an important benefit dinner to help crippled children. Will you be my date, Sue?"

Susan hesitated.

"Well, darling?" Ben prodded. As the silence lengthened, he added, "I know these affairs tend to be superficial and boring, but it's for a good cause."

Susan sighed. She couldn't let Ben down, nor did she want to risk disappointing him by voicing her misgivings. "Sure, Ben."

"Hey, that's great." He hesitated a moment, then added, "There's one other thing."

"Yes?"

"Could you get an afternoon off? I'd like to take you shopping."

"Shopping?"

"It's going to be a pretty glitzy affair. I want to buy you a gown."

"Ben, you don't have to buy me something to wear."

"Susan, it will be my pleasure. You're doing me a big favor by being my date, so the least I can do is to buy you something to wear."

Susan bit her lip. She didn't know what to say. She certainly had nothing in her own wardrobe suitable for such an occasion. "You're making me feel like a kept woman," she grumbled.

He laughed. "Oh, but I am planning to keep you, darling. Permanently."

"Ben—"

"When can you get off?"

Susan sighed. She'd long since learned the futility of arguing with Ben Adams. "Oh, my supervisor is pretty flexible about that sort of thing. It's Monday now, so why don't we shoot for Wednesday afternoon?"

"That's fine with me."

Yet Susan felt troubled as she hung up the phone. Since she and Ben had been together, they'd spent much of their time alone. But now they were venturing forth in the world again—Ben's world. She didn't run in the same circles as he, and she had doubts about fitting in. And attending a glamorous affair such as the benefit Saturday night would certainly be an initiation by fire! Susan well knew that Ben was accustomed to attending such events with far more sophisticated and socially prominent women. And, remembering how he had increasingly spoken of a future for them, she wondered if he wasn't now testing her as "banker's wife" material. She knew his position involved a great deal of social responsibility—and his wife would have to be equal to these demands.

ON WEDNESDAY, Susan got off work at noon. She drove over to the Crescent, a ritzy shopping center near downtown. Ben had asked her to meet him there at twelve-thirty.

Susan parked her car in the basement garage and took the escalator up to the open air mall. She at once fell in love with the delicate setting. The exclusive shops and stores were arranged in two circular levels around a gleaming gray wrought iron fountain. Gray wrought iron archways and railings added lacy elegance to the curved walkways, while pale pink awnings supplied a fanciful contrast. Trees and flowers spilled their fragrance into the warm summer air.

Susan found Ben not far from the center of the mall, standing near a furniture store window. He looked so handsome in his impeccable suit and dark glasses. She wore one of her best work dresses—a white cotton knit with three-quarters-length sleeves and a long, full skirt. Ben's eyes flicked over her approvingly as she neared him.

He took her to lunch first at the Beijing Grill at one end of the mall. The atmosphere of the restaurant was light and airy, with high arched windows revealing a verdant courtyard beyond. The cuisine was fabulous. Susan raved over her cashew chicken, while Ben enjoyed his shrimp with lobster sauce.

"So what do you hear from Jamie these days?" he asked her as they ate.

Susan glanced up at him; she realized she was feeling a little more comfortable discussing Jamie with Ben. "I'm afraid I've heard nothing," she confessed. "Jamie has evidently made himself scarce again. I've been by the apartment a couple of times, and I've also tried calling. So far, no luck."

"Any idea where he might be?"

Susan frowned. "Sometimes, he gets temporary jobs with one of those inventory companies—you know, the types where they put crews in vans and drive them all over the place on assignment. I'll have to call Aunt Florence and see if she's heard from him."

"I know that's frustrating for you, not knowing where he is or what he's doing."

She nodded. "Ben, I try so hard to understand why Jamie is the way he is. The books your friend lent me have helped a lot there. Only—" She sighed. "I've also learned that the prognosis for most compulsive gamblers is not good."

"I'd like to read the books, too," Ben said.

"You would?" she asked, startled.

"Maybe we can decide on a course of action together."

Susan frowned. "Ben, you don't have to feel so ... obligated."

She knew at once she'd chosen the wrong word, as Ben released her hand and scowled. "Is that what you think? Susan, when are you going to realize that I'm in your life because I want to be, not just because of your dad?"

Susan bit her lip. "I'm sorry," she said at last. "I phrased that poorly. It's just that I've always thought of Jamie as *my* problem."

"Then start thinking differently."

"I guess I'm not used to sharing these things with a man."

"Well, you'd better get used to it."

The two were staring at each other tensely when a waiter stopped by, refilling their water glasses. Susan thanked the man and he smiled at her before walking off. She glanced at

Ben to find him frowning even more formidably. "Now what's wrong?"

"Do you realize that everywhere we go, you turn men's heads?" he asked irritably.

"Hah!" Susan laughed. "Then you didn't notice that group of women tittering and gawking at you as the hostess led us to our table?"

"What group of women?" he asked innocently, and they both laughed.

They ate in amiable silence for a few minutes. Both felt grateful for a lessening of the tension between them.

Over coffee, Ben asked, "Susan, do you like your job?"

She raised an eyebrow at him. "What makes you ask?"

"Well, you were complaining the other day. And I don't like the idea of you working at a job you don't really like."

She shrugged. "My position has its frustrations. Most jobs do. Doesn't yours?"

Ignoring her question, he continued, "You could always quit."

"Quit and do what?"

He grinned.

Susan rolled her eyes exasperatedly. "In that case, Ben Adams, I *would* be a kept woman."

"I see nothing wrong with that."

Susan sighed heavily. "Ben, I just don't know about all this—my staying with you indefinitely, you buying me a gown and all—"

"Ah, yes, it smacks of permanence, doesn't it?" His knee nudged hers under the table, and an unexpected jolt of sensual awareness shot through her. Leaning toward her intimately, he added, "Would you quit your job if the right man asked you to stay home and raise his children?"

Susan's heard pounded. "Now that's a chauvinistic question if I've ever heard one," she managed, with a short laugh.

"But you didn't answer it," he reminded.

Susan shook her head, fighting a smile. "You know what, Ben Adams?"

"What?" he whispered in a low, sexy voice, his knee nudging hers again.

"You're a tease."

He laughed. "Who says I'm teasing? And you still haven't answered my question."

At last, she said awkwardly, "Well, I do feel that most mothers who work do so for economic reasons. I know it was true for my mom. I suppose if I ever have children, I'll want to stay home with them as long as possible. My job provides a lot of intellectual stimulation, but it isn't everything I want from life."

"A girl after my own heart," Ben said. Before she could comment on that, he continued brightly, "Finished with your lunch?"

"Yes."

"Then let's go do our shopping. I have plans for the rest of our afternoon." As she glanced at him quickly, her cheeks hot, he added, "You guessed it, darling."

They left the restaurant, holding hands as they walked toward the other end of the mall. About halfway there, Ben pulled Susan to a halt in front of a jewelry shop. On display were several diamond rings. "Which one do you like?" he teased.

"Ben!"

"Come on, we're only window shopping," he said. "Harmless enough activity, isn't it?"

Susan rolled her eyes.

"Which one?" he persisted.

Gritting her teeth, Susan pointed to a modest, old-fashioned set with a small stone. "That one is nice. Simple. Elegant."

"Too common," he said dismissively. He pointed to a diamond solitaire that looked to be at least two carats. "Now, that's a ring that makes a statement."

"Good Lord, Ben," she said with a laugh. "What kind of statement do you have in mind?"

He pulled her close and whispered, "How about 'I belong to Ben Adams'?"

"Now that *is* a statement," she countered noncommittally. Yet the hard pounding of her heart, the slight quiver in her voice, betrayed the fact that her emotions were hardly immune to his passionate words. She glanced at the ring. "But I must warn you, Mr. Adams, that most women would be afraid to wear a rock like that. It would invite thievery."

"Ah, but not if a girl has a knight in shining armor to protect her," he put in. "Don't forget that I talked down three hoodlums with a knife."

Susan laughed ruefully. "They would have cut off my finger to get that ring."

Susan regretted the words as soon as she saw the look of pain flashing across Ben's eyes. He sighed raggedly and pulled her close. "No, they wouldn't have. I wouldn't have let them, Sue. I'd never let anyone hurt you."

Susan moaned as Ben kissed her. The moment was becoming far too emotional.

At last, as a couple of passing teenage boys hooted a catcall at them, they pulled apart, laughing. "Want to go inside the jewelry store and have a closer look?" Ben asked.

"No way," Susan said quickly.

He chuckled as they started off down the walkway together.

The clothing store they entered was the most lavish and elegant Susan had ever seen. It was flowing and spacious, with marble floors and fabulous designer clothing on small, freestanding chrome racks. The owner herself greeted Ben; she turned out to be well-acquainted with his mother. After the introductions and small talk were exhausted, Ben matter-of-factly informed the woman that he wanted to buy Susan an ensemble to wear at an important benefit this weekend. When Mrs. Reese turned her sagacious smile on Susan, Susan could have sworn she spotted dollar signs gleaming in the older woman's eyes.

Susan had known before that Ben had a fastidious streak, but never had she seen him in top form until she went shopping with him. He took charge of the entire procedure and was nearly impossible to please. As the two of them sat on an antique love seat, Mrs. Reese brought out dress after dress—none of which seemed to please Ben. "No, that one's not right," he would say. "I don't want Susan in black. She's quite exotic looking, you see, and she looks great in striking colors. We'll want something to contrast with her vibrant dark eyes—perhaps jade green, I'm thinking."

Susan herself could have crawled under the love seat. She felt a bit miffed by Ben's taking charge of choosing her gown, although she had to admit to herself that it was his money. And as much as she hated for him to spend that money, she couldn't quite spoil his fun, either, since he was clearly having the time of his life. Even when he scowled and waved off another dress Mrs. Reese produced, the devilish glint in his eyes gave him away. He had to have known she felt very much on the spot here, especially since the owner of the shop was well aware that she wasn't his wife. Yet he seemed almost to delight in making her squirm.

However, when he shook his head dismissively at a pale green silk gown, she felt compelled to protest. "Ben, I like that one."

He turned to smile at her. "If you like it, I'll buy it for you, too, but not for Saturday night."

Susan was horrified. She knew that all the gowns they'd seen so far were designer originals that cost a small fortune apiece. She wasn't about to let Ben buy her two dresses. "Oh, on second thought, I don't like it that much," she muttered, watching the owner's face fall.

At last, Ben spotted "the" gown. The design was strapless, the top composed of sequinned, diamond-shaped panels of fuschia and green. The straight-lined skirt and elegant jacket were of jade-green satin.

"Yes, that's Susan," Ben said when he saw it.

"Oh, is it?" she murmured with a laugh. Yet she could hardly take her eyes off the gown. It was divine and Ben was right.

Minutes later, walking about the room in the glittering gown, Susan felt like a model on a runway as Ben scrutinized every inch of her. The owner wrung her hands as she observed his studious frown.

"It will need some minor alterations through the waist and hips, Mr. Adams," Mrs. Reese said at last.

"Ah, yes, Susan's so slim," Ben murmured. He looked straight at her then, and thought of what he loved to do with those lovely, slim hips. And he knew from her sudden, hot blush that she had read his mind. He turned back to the owner. "Can you have the alterations completed by Saturday morning?"

"Certainly, sir," the woman said with a relieved smile.

Then the frustrating ritual was repeated for Susan as Ben selected just the right purse and shoes to go with the gown. When they were checking out, she nearly fainted as she caught a glimpse of the check he was writing. But he forestalled her protests by saying, "Not a word, Susan, or I swear I'll buy you the other gown, too. I know you really liked it, but the color wasn't quite you."

Susan could only stand by in mute exasperation.

In the car heading for his penthouse, she said, "I never knew you were that interested in women's clothing."

He laughed. "I wasn't. Until I met you. Did I embarrass you in there?"

"A little," she admitted. "Actually, I think you delighted in embarrassing me."

He chuckled. "Susan, I knew that if it had been left to you, it wouldn't have gotten done. You never wanted me to buy you a gown in the first place. And besides, our moment in front of the jewelry store told me a lot."

"Oh, did it?"

"You think of yourself in far too modest terms. I want to show you off like the beautiful diamond you are."

Susan was suddenly lost in troubled thought. "But diamonds have flaws, Ben. I think you have to remember that."

He braked for a light, then leaned over the console to kiss her. "At the moment, this particular diamond seems damned perfect to me."

11

SATURDAY WAS quickly upon them. Susan and Ben awoke early, and he asked her to accompany him for a jog along Turtle Creek. The morning was sweet, the air filled with the scent of flowers, the path along the bayou shady and dappled. Susan marveled at the beauty of Ben's body as they moved along. He looked magnificent in his athletic shorts and tank top, his lithe body rippling with power. Even the gloss of sweat on his tanned shoulders and arms was very sexy. She was clad in equally skimpy athletic wear, and he cast numerous admiring glances in her direction, as well.

"Nervous about tonight?" he asked as they rounded a curve near the creek.

She laughed shortly. "And I thought I was doing such a good job of hiding it."

"You've seemed a little tense, a bit withdrawn, ever since I asked you to accompany me," he continued worriedly. "Look, Sue, I didn't want this benefit to come between us. I wanted it to be something we could share."

She was quiet for a moment, taking deep breaths as they continued along. "It's just that I'm not used to—that sort of thing."

"I'll be with you every minute, Sue."

"I'll be okay, Ben," she said, starting to feel defensive. "You don't have to coddle me."

He pulled her to a halt beneath a large oak tree, and both of them panted as he stared down into her eyes, his own gaze filled with poignant emotion. "But maybe I do want to coddle you, to protect you. Susan, I live in a world where everyone is always pretending, playing some sort of game. But you're different. Please don't hide your feelings from me. I think that what I love about you the most is that you're so honest, so vulnerable."

"Oh, Ben," she breathed.

When he kissed her, she felt breathless from much more than the jogging. Yet she also felt sad. She knew she was withdrawing from him in a sense, pulling in to protect herself, uncertain that what they had could last. Things had gotten so hot and heavy between them so quickly. Both of them were caught up in their emotions. Indeed, Ben increasingly hinted of a future between them, of marriage.

But Susan was very much afraid that tonight, he would discover that she just didn't belong in his world.

BACK AT BEN'S apartment, they took a shower together. Afterward as they dressed in the bedroom, Ben asked her what she wanted to do with their day. "We need to pick up your gown over at the Crescent," he said, "but other than that, the docket is pretty open."

Awkwardly, Susan said, "Ben, if you don't mind, I really would like to spend the day at my apartment. It's like every time I get ready to go tackle that place, you have some other design for my time." Watching him grin, she added, "Not that I'm complaining, but I do need to get my mail and start cleaning the place up. And I'm really worried that Jamie has pretty much disappeared."

"I'll come with you," he quickly offered.

But she shook her head. "I can't ask you to help me contend with that disaster."

He laughed shortly. "Do you think it's beneath my dignity to clean an apartment?" Grasping her hands, he continued earnestly, "Sue, do you want to get your apartment back in order so you can leave me?"

Susan avoided his eyes. "Ben, it's my home."

"And this isn't?"

"I—I'm not sure."

Muttering a curse, he released her hands and began to pace. "Susan, what is it?" Before she could answer, he went on tensely, "It's the benefit tonight, isn't it? If I'd known it would have upset you so, I never would have mentioned it. Look, we don't have to go—"

"Don't be ridiculous," she cut in quickly. "Of course you have to go, and I'm not going to back out of it, either."

"Then what is it?"

She bit her lip. How could she tell him she was sure she wouldn't fit in?

He sighed in annoyance. "Look, I want to come with you to your apartment today. Don't argue with me, okay?"

"Okay," she said.

After they picked up Susan's gown and brought it back to the penthouse, they both changed into old jeans and T-shirts. Ben gathered a bucketful of cleaning supplies and they left for her apartment.

They walked in the front door to the heavy door of a pine-scented cleaning compound. A plump, middle-aged woman with neat graying hair stepped out from the kitchen to greet them.

"My stars and garters, Susan!" she exclaimed. "What happened to this place?"

"Hello, Aunt Florence," Susan said with an awkward smile. Setting down her purse and the mail she'd just picked up, she stepped forward and briefly embraced the older woman. "How did you get in?"

"Well, I brought you kids some food, and the landlord let me in." She glanced at Ben. "Who's your friend?"

"Oh, sorry. Aunt Florence, this is Ben Adams. Ben, this is my aunt, Florence Nowotny."

Florence extended her hand to Ben. As he shook it and murmured a pleasantry, she said with a frown, "Ben Adams... You know, that name sounds familiar."

"Ben flew with Dad in Vietnam," Susan explained. "He came to see us not long after Dad was killed. Remember?"

Florence snapped her fingers. "As a matter of fact, I do." She studied Ben in amazement. "You've really changed." As he grinned, she turned to Susan and added, "But how did the two of you get together again?"

Susan sighed. "That's a long story." She glanced about the living room, where a modicum of order had already been restored. "I see you've started cleaning up. You really didn't have to do that, Aunt Florence."

"Which brings me to my initial question. What happened here, Susan?"

Glancing at a pile of papers and other debris her aunt had swept up, she muttered, "Oh, I did my taxes a bit late this year. Chalk it up to last minute panic."

Florence shot her an admonishing glance. "And Jamie tells me you broke your foot?"

Susan distractedly brushed a wave of hair from her brow. "Yes, it was a chicken."

"A chicken? What did you do, trip over it?"

"Something like that." Susan bit her lip. "Aunt Florence, have you heard from Jamie?"

"Yes. As a matter of fact, he came over for dinner last week."

"Do you have any idea where he is?"

"Why, yes. He got a job with one of those inventory crews again. He told me he'd be gone for about ten days."

Susan expelled a relieved sigh. "Well, at least he's okay." At Florence's puzzled look, she added, "He didn't tell me where he was going."

Florence glanced about the room. "Well, dear, I'd best continue with my cleaning. I've got the minister and his wife coming over for dinner tonight."

Susan was about to protest, when Ben held up the bucket of cleaning supplies and said firmly, "Really, Mrs. Nowotny, Susan and I can handle this."

Florence gave them both a meaningful once-over. "Well, if that's the way things are," she said pointedly to her niece. As Susan ground her teeth in silent embarrassment, she added, "There's ham and beans in the refrigerator, dear. Please don't let it turn green like everything else did."

"We won't, Aunt Florence," Susan promised.

"Guess I'll run along then," Florence said. She kissed her niece quickly on the cheek and picked up her purse from the desk. "Nice meeting you, Mr. Adams. You two must come over for dinner some time soon."

"We'd be delighted to, Mrs. Nowotny," Ben said.

After Florence left, both of them laughed. "So that's Aunt Florence," Ben said.

Susan nodded. "I think her mission in life is to feed the world."

"At least she was able to tell you where Jamie is."

"Yes. Knowing he's okay is a big relief."

Ben set down his bucket. "Where shall we begin, Sue? Your aunt made a good start, but . . ."

They worked all morning setting the apartment to rights. Since Aunt Florence had already restored order in the kitchen, they began by finishing up in the living room. Next, they tackled the bathroom. It was a real mess, since one of the thugs had smashed most of the bottles when he rifled through the medicine cabinet. Afterward Ben helped Susan right the furniture in the bedrooms, then he rehung clothes in the closets while she tackled the dressers and made the beds.

The fact that Ben was helping her today made Susan's heart well with tenderness toward him. She would have expected him to offer the services of his housekeeper, but not to come over and help with the physical labor himself. He was certainly full of surprises, she mused.

After finishing up in Jamie's bedroom, she went hunting for him. She found him sitting on her closet floor, staring at some pictures he was neatly replacing in a box. He looked fascinated.

She sank to her knees beside him. "Those are of me and Jamie as children," she said.

He glanced up at her, his eyes strangely awed. "Do you realize what a beautiful child you were? Of course, you're an even more stunning woman. But I remember when I saw you at eight—those big, sad brown eyes of yours. You stayed in my mind long afterward."

"Did I?" A dreamy smile tugged at Susan's lips.

He held up a picture of her and Jamie clashing with rubber swords. "You look so different from your brother. He looks a lot like Jim."

Susan nodded. "I look more like my mom did."

He glanced at her closely. "So that's where you got those exotic good looks."

She smiled. "Mom was half-Italian."

"Was she?" He stared down at a picture of her at about six. She was in a swimsuit, laughing as the sprinkler spurted over her. "May I keep this?"

"Sure," she said, rather touched that he wanted the old photograph.

"You look so happy there, so innocent," he said wistfully, tucking the small snapshot in his T-shirt pocket. "That was before all the bad things happened, wasn't it, darling? Before you lost your mother—and Jim."

Susan swallowed a lump in her throat, touched by the sensitivity of Ben's remarks. "I'm happy now," she said, shocking herself with the heartfelt remark.

He stared back at her tenderly. "Are you?" He reached out, grazing her soft cheek with his fingertips. "I'd like to make you happy for the rest of your life—make up for all of those bad things."

She raised her chin slightly. "You don't owe me anything, Ben."

"That's not what I meant." He sighed exasperatedly. "Susan, why do you keep implying that I'm only with you out of some sense of duty?"

She lowered her eyes. She couldn't bring herself to say, *Because I can't quite believe that you'd want me for myself.*

In the meantime, Ben had picked up another snapshot— of Florence Nowotny standing near a Christmas tree with two sober-looking, sad-eyed children in red flannel pajamas. He sighed, his heart aching as he thought of the pain Susan and Jamie must have suffered after losing both parents. "This had to have been taken not long after you came to live with Aunt Florence," he said. As Susan nodded solemnly, he asked, "What was it like for the two of you, growing up with your aunt?"

Susan sighed. "Aunt Florence is—well, eccentric, I guess. She seems to feel her purpose in life is to fret over other people. She nursed my grandfather for years; then he died, leaving her an adequate, if modest, income. After Dad got killed in Vietnam, I think she took over with Jamie and me where she had left off with Grandpa. She provided us more with neurotic smothering than with real guidance."

Susan paused, a faraway look in her eyes. "After we lost Dad, Jamie and I became very close. Often, he would come into my room at night. He used to sob and say, 'I want Mama. I want Daddy.'" Susan looked at Ben and smiled bravely. "I tried to comfort him, but it was hard. He was only five."

Ben pressed his hand over hers. "And you were only eight, and very much in need of comfort yourself. You had to grow up in a hurry, didn't you, darling? And no wonder you feel so protective toward Jamie now."

"He's all I've ever really had," Susan said, fighting the sudden sting of tears.

"You have me, darling," Ben whispered, and kissed her. Her lips trembled softly beneath his, and he placed his hand intimately on her warm thigh. The sudden catch of sadness she had felt uncoiled in a wave of tenderness toward him.

A moment later, Ben held up a picture of Susan at two, in the bathtub. He grinned his delight, studying the wide-eyed, smiling moppet with her riot of dark curls. "Now that's what I call a beautiful baby. Do you realize what perfect children we could have?"

For once, Susan allowed herself to indulge in the whimsy. She studied Ben's chiseled face, his vibrant blue eyes. "Any child of yours should have your eyes," she said.

But he shook his head. "Any child of *ours* should have your eyes." As she bit her lip, he added, "Then I guess we'd just have to keep trying until we got one of each, wouldn't we, darling?"

Susan sighed. "It's a nice fantasy."

"It's more than a fantasy." Saying the words, he tucked the picture of her in the tub in his pocket, as well.

"Ben, you're not keeping the picture of me in the bathtub!"

He laughed as he stood and pulled her to her feet. Pulling a couple more snapshots from the back pocket of his jeans, he confessed, "And I'm taking this one of you in your Girl Scout uniform, and this one of you graduating from high school." As she tried to grab the pictures, he grinned and held them out of reach. "But I most certainly want the one of you in the bathtub. That way, the next time you balk, I'll have the means to blackmail you into line."

"Spoken like a ruthless businessman," she said, her hands on her hips.

He grinned as he tucked the pictures safely away. Then he stepped closer and whispered, "Perhaps spoken like a man in love?"

Susan stared up at him breathlessly, her lips slightly parted. Ben took full advantage of the moment by ducking his head down and kissing her deeply and thoroughly. Susan moaned and pressed herself into him, drinking in his nearness, his touch, his taste. But she didn't know quite what to make of his near-declaration seconds earlier. He'd spoken teasingly—like the motion of his tongue, which now darted in and out of her mouth like a sweet, titillating flame. Yet she also sensed the seriousness behind his words.

"So, are we through here?" he asked at last.

"Looks like it," she managed over her pounding heart.

He ran his index finger over her wet lips. "Now, I want you to come home with me, Susan," he said solemnly.

"Okay, Ben," she breathed. "Is that why you came here with me today? To make sure I'd come home with you?"

He spoke with husky emotion as he held her tightly against him. "Partly. I want to take you home and make love to you, then maybe we can catch a nap before this evening. We're bound to be out till the wee hours."

"Why don't we make love here?" she asked with a surge of reckless desire.

"Here? On the closet floor?"

"Unless you'd rather try it standing," she quipped with a crooked smile, insinuating her hand under his shirt.

He glanced around. "I could always put you on the rack," he teased.

"That would be exotic."

Ben smiled at her, his eyes full of tender amusement. "And what are we going to do about the stork, darling? Risk a visit from him?"

She laughed. "I came prepared."

He shook a finger at her. "Then you were planning all along to ravish me on your closet floor?"

"*I* was planning to ravish *you*?" she repeated indignantly. She ran her fingertips teasingly over the straining front of his jeans. "You have a hair-triggered libido if I've ever seen one."

"That does it, minx."

Ben glowered menacingly as he wrestled Susan down onto the floor with him. She squealed her delight as he raised her T-shirt and nuzzled her stomach with his face; she sighed with longing as he unzipped her jeans.

There among her childhood mementoes, they made love.

BACK AT Ben's penthouse, they dozed in his bed for a couple of hours. Susan found that all the physical work, and especially their lovemaking on the closet floor, had really taken the edge off her tension. She'd seen a new side of Ben today—a warm, caring, sensitive man who was not beneath physical labor, who was so fascinated with her that he had snitched her childhood photos. All of this endeared her to him. He'd seemed so different from the ruthless business man in the impeccable suit, the sophisticated banker she knew.

But as they dressed for the evening, the tension again built up for Susan, especially as she stepped into the living room in her designer gown and faced Ben in his formal black. He looked devastatingly handsome, every hair in place, every crease perfect. Yet he also looked like an urbane, intimidating stranger standing across from her.

"My God, you're so incredibly lovely," he whispered, feasting his eyes on her in the fabulous jade dress with its fuchsia accents.

"Thanks. You look quite dashing yourself," she responded shyly. Touching her hair, she added, "I should have had my hair done."

But Ben shook his head. "That simple style suits you perfectly. You're so beautiful that no embellishments are needed." He came over and offered her his arm. "You're going to knock everyone dead, Susan."

"Oh, I hope not," she quipped dryly, and they laughed as they swept out the door together.

SUSAN TRIED NOT to betray her uneasiness as they drove downtown to the posh hotel. Ben pulled up to the main entrance, where his Jaguar was whisked away by a smiling valet. Susan felt tense as she walked into the lobby on Ben's arm. They proceeded into a huge room with deep red carpeting and dazzling crystal chandeliers. Elegantly dressed men and women were sipping cocktails and sampling fabulous hors d'oeuvres—caviar, delicate small crepes, pâtés and canapés of every description.

The evening went fairly well at first. Ben's friends and associates greeted him effusively and accepted Susan readily. The almost fawning attitude of many of Ben's acquaintances made her realize what a powerful man he was. She did receive some pointed stares from several beautiful women he introduced her to. From the way these women simpered around Ben, she was sure he'd dated them before. Even as Susan seethed with jealousy, she had to acknowledge to herself once more that there had been a long line of sophisticated, prominent women in Ben's life before she came alone. This reality hardly inspired confidence regarding their future relationship.

Just a few minutes after they'd entered the posh ballroom, a couple came up to join them—a handsome, balding man and his blond, pregnant wife. Ben introduced Susan to Charles and Jessica Marshall. The Marshalls greeted Susan graciously, then Charles took Ben aside, leaving Susan with Jessica.

"So, you're Ben Adams's latest flame," Jessica said.

Susan laughed. She liked Jessica—she had sparkling blue eyes, dimples, and a natural, girl-next-door loveliness. She wore a simple, pale blue gown that suited her wholesome beauty perfectly. Her down-to-earth manner put Susan at ease. "Actually, Ben's an old friend of my family's."

Jessica elbowed her slyly. "Come on. Don't try to fool Jessie. He's more than a friend, right?"

Susan smiled. "Okay, he's more than a friend."

"Don't you think Ben's a dreamboat?" Jessica went on.

"He is that," Susan agreed.

"I tell you what—if I didn't have Charles, I'd be chasing Ben Adams till my Reeboks fell off." As Susan chuckled, Jessica added, "Don't be surprised if you receive some scathing looks from other women tonight."

Susan laughed ruefully. "Oh, I already have."

"Ben Adams has left behind a trail of broken hearts."

"Has he?" This came as no surprise to Susan.

"Every available female in Dallas has tried to latch on to him, but let me tell you, that man is *picky*."

"Is he?" Susan was all innocent attention.

Jessica nodded. "He once brought a date to our house for dinner, and I heard him complaining to Charles because he didn't like the color of her fingernail polish. Can you imagine—her fingernail polish?"

Susan frowned. "Maybe something else about her bothered him, and he couldn't quite put his finger on it."

"Put his finger on it?" Jessica repeated, elbowing Susan. As both of them laughed at the unintended pun, Jessica went on, "You know, I've never seen Ben with a woman who wasn't a knockout. But don't worry, Susan. He's never dated anyone quite as stunning as you. It's easy to see why he looks at you the way he does."

Susan blushed. "Now you're embarrassing me."

"But it's true," Jessica asserted. "I'd say you're definitely the woman Ben Adams has been looking for."

Susan was feeling increasingly put on the spot. Watching Jessica shift uncomfortably from foot to foot, she grabbed an opportunity to change the subject. "When is your baby due?" she asked with a smile.

"Eight more weeks," Jessica said. "The little ball of fire is keeping me up nights, but other than that, Charles and I are really getting excited."

"Is this your first child?"

"Yes."

"I'm so happy for you," Susan said sincerely.

Jessica nodded toward Ben, who was still off conversing with Charles. "You know, I'd say it's about time for good old Ben to start thinking of little Adamses, if he ever wants them. He and Charles are close to the same age, so unless I'm missing my guess, Ben will soon be approaching the big four-o."

Susan laughed. She wasn't about to tell Jessica that Ben already had little Adamses very much on his mind. Then, watching Jessica's eyes suddenly widen, she asked, "Is something wrong?"

"Well, let's just say I don't stray far from the ladies' room these days, hon," Jessica quipped dryly. "Junior just gave me a swift kick—well, a place I'd rather not mention. Care to come along?"

Susan laughed and went off with her new friend.

Later, in the banquet room, Ben and Susan sat next to Jessica and Charles at the table Reunion Bank had bought for the evening. The meal was long, with several speeches given by representatives of the various sponsors of the benefit. Ben himself gave a brief talk in behalf of the bank, thanking all those present for their support of crippled children.

Watching Ben stand before the crowded room, addressing the throng with such polish and sophistication, Susan could hardly believe that this was the same man who earlier today had mopped her bathroom floor and rehung her clothes, who had sat on her closet floor in his jeans and lovingly perused pictures of her childhood. Bits and pieces of things he'd said to her over past days kept drifting back to her. How he'd called her "perfect," how he'd looked at her childhood pictures and spoken of the "perfect" children they could have together. She remembered, too, how Jessica had remarked that she'd never seen Ben with a woman as beautiful as she was. Could it be that Ben was trying to select a wife as he had chosen everything else in his life, finding a woman with just the right eyes, the right body, someone with whom he could make perfect children for his perfect world?

She remembered, too, how he'd promised to make up for the bad times she'd known, and this convinced her that he hadn't completely given up his guilt over her father's death. She was beginning to fear that Ben wanted her for all the wrong reasons.

After all the speeches were concluded, there was an auction to benefit the charity. Furs, jewelry, vacations, even a small Mercedes, had been donated by local businesses. The auctioneer was a colorful oilman who kept the crowd entertained with his down-home humor. Susan was stunned by the affluence of the attendees, the ease with which they spent their money—four thousand dollars for an Alaskan cruise, ten for a mink, over twenty for the small Mercedes.

Then the auctioneer held up a stunning emerald on a gold chain, and a collective "Aaah" rippled through the crowd. "Now this is what I call a Texas-size rock," he quipped with a grin. "Which one of you boys wants to buy this for his favorite gal?"

The bidding was lively, with several men jumping into the fray, amid the delighted squeals of their wives or girlfriends. Once the bid had passed five thousand, Ben shocked Susan by joining in with a bid of sixty-five hundred dollars. Susan was flabbergasted, and tried to catch his eye; but his attention was riveted on the auction, as he listened attentively and continued to top the other men's bids. Susan had a sick feeling that Ben was going to buy the emerald for her. After all, it was hardly the type of thing he'd give his mother. She glanced at Jessica, horror-stricken; but Jessica only smirked and winked back at her.

Seconds later, Ben placed the top bid, and the crowd cheered. He strode to the front of the room and wrote out a check to the smiling woman collecting the auction receipts. He returned to the table with the jeweler's box in hand; he paused in front of Susan. A hush fell over the crowd as he smiled down at her. Susan's heart was pounding so hard she could barely breathe as she stared back up at him. As the attendees looked on in rapt fascination, Ben took the necklace from the box, undid the clasp, and placed it around Susan's neck.

Snapping the clasp in place, Ben leaned over, lightly kissing Susan's lips. That's when the crowd went wild—whooping, clapping and cheering. Susan could have died on the spot. When Ben moved back to smile at her, her cheeks were flame-bright. The emerald was cold against her breast, and yet she burned from its imprint. She realized that Ben had just branded her his, in front of God and everyone. He couldn't have made a more adamant statement had he hired someone to skywrite, Susan Is Mine.

At last he slipped back into his chair beside her, took her hand and winked at her. He looked eminently satisfied with himself as his eyes flicked approvingly over her. Susan could only stare at him speechlessly. The man was maddening, captivating, impossibly endearing.

After the auction, Charles and Jessica left, and Susan had no opportunity to talk with Ben as the chairman of the event took him aside. She stood on the fringe of the crowd, fingering the emerald at her neck and watching couples dance to the lively music of the band.

Then a familiar voice said, "Well, hello dear."

Susan automatically stiffened as she spotted Sybil Sayers standing beside her. The woman looked almost garish in her red, sequinned gown; as usual, she wore too much makeup and jewelry. "Hello, Miss Sayers," she said guardedly.

"I see you and our Mr. Adams are quite the number these days," Sayers said snidely. She nodded toward the necklace. "Ben practically brought down the house when he bought you that rock."

"Ben's a good friend," Susan responded automatically, defensively dropping her hand away from the necklace.

"Oh, come on, Sue," Sayers coaxed, "you can do better than that with Sybil. I've seen you two making ga-ga eyes at each other all night. And that kiss that Ben gave you in front of everyone—" Sayers paused to whistle "—why that little kiss was hotter than the emerald, wasn't it, dear?"

Susan struggled to retain her composure, and didn't comment.

The two women stood in strained silence for a moment, watching the dancers swirl about. Then Sayers murmured, "Dear, I've been meaning to tell you that I found it so tragic, what happened to your mother."

Now Susan couldn't hide her shock. Her eyes were huge as she whirled to face the columnist. "What do you know about my mother?"

Sayers continued nonchalantly, "Oh, you know, dear. That horrid embezzlement scandal concerning the county hospital here, and her being implicated with her boss." Sayers clucked sympathetically. "What a shame your mother never got a chance to vindicate herself. And then she was killed with her boss in his private plane. . . . Well, it did look rather compromising, didn't it, my dear? What with your father being gone in Vietnam and all . . ."

Susan was reeling. "If you'll excuse me, Miss Sayers, I really must go find Ben."

"And it's a shame about your brother, too," Sayers continued, as if she hadn't even heard Susan. "Being dishonorably discharged from the Army for stealing." Sayers flashed her poisonous smile at Susan. "Does Ben know about all this? I can't think his mother would approve. She's so protective of her darling son. But then, Charlotte is in Europe at the moment, isn't she? How nice for you."

White-faced, Susan could only turn and hurry away. She was rushing for the ladies' room to gather her tumultuous emotions when she collided with Ben.

"Hi, darling," he said with a laugh. "Where are you going in such a hurry? I was really hoping you'd dance with me."

"I'm tired," she said lamely.

"Just a couple dances, please," he coaxed. "It wouldn't do for us to leave too early."

"Sure," she said, forcing a thin smile.

As Ben swept her about to a lilting waltz, Susan tried her best not to burst out weeping on his tux. He seemed in grand good spirits tonight, and she hated to spoil the evening for him. But the things Sybil Sayers had said had devastated her, had made her realize that she and Ben were living in a fantasy world. This man was looking for the perfect woman, and yet she knew now that no woman would be less perfect than she, with her scandalous family background. If she stayed with Ben, there would always be someone like Sayers around to dig up the dirt and fling it all over them. She would be a liability to his career—the wrong woman to grace his glitzy world.

Susan's withdrawal was not lost on Ben. "What is it, darling?" he asked tenderly. "Are you still mad about the emerald?"

Susan stared up at him in anguish and love. "Ben, what can I say? I can't accept it, of course."

"Of course you can," he countered. "It's perfect for you, you know."

Susan glanced away, fighting a new rush of tears. There was that word—perfect—again. How Ben seemed to love it. If only he knew how truly imperfect she was! He'd run for sure.

Yet he went on blithely talking, still teasing her. "You know, it was either the emerald, or the baby Mercedes. But I'd prefer that you have a larger car than that."

She sighed. "Oh, Ben. What am I going to do with you?"

"I have numerous ideas—wickedly pleasurable ideas."

"Ben, I can't keep the emerald."

"What if I threaten to show all our friends your baby pictures?" he taunted. He snapped his fingers. "I know, I'll use the picture of you in the bathtub for my Christmas card this year."

He was being so treacherously endearing that Susan wanted to sob again. "Ben, you're impossible."

"Darling, keep the emerald. It's for a worthy cause."

Her eyes flashed with sudden resentment. "Is that how you think of me? As a worthy cause?"

But he only chuckled. "I'd say you're the most worthy cause of all."

As Ben drew Susan closer, he inhaled the captivating scent of her. He realized that he held everything he wanted in life right here in his arms. His sweet, adorable, unspoiled Susan . . . He remembered the moment when he'd given her the emerald, how vulnerable and breathless she had looked as she stared up at him. He remembered how the pulse on her neck had jumped when his fingers had snapped the clasp. He remembered the moment when he had kissed her in front of everyone, how sweetly her lips had quivered beneath his, how much he had hungered to make the kiss very passionate, very deep, and very long. Lord, he was so proud that she was his. He wanted the whole world to know, even if she wasn't ready.

Yet he wasn't about to tell her that he was the one who had convinced the jeweler to donate the emerald necklace tonight. He wasn't about to tell her that he'd intended to buy it for her all along, and had known she would never accept it unless he forced her hand in public this way.

Ben continued to try to bring Susan out of her shell, but she remained withdrawn for the rest of the evening. On the way home, he finally asked, "Okay, Susan, what is it?"

"Nothing," she said, staring out the window.

"You're still mad about the emerald, aren't you?"

"I thought we had that settled. I told you I can't keep it."

"Won't," he amended tightly. "Come on, something else is troubling you. Spill it out."

"It's just that..." Reeling with hurt, she tried to cover with anger. "I just felt that your friends were pretentious and the evening was an extravagant waste."

"Oh, did you?" Now Ben sounded angry, too.

"Yes. I'm not cut out for your glitzy world, Ben."

"Susan, I'm not asking you to go to events like this every day," he pointed out. "But if we're to have a future together, we can't ignore the social obligations of my job."

"That's just it. I'm not the right woman to help you with those obligations."

"Damn," he muttered. "You're not even giving it a chance."

"I did give it a chance. What we've had has been good, but tonight was a big dose of reality for me. I—I didn't care for any of it."

Exasperated, he asked, "Then what do you like?"

"Jeans," she retorted, turning away.

The atmosphere was tense between them as they arrived back at his penthouse. She sat down on the couch in the living room and he stared at her broodingly. "You coming to bed?"

She shrugged. "Think I'll stay up awhile."

"Suit yourself."

Susan sighed miserably as Ben strode out of the room. At last, she succumbed to tears of hurt and anger and confusion. She had acted like a real bitch toward Ben, and she knew it. She'd been wounded, and she had lashed out at him, hurting him and putting distance between them. But it wasn't his fault that Sybil Sayers had confronted her so cruelly. It wasn't his fault that she was the wrong woman for him. Right now, the thought of losing him devastated her, and she knew she would hang on for as long as she could. Soon enough, he'd realize they could never make it together, but for now . . .

Susan got up and went into the bedroom, but Ben wasn't there. She could hear the shower running in the bathroom beyond. She smiled to herself ruefully. He was probably trying to cool off.

Susan took off the emerald necklace, carefully replacing it in the velvet box that Ben had put down on the dresser. She went into the bathroom and spotted him in the shower through the mottled glass. A hard twinge of arousal squeezed deep in her belly as she stared at his nakedness, his vibrant movements shimmering through the glass. He seemed, as yet, unaware of her presence.

Susan went into the closet and carefully hung her gown, then stripped off the rest of her clothing. She emerged and stepped into the shower, closing the door behind her.

Ben whirled, startled, toward her. His hair was sopping wet, his vivid blue eyes piercing. The cold water hit her in a solid blast, and she shivered, thrusting herself eagerly into his arms, her nipples taut against the heat of his chest.

"Susan." His mouth came down hard on hers and his hands took her hips, nestling her against his manhood, which had already sprung robustly to life.

"I'm sorry," she whispered achingly.

"Oh, Susan," he said, kissing her again, hungrily.

"You were so wonderful tonight," she said in an emotional voice. "So sweet when you bought me the necklace. It was the dearest thing anyone ever did for me."

"Will you keep the emerald, please?" he asked tenderly.

"Ben, let's not argue about it tonight."

"Okay."

Welling with the love she felt for him, Susan sank to her knees and took Ben's swollen maleness in her mouth. Ben groaned and almost lost his balance, stunned and electrified by her boldness. The water was cold, so cold as it rushed down their bodies. And Susan's mouth was hot, so hot, engulfing him in a cocoon of wicked pleasure, squeezing him like a vise. Her fingernails were digging into his buttocks, sending him spiralling downward toward shattering ecstasy. . . .

Susan thrilled to Ben's agonized moans as she made love to him with her lips and tongue. After a moment, he tangled his hands roughly in her drenched hair and drew her head back. His eyes blazed down into hers.

"Let me please you, too," he said hoarsely.

"This pleases me," she whispered back, taking him deeply in her mouth again.

Ben exploded in a surge of love so powerful, it hurt.

12

AT WORK ON MONDAY, Susan found it hard to concentrate on the inventory program she was completing. She kept thinking about Ben and the doubtful future of their relationship. While the rest of the weekend had passed without further incident, there'd been a discernible tension between them ever since they'd attended the benefit on Saturday night. They'd been pleasant toward each other outwardly, and as intimate as always in bed; yet the physical closeness simply couldn't banish all Susan's doubts. And she hadn't been able to bring herself to tell Ben about her upsetting conversation with Sybil Sayers.

Susan had lunch with her friend Gloria Watkins at a nearby pizza parlor, and she noticed at once that Gloria was not her usual, effervescent self. Gloria only nibbled at the pepperoni pizza she and Susan were sharing; she kept avoiding Susan's eye and finally, she dumped over her drink.

"Something bothering you today, Gloria?" Susan asked as she helped her friend mop up the mess.

Gloria shrugged. "I'm fine."

"You don't look fine to me. Nor are you usually all thumbs."

Gloria bit her lip as she tossed down a soggy napkin. "Well, actually, Sue, I've been debating something all morning."

"Oh?"

"I hate to be the bearer of bad news, but I guess maybe it's better that you hear this from a friend. You're bound to find out sooner or later."

"Gloria, will you please stop talking in riddles?"

Gloria sighed. She leaned toward Susan and continued in a low voice, "You haven't seen Sybil Sayers's latest column, have you?"

Feeling the blood drain from her face, Susan shook her head. "Let me guess. She's taken aim at me again?"

"Yes. But I'm afraid that this time, she filled her pen with poison first."

"Damn," Susan muttered, glancing around. "I wonder where we can find a newspaper."

"Don't bother. I brought the column along in my briefcase."

Watching her friend lean over to pick up the leather case, Susan laughed ruefully. "I wondered why you brought your briefcase along for lunch."

Sheepishly Gloria handed Susan the folded section of the newspaper. "Sorry, Sue," she said, watching helplessly as her friend read it.

Susan soon discovered that Sayers had pulled out all the stops this time, and she felt devastated by the stinging prose she read:

I ran into that darling Ben Adams, at the benefit for crippled children on Saturday night. Again, Ben had in tow his latest heartthrob, Susan Nowotny, and darlings, you would have killed for the green rock Ben bought for Sue at the auction! Ben nearly caused a stampede when he dangled the emerald around Sue's neck and kissed her in full view of the crowd. Looks like that man has caught a full quiver of arrows from Cupid's bow!

But there may be trouble brewing in paradise. Sue is the daughter of Stella Nowotny, that unfortunate little executive secretary who was implicated with her boss, Samuel Evans, in the Westfield Hospital scandal here in the early seventies. Stella and Sam were killed together when his private plane crashed on the way to state senate hearings in Austin—and all this while Stella's hubby was off fighting in Vietnam! A pity Miss Nowotny's mother never got to vindicate herself—or spill the beans, as the case may be. But Sue has plenty of other woes, too, I hear, as it's rumored that her brother has a big gambling problem. Ben Adams might be well-advised to watch his step. I wonder what his board of directors at Reunion Bank will think of his associating with a woman who lives so close to the seamy side of life. . . .

"Damn," Susan muttered when she finished, flinging down the column in disgust.

"I know, Sue, that witch needs a rabies shot," Gloria commiserated. "I'm so sorry. But Sayers has given the same treatment to a number of prominent people here in Dallas. I read her column regularly and she's one mean bitch."

Susan laughed bitterly. "I'm surprised she's managed to hang on to her job if she's stepped on that many toes." She stared pointedly at Gloria. "But then I suppose many people love sensationalism."

Gloria held up a hand. "Hey, Sue, don't kill the messenger."

Susan sighed. "I'm sorry. I know it's not fair to blame you for her spitefulness."

Indeed, Susan knew she had only herself to blame for thinking she could ever fit into Ben Adams's world.

LATE THAT AFTERNOON, Ben had a drink with his friend Charles Marshall at an exclusive club at the top of a downtown skyscraper. The two men sat before the carved antique bar, with its etched-glass mural of Spindletop.

Both men were in sober moods. They'd discussed a few more details pertaining to the financing of Southbridge Manor; but now, their talk turned to personal matters.

"You're looking a bit down in the mouth today, Charles," Ben remarked as he sipped his Scotch.

Charles laughed ruefully. "Am I? I was about to say the same thing about you, Ben."

"Were you?" Ben shook his head. "You first, then. Why the dour expression?"

Charles sighed as he stirred his gin and tonic. "It's Jessica."

Ben laughed. "Jessica? Our darling little Wife of the Year?"

"She's not quite the wife of the year these days."

Ben was fascinated. "How so?"

"Well, I feel selfish to even bring this up, but a lot of it has to do with the baby."

"You're not happy about the baby?"

"Of course I'm delighted," Charles said quickly. "But Jessica has taken it so much further. She seems almost—obsessed."

Ben chuckled. "This is her first child, Charles."

"Yes, I know that. But already her time is almost completely taken up with the baby—furnishing the nursery just so, buying all the right clothes and toys, plus getting the child on the waiting list at all the right nursery schools. Not to mention attending La Leche League, interviewing pediatricians—"

"Interviewing pediatricians?" Ben asked, trying hard not to laugh.

Charles drew himself up stiffly. "It's not that I'm not for all of that, and of course I'm going with Jessie to the La Maze classes. It's just that otherwise, I'm beginning to feel—left out."

"Ah, jealousy rears its ugly head. A common enough reaction for a new father, I understand."

"If things are this way now," Charles continued exasperatedly, "what's it going to be like after the baby is born?"

Ben chuckled. "Have you thought of hiring a nanny?"

Charles waved him off. "Jessie is interviewing them at the rate of two dozen per week. We might find someone suitable by the time our child is in college."

Grinning, Ben sipped his drink. It seemed that his old friend Charles hadn't been able to find the perfect woman, either. Perhaps *she* didn't exist, he thought ironically.

"Why don't you just tell her?" he finally murmured.

Charles almost choked on his drink. "Tell her?"

"Tell her you feel left out."

Charles blinked rapidly, looking flustered. "Well, I hadn't thought of that. But I wouldn't want to hurt her feelings, Ben, especially not at this critical time."

"But don't you feel hurt and left out? You know, honesty needn't be brutal. You could always bring flowers and champagne, then have a little heart-to-heart chat with her."

Charles grinned. "I'll give that suggestion some thought."

As the bartender handed them another round, Ben mused that he might well take his own advice. It was time to get a fifth of Dom Perignon, take Susan in his arms and say, *Look, lady, what we have is wonderful, but it's not enough. I want a commitment. So if there's anything we need to battle out, let's get it out into the open now.*

"So what about you and Susan?" Charles asked, as if he'd just read Ben's mind. "You know, she really is dazzling, Ben."

"She is that," Ben murmured with a smile. "I want to marry her," he added, recognizing the truth of his statement even as he said it.

Charles grinned broadly, nudging Ben's arm with his fist. "Well, congratulations." Studying Ben's frown, he went on, "But you didn't look too happy when you said that."

Ben sighed. "You know, I'd never have thought I'd be attracted to someone like Susan. She's fresh, unpretentious, unspoiled. Very different from the women I'm accustomed to. And yet she fascinates me, she delights me." He drew a heavy breath, turned to Charles and added feelingly, "I've fallen for her so hard, Charles, it scares the hell out of me."

Charles laughed. "I figured you were a goner when you bought her that emerald Saturday night. So what's the problem?"

"Susan and I are from very different worlds. She lost both of her parents when she was quite young, and her brother's a compulsive gambler she has protected to her own detriment. Although she hasn't said so in so many words, she seems to think that what we have could threaten her relationship with her brother. She keeps telling me she's not right for me, and I can't convince her otherwise, or even get through to the real, gut-level reasons." He took a sip of his drink and sighed heavily. "I don't know, Charles. I've tried my best to accept Susan just the way she is, but now she has rejected everything I have to offer."

"She has?" he asked, looking taken aback.

Ben nodded grimly. "She told me so on the way home from the benefit Saturday night. She said she didn't care for anything in my world."

Charles frowned. "Well, maybe that sort of glitzy affair just makes her nervous, although she seemed quite self-possessed around Jessie and me."

"She told me she likes jeans," Ben muttered ruefully.

"Jeans?" Charles repeated, laughing. "I wish I could say the same for my wife's tastes." He chuckled again, shaking his head. "Jeans! Look, why don't you marry the girl and send her brother to Gambler's Anonymous? She's a bargain."

Ben smiled, but inside, he remained troubled. The solution might be simple from Charles's perspective, but in his heart, Ben knew he'd far from won Susan over.

SUSAN GOT OFF work early and drove straight to Ben's penthouse. When she arrived upstairs, the housekeeper was still there, dusting in the living room. Susan spoke with Mrs. Ramirez briefly as she finished up. The moment the woman left, she hurried into Ben's bedroom and began packing her things. She wiped tears as she worked. She cried in part due to her hurt over the devastating things Sybil Sayers had said about her mother and brother; she hadn't been able to get the woman's cruel comments out of her mind all afternoon.

Yet she cried more because she knew now that there was no hope for her and Ben, and it was breaking her heart. She was sure he'd reach this same conclusion as soon as he read the column. If she stayed with him, she'd wreck his career and probably his life. They'd had a beautiful, emotional affair; but it was over now, and in time he, too, would realize that what they had never could have lasted.

With her suitcase in hand and Rumor clutched in her other arm, Susan hesitated for a moment in the living room, looking around one last time—at the couch where she'd once fallen into Ben's lap, at the dining-room table where they'd shared so many happy meals together, at the glass wall where so often, he'd taken her in his arms and kissed her. For a moment she wavered, almost losing sight of her good intentions. They'd known so much love, so much joy here.

But they couldn't go on ignoring the outside world and its realities.

Rumor meowed and shifted restlessly, and Susan knew she had to get out of here before the cat bolted. Should she leave Ben a note? She shook her head and wiped new tears. She needed to make this a very clean break, and just walking out on Ben Adams was about as final a statement as she could make.

"SUE?" Ben called.

It was twenty minutes later, and as soon as Ben walked into the penthouse, he sensed something was wrong. Susan usually got home before he did, and things were much too quiet. Rumor was nowhere in sight, either.

He went through the rooms hunting for her. Then he swallowed hard, a feeling of dread gripping him as he saw that her toiletry items were no longer laid out on the vanity in the bathroom. He flung open the door to one of the closets and found her clothes were missing, as well, except for the jade-green gown.

She'd gone. He should have known it, after Saturday night. He went out into the living room, grabbed a bottle of Scotch, sloshed some in a glass and raised the drink to his lips with a trembling hand. He should have confronted her yesterday, gotten all their differences out into the open.

Or would that simply have hastened her departure?

Ben slammed down his drink and blinked at eyes that stung bitterly. He was angry. Angry at himself for not doing more to make her stay. Angry at her for leaving and not giving them a chance. Ever since Susan had come into his life, she'd tried again and again to pull away. She was forever like sand slipping through his fingers. He'd chased after her before.

And he'd be damned if he'd do so again.

"Aw, hell," he swore under his breath. He was striding for the door when the phone rang. He answered it tensely, praying it was her.

Yet instead he heard Charles Marshall's voice again, and Charles sounded nervous. "Hi, Ben. Um—is Susan there?"

Ben frowned at the phone. "Not at the moment."

"Well, Jessie and I were concerned about you both."

"Why?"

Charles sighed. "Then I take it you've not read Sybil Sayers' Monday column as yet?"

"No."

"When I got home, Jessie was very upset about it. She really likes Susan and—"

"What did that bitch say about Susan?" Ben practically shouted.

"It wasn't good, Ben. Look, I just wanted you to know that Jessie and I both think it stinks. That woman will never be welcome in our home again, and I'm sure many of our friends will feel the same way."

"Thanks, Charles. Look, I've got to go."

The instant Ben hung up the phone, he ripped into the paper Mrs. Ramirez had laid out neatly on the coffee table. He read the column, then cursed vividly. He knew in that moment that Susan had read it, too; he knew she was terribly hurt, and that he had to find her.

WHEN SUSAN arrived at her apartment, she felt exhausted, mentally and physically. She set down her cat and suitcase in the living room. She went into the bedroom and changed into old jeans and a T-shirt, then she wandered out into the kitchen looking for a soft drink. But as soon as she stepped into the room, she froze in her tracks and turned white.

The cover had been removed from the air conditioning vent! A dark hole gaped in the ceiling, while the vent cover itself had been tossed on the counter top.

In a panic, Susan grabbed a chair and hopped onto it, feeling up inside the ventwork. Her mother's rings were gone!

Fighting tears, Susan stepped down and walked numbly into the living room. She collapsed on the couch, feeling as if she had just been raped. The rings were the only things she had left of her mother's—and now it was practically certain that she'd never see them again.

Should she call the police? She laughed bitterly. She was sure that it wasn't a thief who had taken the rings.

No, she amended, it had been a thief. The thief just wasn't a stranger.

She wasn't sure just how long she'd sat there, reeling with pain, when she heard Jamie's voice. "Hi, Sis."

Susan lurched to her feet to see Jamie standing in the opened doorway. As soon as she saw his face, she knew he was the culprit; his mouth was tight, he was blinking rapidly and avoiding her eyes.

"So you're back," she said woodenly. "Aunt Florence told me you went off with an inventory crew."

"Yeah," he said, shifting nervously from foot to foot. "We have a few days off now. We're leaving for east Texas on Friday."

"You stole Mom's rings didn't you, Jamie?" Susan asked angrily, stepping forward, her eyes gleaming with outrage.

When he didn't answer her, but turned away, running a hand through his hair, she continued furiously, "Mind telling me how you discovered my hiding place?"

He sighed. "I noticed the vent cover in the kitchen had been cleaned, and I figured you'd hidden the rings there."

"Jamie, how could you?" Susan asked brokenly.

"Susan, you don't understand," he said plaintively. "I had a sure thing tip on a race at Louisiana Downs. The odds were twenty to one, Sue. I thought, if only I could score this one big win, I could make up for everything, pay you back and—"

"So what happened to your sure thing bet, Jamie?" Susan asked with a bitter laugh.

He turned away miserably. "I lost."

"Is that all you lost?"

In a small voice, he admitted, "I owe my bookie another couple of thou."

Susan gestured in wild exasperation. "Damn it, Jamie, what am I going to do with you? You'd think you'd learn by now! And to steal Mother's rings from me—"

"I don't know why you care so much about those damned rings anyway," Jamie said defensively, "after all the things Mom did, betraying Dad and—"

"That's not true!" Susan cut in furiously. "Mom never did anything wrong. You're just trying to diminish her in your own eyes to cover your own guilt."

"Hell," Jamie said disgustedly, reaching into his back pocket. "If you want the rings back that bad, here's the pawn ticket."

Jamie was stuffing the ticket in Susan's hand when abruptly, Ben walked into the apartment. "Hello, Susan. Jamie."

Susan whirled, her heart pounding. Ben—tall, solid, masterful as ever—stood near the open doorway, his blue eyes riveted on her. She knew at once that he'd overheard a lot. And she knew how much she loved him for coming after her again. That love hurt as much as the distance, physical and emotional, that stood between them now. He was staring at the tears in her eyes, his own gaze filled with such compassion that she didn't know if she wanted to start screaming out her frustration, or just run into his arms and sob her heart out.

"Ben, what are you doing here?" she whispered at last.

"I came for you—again," he said simply. He then turned to Jamie, taking a card from his breast pocket and handing it to him. He spoke coldly. "Jamie, if you want to straighten out your life, I'll do everything I can to help you. But otherwise, stay the hell away from Susan."

Jamie backed away, as if burned, Ben's card in his hand.

"Ben!" Susan exclaimed.

Ben made no attempt to argue with her. He simply picked up her suitcase, handed her her purse, then tugged her toward the door. To Jamie, he called over his shoulder, "Take care of the cat, will you? Susan and I will come back for him later."

Outside on the walkway, she exploded. "Damn it, Ben! You had no right to say those things to Jamie!"

Ben turned and gently brushed a wisp of hair from her eyes. "Susan, you're not doing him any good."

"And you're not doing me any good!" she railed back. Then, to her horror, something snapped inside her and she began to cry. Ben set down her suitcase and pulled her into his arms. She sobbed brokenly against his chest.

"Jamie hocked Mother's rings," she choked out.

"I know, darling. I heard," Ben whispered. Feeling the sobs wrack her slender body, he rubbed her back and added, "Please, don't cry, Susan. It's okay." And he kissed her tenderly.

Susan clung to Ben, her wet face pressed against his. He held her tight and murmured soothing endearments, brushing the tears from her face with his fingertips.

"I'm making a fine mess of your suit," she managed at last.

"To hell with my suit," he said tightly, kissing her again.

After a moment, Ben pulled back and stared down into her eyes. "I don't want you staying here with him," he said simply.

Susan nodded up at him, sniffling. She knew Ben was right; after Jamie's heartbreaking betrayal, she didn't want to stay here, either. "I'll go to a hotel."

"The hell you will," he said. "You're coming home with me."

Susan felt too broken up emotionally to fight him. She let him pick up her suitcase and lead her off again.

Once they were in his car, he said quietly, "I want you to give me the pawn ticket, Susan."

Susan had been holding ono the ticket for dear life. She shook her head violently. "No, Ben. I'm not going to let you buy back the rings."

"Then I guess we'll just have to sit here until you give me the ticket."

When Susan could only stare at Ben in anguish, he leaned across the console, took her roughly in his arms and kissed her with all the pent-up emotion in his body. As she trembled and kissed him back, he slipped the pawn ticket from her fingers. Then he turned and started the engine.

He stopped at the pawnshop on Mockingbird Lane, and minutes later, emerged. He got into the car and dropped the rings into her hand. She stared at them through her tears, not knowing what to say. Finally, as they pulled back onto the street, she whispered hoarsely, "I'll pay you back every dime."

"Don't be ridiculous," he said gruffly. "What's mine is yours."

Swallowing a huge lump in her throat, she said, "Did you read Sybil Sayers's column?"

She watched his jaw tighten. "Yes."

Stunned, she asked, "And you still came after me? Ben, that column could ruin your career."

"Baloney," he snapped back. He continued speaking with a stinging anger that mirrored the depths of his hurt. "Susan, do you think I'm so shallow that I'd let something like that affect out relationship? I care for you enough to take the heat. But what about you? Do you care enough about me—about us—to see this through? Will you give me and my world a chance? Or are you just going to keep on running?"

Ben's incisive questions stunned Susan into silence. Once they had arrived back at his penthouse, she went over to stand by the glass wall, looking hurt and withdrawn. Her mother's rings were still tightly clenched in one hand.

Ben came up behind her, placing his hands on her shoulders. "Why don't I put your mother's rings in my safe?" he asked.

She turned and handed him the rings. "Yes, thank you. I suppose that would be wise."

He moved to the opposite wall, drew open the door to a picture safe and began dialing the combination. "You can have the rings back any time, of course," he added. "I'll give you the combination—"

"Don't be ridiculous," Susan cut in. "I trust you to give them back to me."

She turned to look out at the city lights again. Ben took off his jacket and tie, then walked over to join her. He studied her back; her posture was straight and brave, but her shoulders trembled slightly. Her T-shirt was old and tight, emphasizing her slenderness, her vulnerability. Her jeans were older and tighter still, hugging her bottom. There was a tear high on one thigh that tormented him, making his fingers itch to touch her there, to rip those jeans off her and claim her with all the desire and aching need in his body. Never had he so yearned to make love to her.

But first... Clearing his throat, he asked, "Susan, don't you think we should talk?"

She nodded, swallowing hard. She found she couldn't turn to meet his eye. "Ben, I'm sorry about the things I said about your friends Saturday night. I didn't mean any of it. But Sybil Sayers took me aside at the party, and it was then I learned that she knew everything about my mother and Jamie. I knew it was only a matter of time before it all got into the papers. I was just so upset, so sure you'd be hurt by all of it."

"But you didn't tell me."

"No. I couldn't, Ben."

Ben groaned and put his arms around Susan's waist, nestling her against his strength. "Darling, don't you know it killed me to think that you could be hurt by all of this, too? If you hadn't met me, then Sayers never would have descended on you that way. I blame myself, and—oh, God—I'd like to strangle that bitch!"

Through her tears, Susan said, "Don't blame yourself, Ben. Please don't ever do that."

Ben turned her in his arms. "Why did you run away tonight? Was it because of the column?"

"Partly. And there's Jamie, and the fact that we're just so different. Ben, I can't see imposing all my problems on you."

He tilted her chin and looked down into her eyes. His expression was deeply troubled. "Susan, why can't you get it through your head that it's okay for you to lean on me? You know, I think before you came along, I never had anyone need me before—not really. And you do need me, Susan. You just won't admit it."

"Do you need me?" she asked quietly.

His eyes flashed with pain. "I needed you tonight, and you just walked out. Do you have any idea how much that hurt? You didn't even trust me enough to share your feelings."

"I—I'm sorry," she said again, helplessly.

He drew her closer and spoke intensely. "We have a lot of making up to do, Susan."

"Ben..."

Susan shuddered with emotion as Ben kissed her. She wanted to tell him they were just postponing the inevitable, but she couldn't bring herself to say the words. She was too vulnerable tonight, and she had hurt him too much already.

Ben took her hand and led her down the hallway. In his room, he sat down on the bed, then drew her between his spread thighs. His eyes blazed up at her as he tugged off her T-shirt and pressed his lips against her lacy bra. Just the heat of his breath through the lacy fabric made her nipples tauten in painful need, and when he caught one nipple with his teeth, abrading it through the fabric, Susan reeled and clung to him to keep her balance.

"You took care of me the other night," Ben whispered as he unzipped her jeans. "Tonight, I want to take care of you."

"Oh, Ben," she whispered, running her hands through his hair. "I do need you tonight."

Ben tugged her jeans down just below her hips. Bracing an arm at her waist, he slipped his free hand inside her panties and pressed upward boldly. Susan gasped as two of his fingers pushed inside her; the pressure was unexpected and very intense. Ben glanced up at her face, watching her reactions raptly. Her breathing was sharp and shallow, and her fingernails were digging into his shoulders. Not satisfied, he moved his fingers in a searching, provocative rhythm, even as he rubbed his thumb ever so gently across the bud of her passion.

Susan bucked wildly and cried out, feeling as if her legs had been knocked from beneath her. "Ben, I don't think I can stand—"

"It's okay. I've got you."

They both knew that it was only his hand that kept her upright now. His touch was wicked—probing, twisting, unbearably erotic. Susan hung there on a shaft of throbbing pleasure, crying out again when the ecstasy grew too intense. Even as she was sure she couldn't stand any more, Ben's teeth again nipped at her bra. Susan tore at the clasp to her bra, flung it off and pressed her right breast greedily into his mouth. As Ben tugged and sucked at the tender globe, pleasure flooded her with such violent force, she arched her back, then sagged against him.

"You okay?" he whispered.

Clinging to Ben, Susan could barely find the strength to nod.

Withdrawing his fingers, Ben rolled her over onto the mattress with him and tugged off her jeans and panties. This time, he pressed his mouth between her thighs. Where before he'd been forceful and bold, now he was slow and exquisitely thorough, his tongue flicking, teasing, darting in sweetly, then retreating. Susan bucked and clawed at the sheet, but he didn't stop the provocative torture until she climaxed again. Afterward, he kissed her wildly, plunging his tongue deep into her mouth. She tore at his clothes, popping buttons on his fine cotton shirt and clawing at his belt. He rolled away and impatiently threw off his clothing. She followed him, drawing her lips down his naked body, then fastening her mouth hungrily on his manhood. He groaned with agonized pleasure, but soon he caught her face in his hands, pulling her away.

"No," he said hoarsely. "I want you to climax again, this time with me inside you."

His words alone practically sent her over the edge. "You know you're killing me," she gasped as he rolled over on his back and pulled her astride him. "I wonder if anyone ever died from too much pleasure."

"Let's find out," he said.

As he caught her hips in his hands and lifted her, she belatedly remembered that they hadn't taken any precautions. Then she recalled that it wasn't a particularly risky time, and decided she couldn't let it intrude tonight, when they needed each other so desperately.

Then further thought was obliterated as Ben slowly lowered her on his straining hardness. She was hot, swollen from his ministrations, and very tight. Feeling the wonderful constriction of her, Ben held her hips and surged deep.

At once, Susan shuddered and cried out. Ben froze. "Am I hurting you?"

She shook her head violently. Her breathing was ragged, her emotions in chaos. "It's just that—I feel you so intensely—after—"

"Good. That's just what I wanted," he whispered, and thrust boldly again. Susan whimpered mindlessly and clutched his shoulders for dear life, instinctively rolling her hips to heighten his pleasure.

A moment later, he whispered, "Turn over, darling." Susan didn't hesitate, rolling over onto her knees. Ben nestled her close and thrust into her womanhood from behind. His inventiveness aroused her wildly, even as the new position realigned their bodies, making the penetration, the friction, exquisite and deep.

"Is it okay for you this way?" he asked roughly.

"Wonderful," she managed. And it was, she thought, as he filled her to bursting with slow, searing strokes. After their estrangement, only such an intense moment of sharing could bring the momentary peace, healing and oneness they both so desperately craved.

Then Ben reached around Susan to stroke her in just the right place. She reacted with such violent pleasure that she actually heard him chuckle, low and deep in his throat. He pressed his mouth against her shoulder and told her in coarse, earthy terms exactly how far he intended to take her tonight.

Even as he spoke, Susan felt the familiar spasms gripping her, and they were so much stronger than ever before. She arched against Ben, triggering the same frenzy in him. Their moans mingled as they grappled together, his fingers stroking, lifting her toward that sweet, agonizing melting point. Susan hung there, utterly shattered till a moment later, he found his own release.

They collapsed on the bed together, both breathing hard. Ben moved aside her hair and kissed her cheek. "How do you feel?"

That question brought fresh tears to Susan's eyes. "Close to you," she whispered in a breaking voice. "So close to you."

"Me too," he whispered back. He pressed his mouth against her ear. "Sue, I love you, and I want to marry you."

"Ben—"

"Just think about it a minute while we're lying here like this. Do you love me, Susan?"

"Yes, I love you." Inexplicably, the words made her cry.

At once, Ben rolled off her, pulling her around into his arms and kissing away her tears. "Was that so horrible, darling? It's as if I had to pull the words out of you with pliers."

"Maybe they're words I'm afraid could hurt you."

"Nonsense," he said. "They're the most beautiful words I've ever heard in my life."

THEY HAD a light supper of cheese, fruit and champagne out in the kitchen. "So, will you marry me?" Ben asked.

Susan stared at him almost shyly. He looked very sexy sitting across from her, his hair disheveled, his robe partially open, a heavy line of five o'clock shadow along his handsome jaw. Studying his chiseled, sensual mouth and remembering just how and where his wonderful lips had pleasured her, she felt her pulses throb. They had crossed some mystical boundary in bed together, and everything seemed changed now. Physically and emotionally, she felt she belonged to him, even if in terms of life-styles, she still recognized the problems they faced.

"Ben, I still don't know," she said at last. "I'm afraid we're too different to make a go of it."

He set down his champagne glass. "What do you want, Susan—a home, love, children?"

"Well, yes."

He reached across the table and took her hand. "Then we're not different at all."

Susan smiled at him, but her eyes were anguished.

Ben looked troubled, too, as he squeezed her hand and added, "Susan, either we're going somewhere with this, or we're going nowhere."

"I know," she whispered back achingly, realizing he was right. Sooner or later, they'd either have to make a permanent commitment, or end it.

Afterward, they took a bath together. Ben thrust into her endlessly as the water swirled about them. It was almost as if he were trying to hold her with his body as his words never could.

THE NEXT MORNING, Susan got up before Ben. She dressed quietly and had a cup of coffee. Then she went out into the living room, sat down on the couch and spent a long time thinking. Idly, she picked up a scrapbook from under Ben's coffee table.

The scrapbook had obviously been given Ben by his mother. She stared at pictures of Ben as a child—riding a pony, performing in the school play. He'd been a beautiful child, yet even then, his smile had been businesslike, his face a shining young mask. He seemed more like a miniature adult.

Then there were pictures of Ben as an adolescent at an eastern prep school—rowing, playing hockey and polo. That's when the girls started coming in. First, bright-eyed debutantes he took to school parties, and later, sophisticated young women he escorted to concerts and benefits. The latter pictures had been just tossed in, she presumed, by Ben. There was a picture of him and Cynthia Courtland standing with an older couple in front of a huge, stately home. Noting the older man's resemblance to Ben, she was sure the other couple were his parents. There were pictures of him with other gorgeous, sophisticated women she'd never even met before. She clenched her jaw as she studied a picture of a grinning Ben in a tuxedo, his lips pressed against the cheek of a stunning blonde.

How many of these women had he slept with? she wondered, reeling with jealousy. Had he felt at one time that they were all "perfect," too? Where were they now? If none of them were perfect, then—oh, damn!—how much less perfect was she!

Then, tucked in the back pocket of the book Susan found a small, faded snapshot of Ben and her father, standing in front of a helicopter in Vietnam. Both men were grinning; their casual pose, and the obvious spirit of camaraderie between them, made Susan's heart twist with poignant sadness. That friendship was the reason Ben Adams had come back into her life again; he never would have been so interested in her otherwise.

Feeling like an intruder, she put the pictures back and shut the album with trembling hands. This was Ben's world, she thought dejectedly as she put the album away. A world where she didn't belong.

Last night Ben had said that he loved her, that he wanted to marry her. But she was afraid that it could be just an infatuation, or that he was drawn to her out of guilt over her father. And she couldn't help but wonder if he hadn't become blinded by the passion between them, as their physical relationship had always been intense and wonderful. She thought of all the sophisticated women in Ben's album, and realized her picture just didn't belong there. She simply didn't possess the qualities he needed in a lifetime mate. He needed someone glamorous, socially prominent, someone without a tainted background. Someone totally unlike herself.

And while Ben's parents were in Europe now, she could easily foresee additional problems arising when the elder Adamses returned. She was sure now that Ben's friends, his family, would never really accept her, any more than Sybil Sayers had. Marrying Ben would only hurt him in the long run, she sadly concluded. She knew now that the best thing she could do for Ben Adams was to let him go.

Susan tiptoed into the still dark bedroom, not even trusting herself to look at Ben as he slept. She quietly picked up her suitcase and clothing from last night. Out in the living room, she placed her clothing in the suitcase, latched it, then set it down near the door.

She was about to leave when Ben sauntered into the room in his robe. "You're up early," he said, taking her in his arms and kissing her.

Susan was stiff in his embrace, avoiding his eyes. "I'm behind on a project due at work. I wanted to get in while it's still quiet."

Then Ben spotted her suitcase near the door; a muscle jumped in his clenched jaw and he turned to her accusingly. He took her chin in his hand and stared down into her guilt-filled eyes. "And you're a damn poor liar, Susan. You just wanted to get out before I got up. Right?"

Feeling miserable, Susan slipped out of his arms. "I never made you any promises, Ben."

He laughed humorlessly. "So you're just going to walk out again without even giving us a chance? Susan, we've only been together a couple of weeks."

"It's been long enough for me to realize that we're just not right for each other." Before he could interrupt, she held up a hand and continued, "Ben, I just don't think we have the basis for a lasting relationship. I'm not the right woman for you. I think you were drawn to me out of guilt, and that you got involved much more deeply than you should have. I think that in time, you'll realize that what we had was a mistake, and that you need someone more like yourself."

"How can you tell me what I need?" he asked angrily. "I never even knew what it was until you came along."

"Then we need some time apart—to see if this is real."

He shook his head, his eyes anguished. "You're not talking about time apart. You're talking about ending it, and you damn well know it, Susan."

She tilted her chin bravely. "Maybe I am, then."

He took a step closer. "What about last night? We didn't take any precautions."

Again, she avoided his eyes. "It's not too likely I'm pregnant. It wasn't a risky time."

"You always have yourself covered, don't you, Sue?"

"And you just wanted to trap me," she accused heedlessly.

"Maybe I didn't see it as a trap, but a commitment."

She shook her head and fought tears. "You wanted to make me over into someone I'm not."

Now he looked bewildered. "What are you talking about?"

"The dress, the necklace . . ."

"Susan, those were external trappings only. They're meaningless. I wanted the woman you are inside."

"You don't even know the woman I am inside."

"How can you say that after last night?" he asked incredulously.

"Our physical relationship has been wonderful," she said, choking on a sob. "But—but we can't build a future on just infatuation and good sex."

"You're wrong," he said with sudden, cutting bitterness. "The sex has been great."

Susan almost fell apart then. She clenched her fists helplessly at her sides and closed her eyes to staunch the flow of tears. "Ben, you're making this so hard."

"You're not even going to try, are you, Susan?" he asked.

A terrible silence fell between them. At last, Susan managed to take hold of herself. Clearing her throat, she looked at him and said woodenly, "I didn't take the dress with me yesterday, and the emerald necklace is on your dresser."

"Oh, so we're going to make this really clean, are we?" Ben cut in. "Do you want your childhood pictures back, too? They mean a hell of a lot more to me than any damned emerald."

She could barely speak. "Please, just keep them."

"What about your mother's rings?" he went on ruthlessly.

She sighed. "You were right. I never should have kept them at my apartment. Would you mind hanging on to them for a few more days? I'd need to arrange for a safety deposit box."

"Fine," he cut in tersely.

She looked at him through her tears. "Ben, I just want what's best for you."

"If you wanted that, you'd stay. So why don't you just get the hell out?"

He turned his back on her, and she walked out the door.

13

THE NEXT FEW DAYS were miserable for Ben. He tried to lose himself in his work, but he was ill-tempered and easily distracted. He snapped at his employees and launched into tirades at the drop of a pin. When he exploded at his secretary, Agnes Miller, for losing a file he himself had misplaced, she resigned on the spot and he had to woo her back with flowers and a hefty raise. He tried to take himself in hand, tried to convince himself that the breakup with Susan was for the best, but nothing seemed to be working in his life with her gone. She had left a big hole in his heart that couldn't be filled. He finally had to acknowledge that he felt damned angry and hurt because she hadn't given them a chance.

When Ben had to entertain an important customer and his wife for dinner, he asked Margo Pershing along for the evening. He was polite toward Margo during dinner with the customer, but he found that everything about her grated on his nerves. He found her laughter affected, her conversation empty and pretentious. There was nothing genuine or warm about her, he decided. She just wasn't Susan.

When he dropped Margo off early with a handshake and a terse goodbye, it came as no surprise to either of them. "I don't know what's eating you, Ben," Margo had snapped, "but it's obvious that you want to be somewhere else tonight."

He knew she was right. But how could he be where he really wanted to be, when Susan was convinced that there was no meeting ground between their worlds?

On a morning about a week after Ben and Susan had broken up, his secretary rang up to say that Charles Marshall was on the line. Ben frowned, then told Agnes he'd take the call.

"Hello, Charles," he began irritably.

He heard Charles whistle on the other end. "Well, hello, Ben. Actually, I've been meaning to ask whether you're interested in doing business with me or not. This is my fourth call to you in so many days."

Ben sighed. "I'm sorry I haven't returned your calls, Charles. It has nothing to do with you. Sue and I broke up."

"I'm sorry to hear that."

"The girl just walked out on me," Ben went on bitterly.

"Guess that's a first, huh?"

Ben glowered at the phone, muttering an expletive.

"Sorry," Charles added quickly. "What do you think caused the breakup, if you don't mind my asking?"

"Susan says our worlds are just too different, but I think her reasons may have a lot to do with the column that bitch Sybil Sayers wrote on Sue's family background. She was certain I'd be hurt by it, and I couldn't convince her otherwise."

Charles sighed. "Well, it was pretty selfless of Sue to think of you first. If she's willing to give up all you could offer her, there's obviously not a mercenary drop of blood in her body. By the way, were there any repercussions for you due to that column?"

"I did receive one call from a board member taking me to task for being involved with Susan. But he's an habitual troublemaker, and I think I gave him a piece of my mind that will keep him quiet well into the next century." As Charles chuckled, Ben added, "I know everyone else on the board is solidly behind me."

"Good. Now all you need is Susan back."

"That's up to her. She knows where I stand."

"Well, maybe Jessie can have a heart to heart talk with her. Jessie's mom is in from Colorado, and she's giving her a baby shower on Saturday afternoon. I know Jessie's planning to invite Susan."

"If Jessica wants to run interference with Susan, more power to her," Ben said. "But if I can't convince Susan to stay, it's doubtful your wife will have any effect on her, either."

Charles laughed. "My friend, you have no idea how determined these women can be when they get their minds set on something. And Jessie and I both want to see you and Susan together. Beyond that, how is the paperwork for the loan coming along?"

"Just fine. Within days, we'll have everything ready to present to you."

"Great. In the meantime, I'd really like to show you our preliminary plans for the ad campaign on Southbridge Manor. Are you free for racketball and drinks later this afternoon?"

"Sure." Ben laughed ruefully. "Maybe some physical exertion will lessen some of my anger and frustration. I'll meet you at the club at five."

SUSAN, TOO, was miserable without Ben. A dozen times each day, she picked up the phone to call him, then stopped herself. Endlessly, she reminded herself that what she'd done was best for him in the long run. Ben would surely realize this soon and get on with his life, she kept telling herself.

When Susan moved back into her apartment, she found that all of Jamie's things were gone, and he didn't appear during the following days. She was sure he must be living elsewhere, but she made no attempt to find him. For she realized now that the things Bill Newcomb had told her were true; she couldn't help Jamie until he was ready to help himself. Every time she recalled how her brother had stolen their mother's rings, the memory of his betrayal reaffirmed her decision not to go after him.

Still, with Jamie gone, Susan's nights and weekends were very lonely. She found herself, for the first time in many years, feeling a keen sense of loss—feeling like a child again, vulnerable and bewildered.

One night as she struggled to sleep, it occurred to her that she had lost everything in her life—first her mom, then her dad, and then even Jamie had betrayed her. Now she'd lost Ben, too. Yet he was the only person in her life who hadn't let her down, and she was the one who had pushed him away.

Why? Was she afraid of getting hurt again? Yet how could she feel more hurt than she did at this moment? Even as this painful realization made her sob into her pillow, the phone on the nightstand seemed to beckon her again. But knowing that going back to Ben would only bring him more pain gave her the will to resist.

About ten days after Susan had broken up with Ben, she received a call from Jessica Marshall. Jessica was brimming with enthusiasm as she invited Susan to her home that Saturday afternoon. "My mom's in from Denver," Jessica said, "and she's throwing me an impromptu baby shower. She's doing most of the calling, but I wanted to get in touch with you personally, Sue. I really hope you'll come—and you don't have to bring anything, of course."

"Don't be ridiculous," Susan said. "Of course, I'd love to come, and what woman can resist shopping for a baby? I really appreciate your thinking of me, Jessica. But I think I should tell you that I've broken up with Ben."

"I know that," Jessica said. "I mean, Charles told me. But I do hope we can still be friends."

"Of course."

"See you on Saturday at three, then?"

"It'll be my pleasure."

While Susan felt touched by Jessica's invitation, the thought of attending a baby shower saddened her, as well. Three days after she'd left Ben, she'd discovered that she was, indeed, not pregnant. The slight risk she'd taken that last night hadn't resulted in any lasting complication. She wondered, then, why she felt so blue and empty.

Since she was on a limited budget, she decided to sew something for the baby. At a craft shop, she selected a pattern and fabrics for a quilted, teddy bear wall hanging. She worked on the hanging for three successive nights, and it turned out beautifully. She also made herself a dress for the shower—a vibrant, flowered sundress with a full skirt, fitted bodice and narrow shoulder straps. Both the dress and the hanging were bright and cheerful, but neither could elevate her mood.

On Saturday afternoon, Susan drove to Jessica's house in Highland Park. She felt rather daunted as she approached the huge, ivy-covered, old-English home. Expensive sports cars were parked everywhere; Susan carefully wedged her battered subcompact between a red Ferrari and a silver Mercedes convertible. As she walked toward the door with her present in hand, she bit her lip as she thought of the surely extravagant presents the other women would have brought.

She was admitted by a maid who took her present and showed her into a huge, lavishly furnished living room. Susan glanced about, feeling taken aback as she spotted several of the beautiful women who had given her such scathing looks at the benefit two weeks ago.

Then Jessica rushed up to greet her, looking lovely in a pink silk maternity dress. She wrapped an arm about Susan's waist and announced brightly to the throng, "Everyone, this is my good friend, Susan Nowotny."

To Susan's surprise, the women greeted her cordially, shaking her hand and murmuring pleasantries. Jessica's mother was particularly friendly, sitting down next to Susan and keeping her involved in a lively conversation about the hazards of Colorado winters. Overall, the atmosphere was animated and filled with laughter; Susan realized that no woman could resist a baby shower.

In due course, Jessica began opening her presents, and Susan found her previous fears were correct. The presents were quite expensive, including a playpen, stroller, car seat and bassinet. Each box of clothing or linens contained enough sets of everything for triplets.

The women ooohed and aaahed as each present was opened, and Susan did find their excitement contagious. Yet her feelings were also poignant as she tortured herself with thoughts of what she and Ben might have had, fantasizing about the child they might have created together. She found it was hard to remain altruistic and think of what was best for him, when right now she simply missed him and wanted him and needed him so badly.

Susan felt quite touched when Jessica opened her present and cried, "Oh, Susan!" A collective gasp rippled through the group of women, as well. Indeed, everyone there was staring raptly at the lovely, quilted teddy bear, with his bright spray of multi-colored balloons. Susan heard comments like "How darling!" and "How precious!" Jessica beamed at her and said, "Susan, how very thoughtful of you! I can't wait to put this up on the nursery wall."

Then Jessica's mother turned to Susan and said, "Dear, do you mind telling us where you bought that? Jessie and I must shop there," and Susan felt herself blushing slightly as she murmured, "I made it."

This revelation brought a new chorus of admiring comments from the women. Everyone was stunned by Susan's talent, particularly Jessica. "I'll treasure this all the more because I know you made it," she told Susan with a glowing smile. Susan felt warmed that the women were truly impressed with her sewing, instead of thinking of the gift as somehow second-rate.

Before long, the women started leaving. Susan was preparing to leave herself, when Jessica took her aside. "Susan, can you stay on a while? I really need to talk with you."

Susan didn't have anything pressing, so she continued visiting with Jessica's mother as Jessica said her goodbyes to the remaining guests. Then a meaningful glance was exchanged between mother and daughter, and Jessica's mother excused herself.

Jessica took off her shoes and collapsed next to Susan on the couch. "Oh, that was fun, but I'm kind of glad it's over now. At seven-and-a-half months of pregnancy, I feel about as full of life as an old tire toasting in the sun."

Susan laughed. "You look radiant, Jessica."

"Thanks," her hostess replied. Frowning at Susan, she abruptly asked, "What happened between you and Ben?"

Susan laughed ruefully. "I wondered if that wasn't the reason you asked me to stay on."

"Well, you must admit that at the benefit, that man couldn't keep his eyes off you. Nor could you keep your eyes off him. And now it's over?"

Susan sighed. "We're just not well-suited."

"Well, you could have fooled Jessie." Carefully, she added, "Does it have anything to do with Sybil Sayers's column?"

Susan sighed. "That's part of the problem. I can't see wrecking Ben's career."

Jessica placed her hand over Susan's. "Honey, you're not going to wreck Ben Adams's career. That man is firmly entrenched in this town, and people like Sybil Sayers have much more to fear from him than he has from them." Confidentially, Jessica continued, "Everyone in Dallas knows about that witch and her poison pen. Don't worry, honey. It will all blow over."

"You really think so?" Susan asked wistfully.

"Yes, ma'am. You just grab Ben Adams and hold on with all you've got. He's the catch of the town, Sue. And furthermore, Charles tells me he's never seen Ben fall for anyone like he has for you." Giving Susan a meaningful glance, she added, "By the way, Charles tells me Ben is miserable without you."

"He is?" Susan asked with forlorn hope.

"So what's stopping you, Sue?"

Susan frowned. "Miss Sayers hinted that Ben's parents will never approve of me."

"Don't be ridiculous," Jessica said. "In the first place, I don't think Ben is even that close to his parents. They're in Europe half the time. And in the second place, I've met the Adamses—they're classy people, and not the least bit stupid. They'll definitely support Ben rather than risk losing their only son and heir." Playfully, Jessica elbowed Susan. "Just give them a grandchild, hon, and you'll have them eating out of your hand."

Susan smiled at Jessica, then fell silent a moment, thinking over her friend's words. Maybe there could be hope for her and Ben. They loved each other, didn't they? And in the final analysis, maybe they did want the same things—a home, love and babies. She missed Ben so terribly, and obviously, he missed her, too. Maybe what they had could be lasting. Maybe their problems could be worked out.

If he would ever forgive her for walking out on him.

"Well, Sue, why don't you give it another try?" Jessica prodded. "The phone's right over here."

"Is that why you invited me here today?"

Jessica shot her a reproachful look. "Susan, I invited you because I like you."

Susan laughed. "Sorry. Look, I appreciate the advice, and I promise I'll think over what you said. Okay?"

The women were saying their goodbyes when they heard the doorbell ring. A moment later, Jessica's mother ushered

Ben into the living room. Susan's heart seemed to leap into her throat as he strode in, looking so handsome in his pale blue knit sport shirt and gray slacks, with the sun glinting highlights in his wavy dark hair. Yet he also looked tired, tense and preoccupied, and her heart twisted at the thought that she might have caused him distress.

"Good afternoon, Jessica," he said stiffly. "I've come for Susan."

Susan hardly heard what was said next. Her heart skidded crazily as the words, *I've come for Susan*, reverberated through her brain. Three times now, this dear man had come after her. . . .

Ben was addressing her, now, and at last his words reached her teeming mind. "When I went by your apartment and found you weren't there, I remembered Charles had mentioned the baby shower today." He looked around the room at all the baby things; then he swallowed hard, a muscle working in his jaw. He turned to Jessica and added with a smile, "I see the shower was a success."

"It certainly was," Jessica said brightly. She stepped over to the couch and held up the teddy bear wall hanging. "Look what Susan made for me, Ben!"

Ben stared at the wall hanging, then back at Susan. The look of naked anguish in his beautiful blue eyes was almost more than she could bear.

"She's very talented," he said at last, to Jessica.

"Won't you have some punch before you spirit Susan off?" she asked.

Ben shook his head. "I'm afraid it's urgent that I speak with Susan alone." He turned to her. "Will you come with me?"

"Of course, Ben," she said, over the pounding of her heart.

Susan felt taut with anticipation as they said their goodbyes and left. Through it all, she had a feeling that something was wrong. As soon as they were safely outside, she turned to him and asked, "What is it, Ben?"

He sighed. "I'm afraid it's Jamie. He's in the hospital."

14

"WHAT HAPPENED?" Susan asked as Ben's Jaguar pulled away from the curb.

He sighed. "Susan, Jamie's pretty well banged up, but I don't think he's in any danger."

"Good Lord, *what happened?*"

"The police called me to say he'd been beaten up and was in the hospital."

"They called *you?*" she asked incredulously.

He nodded. "Remember when I gave Jamie my card two weeks ago? Well, they found it in his wallet."

"But, how did he get beaten up?"

"The policeman and his partner were patrolling a street not far from your apartment when they saw a man beating Jamie up in an alleyway. They arrested the man, who is supposedly Jamie's bookie."

Susan shook her head, fighting a hot rush of tears. "When Jamie hocked Mother's rings, he bet the entire amount—and then some—on a race at Louisiana Downs. He lost everything, including the amount he didn't have. I'm sure that's why his bookie beat him up."

"I'm sorry, Sue."

"Hey, it's not your fault. I don't know why you want to be involved in this, anyway."

"Then you don't know me very well, Susan," he said with sudden bitterness.

She turned away, afraid to meet his eye; her own eyes were stinging with the depth of her fear and anguish.

In due course, they arrived at the county hospital near downtown and were shown into a large, noisy ward. Jamie's bed was near a far window. He was sleeping, and Susan gasped with dismay as she saw him. His face was puffy, a mass of cuts and bruises. He was hooked up to an IV, and his knuckles were bandaged. A young nurse came by to check on him, and smiled at Susan. "Are you his sister?" she whispered.

"Yes."

"He kept asking for you before he fell asleep."

"Is he okay?"

She nodded. "The painkiller I gave him has made him kind of woozy, so don't be surprised if he drifts in and out of consciousness for a while. He's pretty beaten up, but thankfully there were no internal injuries. He should be released tomorrow."

"Thanks," Susan said, wiping a tear with the back of her hand. She felt Ben move up close behind her and place his hands on her bare shoulders. After the long days of their separation, his warm touch was both agonizing and sweet. She dared not look up at him; if she did, she knew she would fall apart. And if he took her in his arms now, she doubted she could ever again gather the strength to leave the shelter of his embrace.

Jamie began to stir, grimacing as he shifted in bed. Ben's hands tightened slightly on Susan's shoulders, and he whispered, "Darling, sit down."

Susan slipped into the chair next to Jamie's bed. Gently, she took her brother's hand. After a moment, he opened one bruised eyelid and grinned at her crookedly. "Hi, Sis," he said in a slurred voice.

"Jamie! Are you okay?" she asked hoarsely.

He nodded, then groaned. "I've been informed that I'll live, though it's hard to believe at the moment."

"Oh, Jamie! What happened?"

He drew a labored breath. "I squelched on a bet and I got beat up. What else can you expect from me? I'm always letting you down."

"Oh, Jamie."

He drew another pained breath, his hand tightening on hers. "Sis, I have to tell you—"

He tried to move upright then, only to fall back in agony, his features white. "Oh, no!" Susan cried. "You mustn't try to move like that! Are you all right?"

He nodded, then spoke convulsively. "I just—have to tell you—that I was wrong, Susan."

Susan's heart twisted with pain and tenderness. "Look, we don't have to talk about this right now."

"But we do," Jamie continued in a breaking voice. "I have to get this off my conscience. You were right about Mom, Sue. I did try to diminish her in my own mind to justify stealing the rings from you. Actually, I've been lying here feeling rotten about everything. I'm so sorry, Sue."

Susan smiled poignantly at her brother. "It's okay, Jamie. I think I'm finally beginning to understand why you behave as you do. The only thing is, you really do need help."

She watched tears fill his eyes. "I'm not sure there's hope for me, sis."

"But there is!"

He shook his head. "You're better off just staying the hell away from me."

Susan squeezed his fingers gently. She remembered the comment Bill Newcomb had made about approaching Jamie when he was really low. She'd never seen her brother feeling as down as he did now. Carefully she said, "Jamie, I've seen someone, a psychiatrist who specializes in treating compulsive gamblers. Won't you please go see him, at least once? I'll pay for it."

Jamie shook his head. "After all you've done, you're still willing to shell out for me?"

"Jamie, you're the only family I have," Susan said. "And I see in you someone very much worth saving. Just give it a try, okay?"

He hesitated a moment, then nodded. "Okay, Sis. I promise to go at least once." He yawned. "But for now, I'm really having a hard time keeping my eyes open."

Susan stood, then leaned over and kissed her brother's brow. "Get some rest. I'll come back and see you tonight."

"Thanks for coming, Sis." He stared up at her, and she was touched to see a glint of hope shining in his eyes.

As Susan left the ward with Ben, she felt close to the breaking point. She'd managed not to lose control of her emotions in front of Jamie, but it had been hard. Seeing him so beaten up, so low, had devastated her.

Out in the corridor, Ben abruptly turned and pulled her into his arms, and that's all it took for Susan. She pressed her face against his shirt and shook with sobs.

"It's all right, darling," he whispered, stroking her hair. "Just let it all out."

She spoke disjointedly. "Ben, it hurt so much to see him that way and know that there was nothing I could do to help him."

"Do you want me to arrange for him to be transferred to a private room?" Ben asked gently. "That ward was pretty depressing."

She shook her head. "Bill Newcomb told me that Jamie must learn to accept the consequences of his actions. And I guess the ward is one of those consequences. Only, it's so hard—"

"I know, darling. But Jamie did say he'll go see Bill. Maybe then he'll start getting his life back on the right track."

"I hope so," Susan said with a heavy sigh. All at once, she felt terribly awkward with Ben, knowing she had sobbed her heart out in the arms of a man whom she had deserted two weeks ago. She moved out of his embrace and cleared her throat. "Thanks for bringing me here, Ben. I suppose I can catch a cab back to Jessica's house—"

"Susan," Ben interrupted firmly, "I want you to come with me to my penthouse. We need to talk."

She glanced away, blinking rapidly, and he caught her chin in his hand, forcing her to look up at him. "Susan?"

She nodded and said in a small voice, "Okay."

He took her hand and they left the hospital together. Once they were in his car, he stared at her for a long moment. "So Jamie's the only family you have," he said at last. "You know, I wanted to be your family, too."

Susan turned desperately toward the window, fighting a new rush of tears. If only Ben had railed out at her. He certainly had every right. Instead, his tenderness was killing her.

After a moment, she heard Ben sigh. "You look beautiful today, Susan."

"Thanks," she said in a strangled voice.

The engine revved to life, and they pulled out of the parking lot. They said only four more words on the way to his penthouse. At a stoplight, he turned to her and asked, "Are you pregnant?", and she said, "No."

15

IT WAS EARLY EVENING by the time they arrived at Ben's penthouse; the living room was cool and shadowy.

He set down his keys on the coffee table, then turned to Susan. They exchanged a long, intense look. Suddenly Susan could not endure another instant of the aching chasm between them. She whispered Ben's name through her tears. Even as she rushed toward him, he met her halfway, crushing her in his arms.

Susan felt as if she'd come home after a long absence. The feel of his arms about her, his lips on hers, was heaven.

"Oh, Susan," he whispered, kissing her cheek, her neck, then her mouth again. At last he drew back and said, "Darling, we must talk."

She nodded, letting him lead her to the couch. Once they were seated, she stared at him starkly. "I've been miserable," she said.

"Me, too." He drew a ragged breath. "Susan, I'm so sorry I told you to leave two weeks ago."

"Please, Ben, don't apologize. I'm the one who walked out on you."

"Won't you please give us another chance?"

Susan was quiet for a moment, then said, "Ben, I realized something while we were apart. Remember that night when you told me I didn't want to need you?"

"Yes."

"You were right. I wouldn't let myself need you. And I guess it's because everyone in my life that I needed, I lost." Susan's voice began to break, but even as Ben leaned over to kiss her, she held up a hand and she forced herself to press on. "I always had to be so strong, for Jamie's sake. But inside, I wasn't strong at all, only scared of getting hurt again. Then you came along, and I guess you were just too good to be true."

"You're not going to lose me, Susan," he said quietly.

She looked up at him, her expression stark and vulnerable. "Are you really sure? Are you certain you're not mistaking guilt for something more lasting?"

He pulled her close and kissed her lips tenderly. "Susan, I'll admit that guilt may have drawn me to you in the first place. But knowing you has helped me deal with those very feelings, and to put them to rest, once and for all. It's definitely love I feel for you, now."

"Oh, Ben." Susan pressed her cheek against his chest, listening to the comforting sound of his heartbeat. "I love you, too. So much. But I'm still not sure I'm right for you. Perhaps a woman more glamorous and sophisticated would better fulfill your expectations."

Stroking her arm, Ben laughed and repeated, "'A woman more glamorous and sophisticated.' Do you know that before you came along, I had my pick of glamorous sophisticated women, and none of them seemed right for me? I'm only now realizing that I never found that perfect woman before, because I never really knew what I wanted until you came along. I had all these crazy misconceptions about womanhood, and you've shattered them, totally. I want you, Susan—warm, genuine, loving person that you are." Tilting her chin with his hand, he looked down into her lovely face. "You've totally transformed my ideas of perfection—for the better."

Susan's eyes gleamed with new hope. "Do you really mean it?"

"Lord, yes." He laughed ruefully. "You know, I had my life so perfectly organized before you came along. And you know what? It was boring as hell. But since I've met you, I've had my life threatened, my best suits slashed by a cat named Ru-

mor, I've visited pawnshops and chased you all over Dallas.
What more could a man ask for?"

Susan had to laugh there. Still, she bit her lip and asked,
"But what about ten years from now? What about when the
next innuendos appear in the newspaper? What about when
your parents return from Europe?"

"Darling, if we love each other, we'll work it out. All we
have to do is to be willing to try." Seriously, he added, "Susan, what about you? If we're to make our relationship work,
it will mean some compromises. I won't lie to you about the
demands of my career. Perhaps, at times, you'll have to go
places you don't want to go, be with people you may not like."

"Ben, standing by someone you love is never a compro-
mise. You've always stood by me, as much as I've doubted
you. And, as far as your career is concerned, I intend to back
you every step of the way."

"Are you sure, Susan? It will mean a real commitment."

She nodded. "I'm sure. I wasn't ready to give that commitment two weeks ago, but I am now."

His eyes lit with joy. "Then marry me, Susan. I can't live
without you."

She hugged him close. "Oh, Ben. I can't live without you,
either."

"I think I'd like to have that in a blood oath," he added solemnly.

She drew back. "I beg your pardon?"

"Blood tests," he said with a grin. "First thing Monday
morning."

"Oh, you," she said with a laugh. "You're still a perfectionist, a martinet."

"Oh, am I?"

"Already giving me orders."

He pressed his forehead against hers and chuckled. "So
how about another one?"

"*Another* order?"

He drew back, ruffling her hair affectionately. "Come with me, darling. There's something I want to show you."

Ben helped her up and led her to her bedroom. She gasped as she looked at his dresser; the childhood pictures he'd kept of her were framed and placed about. Tears filled her eyes again. Why hadn't she been able to see Ben for the genuine, loving man he truly was? She remembered his saying that the pictures meant more to him than any emerald. But she hadn't been ready to listen then.

She turned to stare at him with her heart in her eyes. "Oh, Ben. You're so sweet."

"There's something for you on the nightstand," he said with a grin.

She went over to the nightstand and picked up a small velvet box. She opened it to see the diamond ring she'd admired in the jeweler's window. "Ben! You got the one with the small stone!"

He nodded. "I knew it was the one you really liked."

"When did you get it?"

"Right after we bought the dress. But I knew you weren't ready for the ring then, so I've saved it for you."

She shook her head slowly. "You know, I've really misjudged you."

He came to her side and solemnly slipped the ring on her finger. "I'll talk you into a big diamond later on."

"But not for this ring," she said, happily gazing at it on her finger. "Believe me, you'll never get it off my finger for that long."

"Okay, not for this ring." Winking at her, he added, "We'll hook a big, fat rock right through that adorable little nose of yours."

Susan laughed, but Ben's eyes had suddenly turned dark and smoky. His head ducked down, and Susan moaned in ecstasy as his lips claimed hers. A moment later, he groaned and pulled her down on the bed with him.

"Now?" she said, laughing as he unzipped her sundress. "You certainly don't waste any time, Mr. Adams."

He grinned wickedly. "No lie. In fact, if you try to run away again, I may chain you to my bed."

Susan met his gaze fully. "I'm through running, Ben."

"Promise?"

"Promise."

He kissed her quickly and possessively, then began tugging down her sundress. She sat up to facilitate his efforts.

"Is it a risky time?" he asked with such a sexy, devilish grin.

She giggled. "Now that's a loaded question if I've ever heard one."

"Well?"

"Getting riskier every day," she admitted.

"Good," he said, swooping down to take her nipple in his mouth.

Susan moaned and thrust her hands into his thick, shiny hair. "Then I take it you want a family right away?"

He pressed his hand low on her belly and growled contentedly. "Unless you'd rather wait."

She shook her head, clutching him tightly to her. "I want your children, Ben."

"Oh, Sue." He had eased her sundress down over her hips now, and was removing her panty hose. "I want to take you off on a long honeymoon. Somewhere isolated, with lots of beach. Perhaps the French Riviera or the Caribbean."

"And what are we going to do with all that time?" she breathed, tugging off his shirt and running her hands over the smooth, taut muscles of his chest.

"Guess," he whispered, rolling onto his back and pulling her on top of him.

They came together sweetly, tenderly. Then they held each other close, the diamond on Susan's hand sparkling in the afterglow of their loving.

Epilogue

"WELL, I HOPE you're satisfied, Mr. Adams."

It was a year later, and Ben stood at the front door of his penthouse, trying to calm down his irate neighbor, Miss Hennessey. He'd been listening to the elderly spinster's harangue for ten minutes now.

"I'm sorry, Miss Hennessey," he said feelingly. "How many times can I apologize?"

The woman shrugged and shoved a large basket toward him. Mewling sounds emanated from the basket's interior. "And to think that their father is named Rumor! Rumor, of all things! Why, my Priscilla hails from a bloodline of champions! And now she's been ruined by—by little more than idle gossip!"

Before Ben could respond, Miss Hennessey dumped the basket into his unwilling arms and continued imperiously, "I did allow Priscilla to nurse them—it wouldn't do to let the foundlings starve. But enough is enough. Let their father rear them."

The woman squared her shoulders, turned on her heel and left. Ben closed the door and sighed, heading off for the bedroom with his basket. As he moved, he glanced approvingly at the penthouse. It was filled with color now, vivid blues and greens and sunny splashes of yellow. Susan had redecorated the penthouse, just as she had redecorated his life.

He entered the bedroom, grinning as he spotted Susan on the bed. She was nursing their three-month-old baby boy and talking on the phone. Rumor was at the foot of the bed, non-chalantly licking his chomps.

"Lecher," Ben muttered to the cat.

"Jamie, that's wonderful!" Susan was saying. "Congratulations again, and don't forget that you're having dinner with us on Saturday." She winked at Ben. "Look, Ben just walked in, so I'm going to run."

She hung up the phone and said brightly to Ben, "Jamie just got his six-month chip in Gamblers Anonymous. And he says his new job is working out great."

"Hey, that's wonderful, darling."

Susan glanced at the wicker basket he held and frowned. "What's in the basket? Another baby present?"

Ben laughed as he set the basket down next to Susan. He joined his wife on the bed, wrapped an arm about her and kissed the baby's head. "Well, it looks like Rumor did more than just chew on my plants all those nights we kicked him off the bed."

Susan stared at the basket, her eyes growing huge. "Kittens?" she exclaimed, watching four precious little furballs cavort about. One was black, one was silver, the others somewhere in between.

Ben chuckled. "Miss Hennessey just informed me that Rumor ruined her silver Persian." At Susan's amazed glance, he added, "It seems Rumor leaps across balconies in a single bound."

Susan laughed. "And here I thought Rumor and Priscilla hated each other." She frowned reproachfully at her cat, whose ears had perked up at the sound of his name. "Why, Rumor, you old reprobate."

At his mistress's rebuke, Rumor got up and moved indolently toward the head of the bed. After giving the kittens a brief, cursory glance, he tossed his nose disdainfully and hopped off the bed.

Susan and Ben fell into spasm of laughter. "Typical father," Susan said, watching Rumor exit the room. "Do your damage and leave 'em to weep."

"Not this father," Ben added meaningfully.

"I know," Susan said, staring at him with eyes filled with love. "Not this father." She glanced at the basket, petting a silver ball of fur. The kitten wrapped itself playfully about her hand. "You know, they're kind of cute." As Ben laughed, she leaned over and whispered to the baby, "Hey, Sweet Pea, look at the kittens."

Three-month-old Ben Junior rolled his blue eyes momentarily toward the kittens, then went straight back to lusty nursing. Watching his son, Ben grinned with pride. Already, Ben Junior was a chip off the old block—all business. "You know when the doorbell rang, I did think it was another baby gift. My mother has Junior's room looking like a toy store."

Susan laughed. "Jessica Marshall once told me that if I gave your parents a grandchild, I'd have them eating out of my hand."

Ben laughed. "You had them eating of your hand from the moment they met you."

"They're good people, Ben," Susan said, suddenly serious. "You should give them more of a chance."

"You don't give me much of a choice there, as often as you invite them over," he said. But the words were gentle, without a trace of bitterness.

A shaggy black kitten now climbed out of the basket onto Ben's leg, snagging the fine fabric of his trousers. He scowled down at the kitten, which took no note. "I'm glad we're looking at houses, Sue. Between Junior, Rumor and all these kittens, we're bursting at the seams."

Susan laughed. "I agree that a high rise isn't the best place to raise a child. Of course, Sweet Pea's too little to know the difference now. But Jessica has warned me that he'll be a handful before long. She should know. In fact, it's hard to believe their little Jennifer is already eleven months old. But she *is* into everything."

Ben chuckled, nodding at the now-sleeping baby. "Well, I see our future champion has drunk his full. Here, let me take him."

Susan lovingly transferred the baby into Ben's arms. As she righted her clothing, he straightened the baby's pale blue T-shirt, which read Sweet Pea. He smiled tenderly at his dark-haired son, lovingly stroking his smooth little forehead and inhaling the wonderful baby smell of him. To Susan, he whispered, "We're so lucky, darling."

"I know."

"Are we ever going to tell Junior that he was conceived on a beach in St. Thomas at midnight?"

Susan chuckled. "By the time Junior's old enough to ask, he'll care less about what his old fogey parents did." She wrinkled her nose at Ben. "But I must say, Mr. Adams, you did make my head spin, the way you whisked me off on that honeymoon so quickly."

He glowered at her. "You put me in no mood to wait around, lady."

She sighed dreamily. "As I recall, it was blood tests on Monday, the wedding on Wednesday afternoon, and on Wednesday night—"

"Paradise," Ben put in with a deliberately prurient grin.

They fell happily silent for a moment, listening to the soft sound of the baby's breathing. "The pediatrician says Sweet Pea's going to keep your blue eyes, Ben," Susan murmured after a moment.

Ben glanced at her in delight. "That's great, darling. But now we *will* have to keep trying till we get that brown-eyed little girl, won't we?" Thrilled by Susan's sudden blush, he looked her over thoroughly. She looked adorable in her tight jeans and a T-shirt that read, I Belong to Ben Adams. He'd bought the T-shirt for her on their honeymoon. "You're getting awfully slim again, my dear," he added meaningfully.

"*Awfully* slim?" Susan repeated, rolling her eyes. "Hah! Don't tell me I'm already giving you ideas again? You must like me fat."

"I like you fat with my child."

Ben leaned over to kiss Susan, thinking of how full and rich his life was. The silver kitten had joined the black one on his pant leg, and the two were now battling wildly, their needle-sharp little claws doing a fine job of ruining his trousers. But Ben didn't care. Everything he loved was right here in his arms.

As he and Susan drew apart, he chuckled.

"What?" she asked.

"I was just thinking of something Miss Hennessey said. She told me she hoped I was satisfied now."

"And are you satisfied, Mr. Adams?" Susan asked with a smile.

"Oh, I am," Ben replied. "Perfectly satisfied, Mrs. Adams."

Spoil yourself next month
with these four novels from

— TEMPTATI❤N —

THE DREAM UNFOLDS by Barbara Delinsky
(Second in a stirring trilogy)

Gideon Lowe was more than just some macho construction worker, and the Crosslyn Rise building contract would prove it. The last thing he needed was Christine Gillette tromping onto his work site, disturbing more than his men . . .

CUPID CONNECTION by Leandra Logan

Cupid Connection was no ordinary dating service, and Abby Shay was determined to prove it. But her investigation was being hampered by the charismatic Nick Farrell.

THE JADE AFFAIR by Madeline Harper

As far as Clea Moore's family were concerned, Reeve Holden had come from the wrong side of the tracks. Maybe now was the time to show them just what he was made of, because Clea had been daddy's little girl for too long.

SLEIGHT OF HEART by Kara Galloway

Proving Garrett Brody was a con artist was going to take all the tricks up illusionist Kate Christopher's sleeve. And what if Garrett found out that she had used trickery to deceive him?

BARBARA DELINSKY

 CROSSLYN RISE

Crosslyn Rise – Six lives linked
by an all-consuming passion.

Read Barbara Delinsky's latest compelling trilogy.

Three powerful romances for the summer.

JUNE   *The Dream*
JULY   *The Dream Unfolds*
AUGUST *The Dream Comes True*

**Don't miss these special books from one of
Temptation's most popular authors.**